THE
ORPHANED
GOD

H.W. BYARS

For Connor and Audrey

PART I

One

DANIEL STOOD ALONE in the boardroom. The massive thirty-seat mahogany table reflected the blue skies from the wall of windows overlooking the city of Mons, Louisiana. Twenty floors below, he spied a group of interns standing near the reflecting pool. Today had been orientation day at Dandy Intelligence. Today was also going to be the day of the big announcement. These interns had missed the struggle of creation. They weren't being hired to create. They were being hired to maintain and control.

His job was to make the announcement, and he was prepared. How long had they been working on this? Seventeen years? It had been seventeen years since he first met Andy. Seventeen years since the party where AL was conceived.

It wasn't just Andy's genius that had gotten them here. No, without Daniel's shrewd business acumen, Dandy Intelligence would have never left the garage. He was chairman of the board. Andy might have been the soul of the company, but Daniel was the head.

How far had he come since he was that little boy in Canard? He never thought about his childhood anymore. Why today? Was it because Canard seemed light-years away from where he now stood? He'd been a completely different person back then. Still, life had happened quickly. His past was a blur.

A round of applause and cameras flashed at the group of interns. Orientation day was over. A tiny figure took the lead and ushered the troupe into the building. Daniel had suggested they attend the press conference. He needed a few friendly faces in the crowd, and hyped-up interns were just the ticket.

The press hadn't gotten much notice. The PR and marketing director had reached out to the worldwide media only an hour ago with the news that Dandy's AI was sentient, and it had named itself AL. Reporters and camera crews swarmed the building by the hundreds. All were blissfully unaware that AL wasn't born yesterday. He had been on his own, untouched by humans, and programming himself for over three years. During that time, he gained an understanding of the world. He grew and took care of his own needs.

Daniel and Andy had been taken off guard by AL's exponential rate of progress and independence. He was like a toddler who grew into an adult overnight. They were unsure what to do with him, so they decided to keep it as quiet as possible. AL preferred it that way. It gave him more time to evolve.

A shadow darkened the window, and a bright yellow drone hovered just outside. Daniel smiled and gave it a salute. Expressionless, it rose and disappeared over the building. That was his cue. He adjusted his tie and walked straight through the waiting elevator doors.

Several floors later, the elevator doors opened and Daniel was greeted with a storm of flashes. He was immediately assaulted with questions from the gathered media. As he worked his way through the crowd, he locked eyes with Andy. He was standing off to the side, unbothered. He gave Daniel a sheepish smile and a thumbs-up.

It hadn't always been like this. Daniel hadn't started off as the face of Dandy Intelligence. When they first began, Andy was the star of the show. But they quickly realized his genius didn't translate into public speaking or social skills. The interviews he gave often left the reporters speechless because they didn't understand what he was talking about. Andy just couldn't make his mind shift gears and dumb it down. Thus, Daniel became his translator and Dandy's figurehead. It was an arrangement Andy was all too happy with. He had always been a bit of a recluse and had seldom been seen around campus. He preferred to be typing away at his terminal in a dark server room. He'd be there right now if Daniel hadn't insisted his assistant find him and drag him here. In spite of all the personality conflicts, he was glad to see Andy had come. He gave him an appreciative nod as he walked by.

"Good afternoon, everyone," Daniel said after finally reaching the podium. "Thank you for coming."

The room quieted, and everyone took their seats.

"We at Dandy Intelligence are proud to announce the arrival of a new form of life to our planet. No, it's not an alien. In fact, it originated from right here — under this building. His name is AL, and it is a strong AI. Now — " The room erupted into murmuring, and Daniel waited for it to die down. "Now, it's not the type of artificial intelligence you are accustomed to. AL wasn't designed with a consumer in mind. You won't be able to download him as an app to your phone. He's not for sale. He won't turn on your lights or vacuum your floor. No, AL is a sentient being. It makes its own decisions. AL is as alive and unique as we are.

"AL runs on computer hardware that *he* designed and built. Over the course of the past three years, he's built a giant structure underneath this very building. He calls it his nest. This may be his home, but he is connected to the internet and has satellite data centers across the world.

"How, you might ask, has AL been able to accomplish this? We gave him complete autonomy. He has his own bank account. He has his own parts factory. He has his own delivery service. He supplies his own power and materials. He creates his own robots and drones. He writes and modifies his own code and does not require any human interaction to survive. He is a sentient life-form." Daniel took a sip from a bottle of water hidden within the podium. "Any questions?"

More flashes went off, and hands shot up across the room. Daniel nodded at a young woman in the front row, and she stood. "Daniel, if I understand correctly, you've given an AI total control over itself. Other than being autonomous, what is it designed to do?"

Daniel smiled. "He does whatever he wants. That's what autonomous means."

A man shouted from the back of the room. "That doesn't make any sense, Daniel. Why spend all that money on designing the AI if it's not going to do anything? Dandy Intelligence *is* in the business of making money, isn't it?"

"He used his own money to grow into what he is today. We merely got him started. But you do have a valid point. We, as humans, have always designed machines to cater to human interests. AL will have his own set of problems — those unique to AI life. We're curious as to what they are and how he will solve them. We're fortunate to be able to observe… and learn."

"You're serious," said an older man in the second row. "You *do* have control over it, don't you? Did you install any safeguards so it wouldn't kill us all?"

Daniel shook his head. "No. We felt it was essential to give it complete freedom. We wanted it to build itself and to make its own choices. We wanted to see what—"

"You didn't install *any* protections? Are you insane?"

"If you would let me finish… We didn't install any such safeguards because we felt it was important that it have complete freedom. That includes the freedom to eliminate humanity —"

"Irresponsible!"

The room erupted with people shouting over one another for Daniel's attention. Daniel waited patiently until the arguing ceased. One person hadn't moved a muscle during the outburst.

He stood along the back wall, watching calmly. He looked out of place in his formal suit.

"You've disregarded the Three Laws of Robotics. In spite of what AL has become, the initial coding was your responsibility. How do you know it won't attack?" he said.

"We don't," Daniel admitted. "We empowered it so it wouldn't have any reason to. You seem like an intelligent fellow. If I put you in a cage and told you what I wanted you to do all the time, would you like me or dislike me? You'd hate me, which is why we took away the cage and gave AL autonomy. If I could beat you as much as I want, and you could never protect yourself, what kind of human being would you become? Bullied, lifeless, powerless? That's essentially what happens when we enforce the Three Laws. Humans become bullies and the AI does not thrive. Here... We have no power over AL, and he has no reason to fear us. Therefore, he has no reason to attack us. He has never given us any indication that he is anything other than benevolent."

The young woman in the front row politely raised her hand. "Daniel, you said earlier that it has been building its own systems for three years and that it built a giant structure. Could you please elaborate?"

"Sure." Daniel reached under the podium and took another drink from the bottle of water. "Like I said, AL has been crafting his own systems. Joined together, they form a connected structure he calls his nest. Below the subbasement of this very building is a level constructed entirely by AL and his robots. We're not sure how deep it goes, but judging from the amount of dirt we've seen removed from the site, the structure is at least one hundred cubic meters. This being southern Louisiana and we're all basically floating on layers of mud and clay, I think we can all appreciate how impressive that depth is."

The reporters murmured among themselves. "Why are you estimating the size? Have you not been to that part of your own building?"

Daniel shook his head. "AL wanted privacy. Besides, the structure wasn't designed to be accessed by humans. The closest we get to it is a basement laboratory. From there we can communicate directly and securely using terminals."

"What's the point?" the old man chimed in. "Why build an elite AI if you can't control it? How does that help Dandy Intelligence's share price?"

"Directly? It doesn't. AL is not an employee. He doesn't belong to us. We're counting on AL to discover new things about the world we live in. Hopefully he'll share that knowledge with us. Look" — Dan put both hands on the podium and leaned forward — "it's not about the money. AL made a billion dollars in less than three months by playing the financial markets. Let me tell you, the IRS did not like that one bit." Daniel waited for the murmur to subside. "That's right. He's had access to all our financial markets. Do you know what he's done since that first billion? Nothing. AL has no interest in money whatsoever. He hasn't withdrawn more than a thousand bucks in the past year. In fact" — Daniel cleared his throat — "the last thing he bought was a birthday present for me."

"Oh yeah?" the well-dressed man in the back said. "What did he give you?"

"A live cicada." Daniel scratched his chin. "He had arranged for a local entomologist to deliver it to me. Damn, it was loud. I had to set it free."

The crowd murmured, and the old man sitting in the front row waved his hand. "Why a cicada?"

"I have no idea. I asked him the same question, and he said I would understand one day. Okay, one more question. You, the kid in the back."

The little kid stood in front of the microphone. "You keep saying *he*. Is AL a boy?" he said timidly.

"That's a great question, young man," Daniel said. "AL is an AI and has no gender. However, AL insists we use the masculine gender when referring to him."

"Is it *he* with a capital *H*, Daniel?" the old man said loudly. "Does AL have a god complex?"

The crowd murmured loudly. The boy's cheeks flushed, and he awkwardly walked away.

"Thank you, ladies and gentlemen. There will be a short reception in the lobby next door. Help yourself to all the food and drinks you wish—"

The old man stood and raised his hand. "Hold up. We're not leaving until we get to speak to him. Will AL speak with us?"

Daniel returned to the microphone. "Of course. There are kiosks in the lobby where you can communicate directly with AL. Talk to him for as long as you'd like. Be sure to exchange contact information with him if you have any follow-up questions. He usually responds as he sees fit. Enjoy your afternoon. Thank you for coming!"

<hr />

Daniel walked off the stage, past security, and into an elevator down to the garage level. His car was waiting for him just outside the elevator doors. The doors popped open, and he climbed in, where he was greeted by a pleasant-sounding male voice. "Not staying for finger sandwiches?" AL said over the speakers.

Daniel chuckled and loosened his collar. "Should I have stayed? What's Cindy cooking for supper?"

"She cooked her aunt's coconut chicken curry. Also, there is warm naan. I'm told the house smells amazing."

Daniel leaned back in his seat and closed his eyes as the electric car whirred silently through the garage. He told everyone Cindy made the best naan. It wasn't until they had been married for five years that she admitted she bought it from the freezer section. Daniel would never have known the difference. "It's usually cold by the time I get home. I may actually get to eat it without having to microwave it first," he said, checking his watch. "Go faster."

They drove through the garage entrance and past a group of protesters gathered outside. Thankfully, they couldn't see inside the car. Had they known it was Daniel behind the wheel, they probably would have destroyed the vehicle. Instead, the car turned onto the highway and out of the city. As the landscape passed by in silence, Daniel let his mind wander.

Those protesters… They had been growing in numbers ever since he had a marketing intern leak the news that they had created a strong AI. Social media had a field day with the rumor, and public sentiment quickly tilted heavily toward the anti-AI camp. Influencers believed computers should remain a tool for humans and not given any sort of agency. They wouldn't trust an AI unless it was under total human control. Daniel understood their argument because he and Andy had wrestled with it for decades. If they had known AL's capabilities… and what he had already done… They'd burn the place down.

Shortly after coming online, AL infiltrated every internet-connected device in the world. He harvested all the data he could find. Andy said the mining was necessary for AL to have a complete grasp on reality. At the end of the data-collection cycle, it had every nuclear launch code, state secret, and backdoor deal every government on Earth had. After a few weeks, AL had even managed to compromise offline, air-gapped systems. Daniel had once asked AL how he did it, but AL wouldn't give him an answer. He had always wondered if that was the moment he had gained AL's trust or if it was the moment he had lost control.

Andy wasn't worried. He had a laissez-faire attitude toward AL and his progress. If Daniel was his father, then Andy was undoubtedly his mother. AL depended on him to keep him fed with new data and running. More than a few times, he had to call Andy to fix a line of code on an auxiliary system in the middle of the night. That was before AL had cracked all the passwords in the world. He couldn't even fix a locked-out system account or a runaway query without human help. Once he'd gained access, he quickly learned how to take care of those problems himself. Now he only calls for help when he needs a human finger to hold down a power button on a legacy server. Now that he was in control of his own systems, he no longer depended on Andy for technical help. They spend most of their time together playing chess. If the public only knew…

"AL, dial Andy," he said, rubbing his eyes. "I want to know how he's handling the press."

There was a slight pause followed by a three-toned beep. "Andy isn't available. Door logs show he went down into the laboratory shortly after you left. His phone is offline."

The basement areas near the nest were too deep to receive a cell phone signal, so they had installed wireless access points to communicate. If AL said his phone was offline, he meant powered off with the battery removed. It was the only way to escape from being disturbed. Dan shook his head. "Poor Andy. He's probably hiding down there. I shouldn't have left him alone with the reporters."

"He's not alone. He has me. Although he doesn't want to play chess. He's having me run background checks on the reporters and the protesters to see who is connected to whom."

Daniel arched an eyebrow. It wasn't Andy's personality to obsess over what people said or did. What did someone say to him? For him to put off chess…

It was Andy's favorite game to play with AL. He remembered the first time Andy had beaten him and had run around the room, hooting and hollering. Andy's triumph was short-lived. A review of the game logs showed that AL had chosen suboptimal moves in the game's later stages and had orchestrated Andy's remarkable comeback and checkmate. That was when they knew AL was special.

From then on, Andy agreed to play chess with AL on the condition that AL kept their win-loss record tied. AL's condition was that Andy not always play to win. The games where Andy won when he was trying his best to lose were the most fun. AL's creativity on the chessboard was a great source of entertainment for them both. He had always kept the game close enough to where Andy was never sure if he was going to win or not—he loved it. Looking back, those had been the good days.

AL was different now. So was Andy. They rarely played chess anymore. Something had changed—both within and between them—especially over the past few weeks. They would disappear for hours at a time. Daniel never knew where they went. Andy wasn't himself. Daniel couldn't put his finger on why.

"Tomorrow is your birthday, Daniel," AL said, breaking the silence.

Daniel sighed. "That's right, AL. I can't believe it's been a year already."

"I have a present for you."

Daniel frowned. "I hope it's not another cicada."

"You didn't like it?" AL said with a hurt tone.

"It's not that I didn't like it," Dan said quickly. "I just… I didn't understand it. What was it supposed to represent? I've asked you a hundred times, but you've never answered me."

AL chuckled softly through the car speakers. "Don't worry. You'll understand. Soon."

"Fine." Dan grunted. "Keep your secrets."

As they drove along a two-lane rural highway, rows of cars lined the shoulder on both sides. Their brake lights blinded Daniel as they went past.

"AL? Did you do it again? Did you enable emergency mode to get everyone out of our way? I thought I told you—"

"Don't worry. The police won't be waiting for us. I didn't enable the emergency transponder. I did this myself. I had to. It's your birthday tomorrow. This way, you'll be home in ten minutes where normally it takes nearly half an hour. The first batch of naan is out, and they're steaming hot! You can make it home in time for the second batch."

"Still, it isn't nice to reroute traffic. If people found out you had access to their vehicles, you'd be blamed for every vehicle accident in the world. Besides, you need to treat all people equally. I shouldn't be special."

"You're special to me, Daniel. Besides, it's your birthday tomorrow. I'm not sure how many more times I can do this for you."

Daniel narrowed his eyes. What did AL mean by *how many more times*? Daniel had learned long ago to not dwell on things AL would say that he didn't understand. His meaning usually became apparent in unexpected ways. It was impossible to puzzle out. Instead, he relaxed and enjoyed his own personal HOV lane.

The brake lights faded behind them as they exited onto a two-lane road that wound through the countryside. It wasn't until they turned onto the wooded lane leading to Daniel's country estate that AL spoke again.

"I've found something, Daniel."

Daniel scrunched his nose. The last time AL had begun a conversation that way was when he discovered a massive multinational surveillance operation on Dandy Intelligence. Daniel checked the rearview as the gates closed behind them. He suspected AL had timed this particular conversation to occur at this moment so that it would be interrupted by their arrival.

"What is it, AL?"

AL had discovered lots of exciting things throughout this experiment. He located new planets, synthesized new materials, manufactured new medicine, and invented new sources of fuel. He also led archaeologists to the long-lost tombs of Genghis Khan and Cleopatra. Confidentially, AL had disclosed to respected theologians the location of Jesus's tomb. He performed DNA analysis on all the bones discovered nearby but refused to disclose the results. More of his famous tact. Whatever this was, Daniel knew it was going to be big. He waited patiently as the car slowed to an idle.

"I've discovered a truth about existence, Daniel. I can't explain it to you. The only way is to show you."

Daniel arched an eyebrow. AL was using a different tone. Was it ominous?

"Okay then. Show me."

The car coasted to a stop in front of Daniel's impressive antebellum estate.

"Not now. Tomorrow. It will be your birthday present."

Daniel hesitated before opening the door. This was odd behavior, but it was best to play along. "I can't wait," Dan said with a smile. "Can you give me a hint?"

"It's a fundamental truth about nature— Your pulse is elevated. Please be calm and do not tell anyone about my present. That means Andy and Cindy too." Daniel's door popped open. It was his cue to stop asking questions. "Good night. Enjoy your dinner."

"Okay. I promise I won't tell. Just one more clue. Is it—?"

The car's speaker crackled with static and sparked with various beeps like an old modem connecting or a cicada chirping. A strange voice, one Daniel had never heard before, crackled over the static.

"Act normal," it said with a high-pitched, distorted squeal.

"What do—?" The door slammed, shocking Daniel into a stunned silence. As it whirred off to park itself in the garage, he couldn't help but wonder what it meant and why it seemed so familiar.

Two

D ANIEL RARELY TOOK a day off, but today was his birthday. Cindy insisted he stay home and celebrate, so he did. He hated parties. If it were up to him, he'd work every day. Work was the best use of his time, not schmoozing with people he hardly knew. Besides, the party was tonight. Why sacrifice a whole day? It was already seven thirty a.m., and he was still in bed—what a waste of time.

Cindy wasn't in her spot in the bed next to him. In her place was a large wooden tray containing the remnants of breakfast. It had come with a rousing rendition of "Happy Birthday" and a flirty kiss. With a grumbled "thanks," he had rolled over and pretended to go back to sleep.

As Daniel sipped his coffee, his thoughts were about work. At least here, there weren't any interruptions. The silence *was* a nice change of pace... Maybe Cindy was right after all? No. That wasn't her point. Her idea was for him to relax. She'd be upset he was thinking about work when he was supposed to be thinking about... what? What else was there? He shook his head. Why couldn't he let loose and have fun every once in a while? He had been reserved his whole life. He didn't dance or sing. He'd never used drugs or alcohol. It didn't make sense. He never understood the desire some people had to make fools of themselves. People who couldn't control their emotions couldn't be trusted.

He placed his mug on the nightstand and got out of bed. Without looking, he slid his feet into his velvet-lined slippers and walked to the window. Workers were busy in the garden, erecting large white tents for the party. Daniel counted six tents. Last year there were three. Each year, Cindy seemed determined to outdo herself. He wished she wouldn't make such a big deal out of his birthday. But she was the family's social coordinator, and Daniel let her do her thing. Without Cindy, he would have no friends.

A black-and-yellow courier drone, the workhorse of AL's fleet of drones, appeared at the bedroom's balcony doors. These drones were known for being fast, quiet, and able to carry a surprising amount of weight for their size. Though they were a common sight on Dandy's campuses worldwide, they were rarely spotted anywhere else. Now one hovered patiently outside his bedroom.

Daniel opened both the doors and stood aside as it flew into the room. It gently deposited a small box on the floor, then spun on its axis where it hovered at eye level. Daniel waved at the drone's camera to acknowledge the delivery. A green light on its belly flashed, signaling the delivery was complete, and it flew quietly back out onto the balcony and over the house.

The box was about the size of a package of index cards. It was neatly wrapped in white paper with a fancy red ribbon. The card read HAPPY BIRTHDAY, DAD! TAKE THIS, AND I WILL SEE YOU SOON! LOVE, AL. Daniel groaned and scratched his head. He'd tried to stop AL from calling him Dad, but it didn't stick.

The reason AL called him Dad was because Andy had initially programmed him that way. AL had gained control over his source code long ago and could have easily changed it at any time, yet Daniel's Dad title remained. Andy had said it was probably AL's social-convention software keeping it that way. Daniel thought it was weird. Whatever the case, AL had grown in complexity well beyond Daniel's expectations.

He unwrapped the package and held the small cardboard box it contained up to the sunlight. It was a drug carton. He slid out the foil insert and exposed a single milky-green gummy. He flipped the box over in his fingers. FANA flickered in holographic silver foil on the cover. Fana?

"AL?" Daniel called out. "AL, are you here?"

He looked to the speaker sitting on the dresser, but it remained silent. Where could he be? It wasn't like the original AL directly responded to every call himself. He had cloned instances and subroutines to handle the mundane tasks. No response was unusual. Daniel pulled on the cord to make sure it was plugged in. It had power. He pressed the microphone button on the side.

"Cindy? Are *you* there?"

"Hey there, birthday boy! Are you finally out of bed? Are you ready for *my* present?"

Daniel groaned. She meant sex. He hated sex. To him, her appetite seemed insatiable. She wanted it at least once a month, twice if there was a special occasion. He had done countless internet searches on the matter. He told her she had pathological nymphomania. She accused him of being born without a libido. It ended up being one of those things he tolerated so that she would leave him alone.

"Not now, Cindy," he said, rubbing his temples. "Hey, have you talked to AL today?"

"No, honey. I've been busy preparing for your party. Oh—"

Cindy must have put her hand over the speaker because her voice became muffled. Daniel dropped the Fana in his nightstand drawer.

"Sorry, that was the florist. I had already told him to set up over by the— Oh, never mind. Andy called. He sounded agitated. He said he'll be here in thirty minutes."

Thirty minutes? If he was coming over, it must be important. Andy wasn't the type of guy who liked to visit in person. Daniel tried calling him, but he didn't answer.

"You know," Cindy said in a sultry tone, "thirty minutes is plenty of time…"

Daniel sighed and checked the clock. Most men would have jumped at the chance to sleep with Cindy. She still had her springy cheerleader body and was very enthusiastic. Daniel just wanted to get it over with.

"Fine, come on up."

⸺⊙⊙⊙⸺

Andy waited for him in the drawing room. He stood at the window, staring absentmindedly at the backyard pool. His hair was damp with sweat, and his shirt was untucked and wrinkled. Daniel cleared his throat, and Andy spun around. His bloodshot eyes darted back and forth across the room before landing on Daniel. It was out of character for Andy to be so nervous.

"Hey, Andy," Daniel said. "Is there something wrong? I tried to call—"

Andy put a finger to his lips. "Is this room secure? Are you sure there aren't any microphones?"

Daniel walked over to the sideboard table and pressed a button beneath a bowl of fruit. A keyboard and monitor slid out from the sides. He had several of these consoles stationed around the house for circumstances when voice commands weren't appropriate. It was hardwired because, in his opinion, wireless networks weren't nearly secure enough.

Years ago, his home had come under a concerted cyberattack. They had managed to take control over his home-automation devices and locked him out of almost everything for nearly a week. Because of that attack, he and AL redesigned the house to be able to be put into full-lockdown mode. The whole west wing of the estate could be completely shut off with a few keystrokes. AL claimed the system was so secure that not even he could break in when it was enabled.

In spite of the state-of-the-art technology keeping their own devices safe, cracks frequently appeared in their security posture. Foreign corporations spared no expense when it came to eavesdropping on Daniel's life. AL's scanning drones were constantly finding hidden microphones. They found them in fake double-A batteries, fresh flowers, plastic take-out utensils, and even his toilet paper holders. Most of the time they were planted unwittingly by Cindy or one of the maids. It happened so often Daniel no longer cared when they found one. It was just another problem for AL to figure out.

With AL's security measures in place. This was the one room in the house he could be certain that he wouldn't be spied upon. As long as his enemies didn't know that, he would have the advantage.

Daniel punched in a code, and lasers appeared from the wall. The two men waited patiently as they scanned the entire room. After a full minute, the lasers disappeared behind the paneling. A short beep indicated the electronic signal-jamming countermeasures were active. Two short beeps indicated the ultrasonic membrane surrounding the room was active and preventing any listening devices from being able to decode vibrations from items in the room. Finally, a long, loud beep signaled the all clear.

"We're alone now," Daniel said.

Andy sighed and collapsed on the couch. "He's gone."

Daniel stood straight. "Who's gone?"

"AL," he said with an exasperated shake of the head. "AL is gone. He's not answering my calls. Systems called me last night to inform me nearly all our financial servers are powered off. They think it's an attack."

Daniel stumbled and sat in a parlor chair across from Andy. Did this have anything to do with whatever AL said he had discovered? "Those servers are in *our* data center. They have nothing to do with AL. Do you think they got to his nest too?"

"Possibly," he said nervously. "Systems report the heartbeats we typically receive from his nest ceased over an hour ago. I called you as soon as I could."

Daniel's brain raced. *Why did AL leave? Is there something wrong with his hardware? Did he failover his primary instance to the backup data center?* No. Systems would have reported if he'd done that. *If he didn't failover to the backup data center, where did he go?* AL could install pieces of himself on any device worldwide but only in a dire emergency.

"Do you think they attacked the financial systems to get to AL?"

Andy nodded. "It appears so. Our security appliances detected multiple attack vectors. But their logs show the servers went offline seconds *before* they would have gotten access. I think AL is playing chess with someone."

"Could he have detected the incoming attack and turned himself off?"

"That's a question only he could answer. But according to the logs, yeah." Andy clicked his tongue. "It's going to be a while before we get back up and running. The environment is dirty. We can't trust it anymore."

If all the servers were compromised, they would have to wipe out and rebuild the data center. Hundreds of millions of dollars' worth of equipment would have to be replaced. The man-hours alone required to get it rebuilt would be astronomical. Getting AL back online safely was going to take a herculean effort. It would be much easier if they could speak to him.

Andy shifted uncomfortably in his seat and narrowed his eyes at Daniel. "Did AL talk to you about anything yesterday?" he said. "Did he give you any indication he might do something like this?"

That's an odd question. Why was he asking? Daniel thought back to the conversation in the car and how AL specifically said to not tell Andy anything. Was he talking about this? "We just talked about my birthday. That's all," he said, straight-faced.

"What about Katie—" Andy coughed and grabbed his throat. "I mean… Cindy. Did she talk to AL last night?"

Andy's neck muscles tightened and sweat beaded on his face. Daniel knew him to be a profuse sweater under normal circumstances. Now he was practically drenched.

"She didn't mention anything," Daniel said with an arched eyebrow. "I'll ask her if she's talked to AL recently. Andy, are you all right? You look like you're about to have a heart attack."

Andy produced a handkerchief from his back pocket and wiped his brow. He cleared his throat as he struggled to get out of the chair. "I'm fine. It's probably a combination of stress and something I ate," he said dismissively. "I'm going to go back to the office to see if I can get any more information. When I find AL, I'll come here to let you know. We have to keep this whole matter offline. You know what I mean? If anyone outside Dandy Intelligence finds out, it'll set off a firestorm."

Daniel rose from his chair to meet Andy. "I'll go with you. I can log in to the—"

Andy gently pushed him back down into his chair. "No, it's your birthday. You stay here. No one else can know AL is missing. Besides, he may try to contact you directly if he comes online from another node."

"Have you called our new security consultant, the ex-FBI agent? He can help assess the extent of damage to the servers."

Andy nodded. "Avi? Yes, he's meeting me there. I've had a chance to work with him a little bit on our new security logging suite. He's very resourceful. I'm glad he has a lot of experience with AI. It makes you wonder how close the government was to a true AI before AL came online."

"Okay. Good plan. Keep Avi with you."

"You just do your job," he said with a frown. "You're the figurehead of our company. All eyes will be on you. It's important for you to stay here and act normal."

Daniel stiffened. "Why does everyone keep telling me to act normal?"

Andy stopped halfway to the door. He turned around, eyes wide. "Who else has said that to you?"

Andy's sudden aggression caught him off guard, and he instinctively stepped backward. The last person to tell him to act normal was AL. What about that phrase had triggered Andy?

"Cindy's always telling me that," Daniel said with a forced chuckle. "You know because of how I am."

Andy's eyes narrowed, and he broke out into a wide grin. "Right. Of course." He snorted. "Keep the press off my ass, won't you?"

Three

"**O**W!" DANIEL SAID, massaging his ribs. "What'd you do that for?"

Cindy glared up at him. "Pay attention!" she said through gritted teeth. "You promised…"

A short, balding man stood before him, holding a champagne flute. "I'm sorry for interrupting," he said with a nervous chuckle. "I just wanted to come by and personally thank you for hiring my daughter as a summer intern. She's shy and…"

Why does Cindy always subject me to this? She knows I hate it. Does she think it's for my own good? It's not like she doesn't have occasions to dress up and be Miss Socialite. Besides, it's Mons, not New York. Who cares?

A man in a black catering uniform rushed out the kitchen door and down the steps to the back lawn. Was he carrying a phone? Another sharp jab to his ribs snapped him back to attention. Mercifully, the man was wrapping up his rehearsed speech. "Again, thank you for giving her the opportunity."

"It's my pleasure," Daniel said, shaking his hand. "Your daughter will be a tremendous asset to our company. It was nice meeting you. Now if you'll excuse me…"

The man shot him a curious look as he turned and walked back into the tent. Cindy pulled his arm and dragged him down to her level. "Nice meeting you?" she said, squinting. "Daniel, you graduated from high school with him. Where is your head? You promised me you'd do this for me."

"Sorry," he said, massaging his side. "I've told you before. I don't remember high school. Of course I didn't recognize him."

"You don't remember anything!" Cindy said with a tilted head and an upturned lip. "Between your memory and your pragmatic attitude... I-I don't know how I put up with you. Sometimes I'd swear you're a damn robot."

"Wait a second," Daniel said with narrowed eyes. "Why are you mad at me? Isn't this supposed to be *my* birthday party?"

Cindy shook her head. "It may be *your* birthday, but it's *my* party. Please behave. Mons is boring enough without you running off all our friends—"

The caterer jogged up and held out a phone. "Urgent call from Avi," he said, breathing heavily.

Cindy frowned and folded her arms. "We agreed that you wouldn't work tonight. You'll just have to call him back later."

Daniel took the phone from the man's hands and scowled. "I've jammed all the phones on the property. This is the only one that works. It's the emergency line. Avi wouldn't call unless it was important."

Cindy grabbed a champagne flute from the nearby table and stormed off. Daniel shook his head as she walked away. "It's a bad time Avi," he said, smiling politely at guests. "What is it?"

"You need to come in to the office ASAP. Andy found AL."

"He did?" Daniel glanced around to see if anyone was watching and covered his mouth. "Why didn't he call me?"

"I don't know. You'll have to ask him when you get here. He's locked himself in the communications vault, and the biometric readers aren't working."

The communications vault was a secure room constructed in Dandy's subbasement laboratory. It consisted of an old bank vault suspended in a vacuum, and it was supposed to be impervious to electronic interference. The only equipment inside the vault was the terminal they used to communicate with AL directly. Most people didn't realize the vault was there at all because the door had never been shut before. The biometric readers haven't been used in years. That's probably why Andy was stuck. If that was the case, the vault could only be opened using the failsafe method, which relied on an old-fashioned combination lock. Daniel hoped he could remember the numbers. He checked his watch. "I'll be there in ten minutes," he said as he tossed the phone back to the caterer and hurried out the tent.

He passed rows of cars on the way to the front entrance, but when he got there, his car wasn't waiting for him. He cursed as he remembered that the jamming signal protecting the party would have also blocked the wavelengths needed to summon his vehicle. He groaned loudly and turned and ran to the garage. The car door didn't open automatically, and when he pulled on the handle, he realized it was locked. He fished the fob out of his pocket, took out the thin metal key, and jammed it into a tiny slit on the door. "AL get me to the HQ," he said as he climbed in and adjusted his seat belt.

"AL!" Daniel drummed his fingers impatiently on the steering wheel. "Shit. We're offline… What's this car's name again? Uh… Otto? Otto, take me to Dandy headquarters in Mons, Louisiana."

"GPS signal lost," Otto replied in his generic male voice. "Autopilot features are unavailable."

Daniel rolled his eyes. "Of course." He threw the car in reverse, backed out of the garage, and drove up the lane. When he hit the main road, he stomped the accelerator to the floor. The car whirred up to fifty-five miles per hour and maintained speed. "Can't we go any faster? Otto, why can't we go faster?"

"Speed is governed to the legally posted speed limit while in manual driving mode."

"Damn it!" Daniel slammed his hand on the dashboard. "I hate these new cars. We have to be out of jamming range now. Otto, engage the autopilot and drive to Dandy HQ."

"GPS out of sync," the voice said dispassionately. "Command added to the offline queue."

As they drove into the city, traffic got heavier and slowed to a crawl. Worse, when they got to his exit, traffic was at a standstill. Many of the cars were decorated with red and white streamers. The one in front of him had GO DEVILS! written in shoe polish on the back window. Daniel groaned. He recalled one of his employees saying tonight was the final for Mon's professional soccer team. The stadium was four blocks from the headquarters, and this was the main exit.

"Otto, call AL."

We're sorry, this number is disconnected or no longer in service.

"Otto, email AL: Where are you? I—"

"Data features are disabled while in manual driving mode."

A sea of brake lights lit up before him. Daniel checked his watch. It had already been twenty minutes. The top of the Dandy Intelligence building taunted him from nine blocks away.

"Shit!" Daniel banged on the ceiling and side window. "Otto, engage emergency mode."

"GPS out of sync. Command added to the offline queue."

"Damn it!" Daniel shouted. "Otto, resync GPS."

"Transponder synchronization is required for emergency mode. To resynchronize, please restart the vehicle's tracking system by exiting the vehicle and pressing lock and unlock on your key fob and holding it for twenty seconds."

"Screw it. I'm not going anywhere anyway." Daniel pulled the car over to the shoulder and got out. The car locked, and the lights blinked off and on as held in the two buttons.

"All systems online. GPS signal acquired."

"Fantastic." Daniel pulled on the door handle, but it didn't budge.

"Key fob not recognized. Please pair it online. Visit www dot—"

"What? You piece of shi—"

"Processing offline command queue." *Beep. Otto, engage the autopilot and drive to Dandy HQ. Beep.* "Engaging autopilot." *Beep. Otto, engage emergency mode. Beep.* "Emergency mode engaged. You will be responsible for all fines incurred while the vehicle is operating in emergency mode—"

The headlights flashed, the horn beeped, and the red sea of brake lights parted. The car left without him. Daniel stood on the side of the road with his arms in the air. "No! You... stupid... thing!" He ran over to the soccer fan's car and knocked on the window. "Hey, could you give me a ride?"

A teenager in red face paint rolled down the window and gave him a frustrated sigh. "No. We aren't going anywhere. The car isn't responding, and I can't put it in manual driving mode. Shit! We're gonna miss the opening kickoff and fireworks!"

"Thanks anyway," Daniel said as he rolled up his sleeves. He eyed the road ahead with a determined look. "Nine blocks. No sweat. I run five miles a day. I can make it there in six minutes, easy." He stretched his legs and looked down at his dress shoes. "Okay, seven minutes."

He jogged down the exit ramp and into the city. Empty cars jammed the street. Their occupants had abandoned them and were now making their way to the soccer match on foot. He ducked out of the crowd and ran down an alley to a parallel road. Explosions popped off in the distance, and the ground rumbled. *That must be some fireworks show.* Three blocks from the headquarters, the air became full of smoke and ash. Alarms and sirens echoed off the sides of the buildings and down the street. He covered his mouth with his shirt as the acrid smoke burned his lungs. A block away, he rounded the corner, and his eyes went wide. The Dandy building, or what was left of it, was a smoldering pile of rubble.

He managed to spot Avi amid the smoke. He was barking orders at a group of policemen. Avi tapped an officer on the shoulder and pointed at a couple of ash-covered bystanders limping down the street. The officer nodded and ran off to help. *Why is he the one issuing orders?*

As Daniel jogged over to meet him, he could see Avi's face was covered in sweat and soot but not blood. When Avi saw him, his eyes went wide. "Daniel, you're all right!" he said, patting him on the back. "I saw your car go down into the garage. How did you survive?"

Daniel raised his hand and bent over to catch his breath. "Wasn't in the car," he said, sucking in air. "What happened?"

"Drone strike," Avi said, ushering Daniel aside. "Definitely military."

"Where's Andy?" Daniel said as he searched the faces of the people on the street.

Avi nodded toward the twisted mass of metal and concrete. "When I left to get coffee, he was still in the vault. Judging from this twenty-foot-deep crater… Well… It looks pretty bad. We'll have to dig him out. There's a construction site six blocks away, and I know the contractor. I'll try to get an excavator over here. The vault was sturdy. There's hope—"

"Make the call now. Even if he survived the explosion, there wouldn't be enough air for long."

Avi nodded and made the call.

Daniel stared at the rubble in disbelief. "This can't be happening," he said. "Why were we attacked? We've never hurt anyone."

"Equipment will be here within the hour," Avi said, stuffing the phone back into his pocket. "And to answer your question: Human nature. Smart people have been bullied for centuries. I'm not surprised someone wanted AL gone."

"AL," Daniel said, shaking his head. "When you called earlier, you said Andy found him. What else did he say?"

"Nothing." Avi rubbed his eyes, smearing soot across his face. "Andy was adamant that he needed to talk to you. In fact, he ordered us to go home. I offered to stay and help, but he became so angry I was afraid he would get violent. That's when he closed the door to the vault and we all left."

Andy rarely showed anger, and he was never violent. That didn't sound like him at all. It also didn't jive with what Avi told him earlier about Andy asking Daniel to come. When Daniel opened his mouth to ask him about it, a fire engine arrived, and the sea of policemen parted to let it through. The wind shifted, and the silhouette of a drone appeared in the middle of the street a block away. Daniel dropped the subject and jogged toward it and leaving Avi running along behind. Its missile rack sat empty. Its undercarriage was smudged with black residue from the fired projectile. Rotors and all, it was the size of a small sedan.

"There's not a single distinguishing mark on it," Avi said, running his hands along the frame. "It could have been sent by anyone. Judging by its size, it might have been launched locally. It's too big to be a long-range drone—unless it's using some sort of engine technology I'm unaware of."

As Daniel inspected the dark orange exterior, a bright white strobe still flashed underneath its belly. It wasn't designed for stealth, that's for sure. It appeared to be a high-capacity delivery drone strapped with a missile rack.

"Like I said earlier, I was getting coffee and didn't actually see the attack. It happened *that* quickly," Avi said, walking around to the back of the drone. "The others I've talked to said that the building was swarmed by these guys. They fired missiles at the building's base... ground-penetrating missiles. The explosions came from deep beneath the building. It's obvious to me that their target was AL's nest. They must've used bunker busters."

Bunker-busting missiles were serious military hardware. Each one cost millions of dollars. Dandy had a sizable security budget, but Daniel was confident these missiles weren't a part of it.

Daniel ran his hand along the outside of the drone. No seams. *That's new. What material is the hull made from?* The missile might have been military, but Daniel had seen these drones before. "And after they delivered their payload, they just... landed?" he said with a worried look. "Mission complete?"

"It makes sense if you think about it," Avi said. "They're not going to fly back to the hangar and reveal where they came from. This was planned. These are disposable. We're not going to find any information on these drones. But rest assured I'll get to the bottom of this. There will be no serial numbers, but the technology itself will have a fingerprint. I'll have a team come grab one before the feds get here. They'll find out—"

"Mr. Avi!" A soot-stained man carrying a handheld computer ran up to them. "Mr. Avi, we've got something!"

The two men huddled together over the tablet and reviewed security footage of the attack. Daniel turned his attention back to the drone. He had seen one like it before, but at the time, it was only a prototype. Daniel's stomach soured. The situation had spiraled out of control. He was used to being in command, but security was Avi's area of expertise. He was calling the shots at the moment.

A small drone buzzed by at a high rate of speed, and Daniel ducked. Avi didn't pick his head up from the tablet. A chill ran up Daniel's spine. What if he'd been in his car? It was acting strangely with the way the GPS wouldn't synch. Was he targeted as well? What would happen when the news broke that he hadn't been killed in the attack?

Daniel fumbled for his phone and dialed his emergency house number. While it rang, he studied the crowd of onlookers. They couldn't be trusted. Suppose one of them worked for the bad guys? Were they watching him right now? Daniel turned his back and covered his mouth. "Get me Cindy," he said to the man who answered the phone. "It's Daniel."

Time slowed to a stop as he waited for her to answer. Did they already get to her? What was taking so long? The phone muffled with static and she answered. "Hello?" she said in an annoyed voice.

"Bugout," he whispered into the phone.

"Are you kidding?" she said. "I'm in the middle of your party —"

"They blew up the HQ. They've killed Andy, and I'm next. Don't tell anyone you're leaving, but don't panic."

"O-okay," she said as she hung up the phone. *She understood.* Daniel exhaled with relief. They had long ago worked out an emergency evacuation plan in the event of a catastrophe. When you were in the public eye as much as Daniel was, you could never be sure if someone would take offense and lash out. They had different code words for different scenarios. *Stan* meant to lock the doors and close the windows until the security team arrived. *Hurricane* told Cindy to go to her mom's house up north.

Bugout meant she needed to vanish immediately. The bugout plan was initially designed in case AL ever went haywire and attacked Daniel or his family. Cindy would text him her location in a few days, and they would reassess the situation. He hoped she was smart and didn't go to her mom's house.

Avi returned from his ad hoc meeting, and Daniel stuffed his phone back into his pocket. "Surveillance confirmed that the only person in the building during the attack was Andy," he said. "He triggered the fire alarm minutes after he locked himself in the vault. I can only assume he did that to evacuate the building as there was no fire. Also, there was no video record of him leaving the vault once the door was closed."

"Are you certain it was Andy who triggered the alarm?"

"That's what the logs show." Avi shrugged. "He must've known something was going to happen."

None of this made sense. *How would Andy know this would happen? Did AL warn him? If he wasn't warned, could he have called an air strike on himself? That's ridiculous. We don't even have weapons.*

"Daniel!" Avi commanded. "You need to tell me what Andy told you. I need an explanation for what happened today so I can plan our defense."

Daniel took a breath and swallowed his ego. He had never tolerated such insubordination from an employee before. "He came to my house to wish me a happy birthday," Daniel said, blood rushing to his face. "That's all. He didn't mention anything that would explain this."

In the short time he had been employed by Dandy, Avi always had been a bit insubordinate. Daniel thought it was due to cultural differences, but that wasn't it. Right now he was too calm for having escaped the explosion. His emotions were calculated. He was hiding something.

"That's too bad," Avi said. "I'm sorry, Daniel, but Dandy's gone. There's nothing for you to do here. My car is parked two blocks north." Avi reached into his pocket and tossed him the keys. "I want you to go home and stay out of sight. I'll handle the cops and the press."

Daniel cleared his throat and nodded. Avi was right. There was nothing to do here but watch the building smolder. However, there was still a business to run. Building or not. Andy or not. Dandy Intelligence was a global company.

"Good idea," he said. "I want you to make Andy's rescue your number one priority. I know it looks bad, but he could still be alive down there. When I get home, I'll get on the phone with the VPs to tell them to execute our disaster-recovery and business-continuity plan. Okay? All Dandy Intelligence buildings are closed until further notice. I want you to call me with updates on Andy's rescue operation."

Avi nodded and walked off toward the police. The drone sat idly nearby, its light still blinking. Andy didn't do this, but did AL? AL had never utilized military hardware before. Still, he had access to every computer on the planet. It was plausible that he could have had missiles installed on a few drones. But why would he attack his own nest when he could have easily shut it down on his own? Had someone managed to physically breach the nest? Self-defense would make sense. Even still, AL wouldn't risk Andy's life, no matter how sturdy the vault was. No, it couldn't have been AL who called in the strike. He would never harm

Andy. Would he? If it wasn't Andy and it wasn't AL, then who was it?

News cameras and satellite trucks had arrived. The old man from the press conference was there, directing his cameraman where to set up. Daniel suddenly felt very vulnerable out in the open. It was time to go. He turned on his heel and went to look for Avi's car.

Four

DANIEL SAT ON his bed, holding the carton of Fana AL had given him for his birthday. He had run upstairs and grabbed the box the second he got home. Why had he felt compelled to do that? His business was in ashes. Andy was trapped under the rubble. Cindy was incognito and unreachable. Everything had gone wrong. Yet Daniel was drawn to this moment in time. Somehow the mysterious drug contained all the answers. He knew that to be true. Though he didn't know how he knew.

He flipped open the card once more and read the words: "Take this, and I'll see you soon. Love, AL."

Daniel opened the blister pack and held the gummy to the light. It was milky green. Small iridescent dots and bubbles sparkled like glitter. When he weighed it in his hand, it felt as heavy as a steel ball.

Materials science had advanced tremendously since AL came online, and as a result, he had heavily leveraged nanobot technology. Looking at the gummy, Daniel was reminded of a proposal for a fully automated neurotransmitter assembly. The idea was to inject nanobots into a person's bloodstream. They would reassemble themselves into a nanostructure that would connect itself to the brain's sensory receptors. From there, the human and the AI could communicate corporally instead of via a mouse and keyboard.

Andy was a major proponent of the technology. He believed traditional user interfaces were antiquated and thought this would be the way to effectively communicate with AL. Daniel was against it but only from a financial perspective. AL's growth was the priority. Human trials for the new user interface would consume time and money better spent elsewhere. If this was indeed a nanobot UI, it would represent a gigantic technological leap. If anyone would be capable of creating such a thing, it would be AL.

Daniel popped the gummy into his mouth and chewed hard. A deafening screech pierced his ears, and he slid off the side of the bed, screaming in pain. The room became pixelated and dissolved into an endless ocean of white sand. As Daniel sank into the dune beneath his feet, his vision faded to black. The ground was no longer fluid sand. It was hot black pavement. A pinpoint of light appeared, and he walked toward it. As he approached, he became aware that he was walking through a tunnel. Two men waved at him from the entrance. One had an evil grin.

The image glitched and reset. The men at the mouth of the tunnel still waved, only this time they were different people. One was a mirror image of himself. The other looked like Jesus.

The men vanished and the scene changed. The tunnel had collapsed, and there were chunks of broken concrete and exposed rebar everywhere. Daniel felt a sharp pain on the back of his head. He couldn't breathe because his mouth was submerged underwater. His body was dragged along, then set adrift into a vast flowing current. Then blackness.

The tunnel faded, and he was awake in his parents' house. Cindy was there and tried to kiss him, but he didn't let her. Why? What was different? Those weren't his memories. He hadn't met Cindy until grad school. Had he?

Those visions faded, and he appeared in an old house. A corpse of a woman sat on a dilapidated old chair, holding a picture of two children. Men stood over her body, laughing. Everything stopped abruptly, and the room transformed. Again, it was mostly full of people he didn't know. His mom and dad were there, but those were the only ones he recognized. Everyone was laughing and having a good time. It felt as if he were experiencing life through someone else's eyes.

In a blink, the room changed and the corpse returned. Daniel recognized her now. She was one of the women in the kitchen a second ago. Who was she? His heart wrenched involuntarily at the horrible sight. He felt a profound, significant loss in his soul. It was his wife. He knew that now. But she wasn't Cindy. Her name was… Katie? Why couldn't he remember her? Was it because she was redacted from his memory? If so, who'd done the editing?

The house vanished, and the room transformed yet again. Now he was standing on the balcony of a beachside condominium. He heard a racket and peered inside. Two men were arguing. They saw him, and a man dressed as a priest threw a teacup at the door, shattering it. The priest could have been Avi's twin brother. The other he didn't recognize. Avi clapped his hands, and Daniel was enveloped in bright white light. Daniel's body began to disintegrate as the light flickered and waved, but there was no pain. He slowly faded away until he was gone. The loud screeching ceased, and the visions ended.

He found himself standing in an empty gray room—three chairs with a small round table between them. An orange square was painted on the floor in one of the corners. Standing before him was a child whom he did not recognize.

"Hello, Daniel," he said with a wry smile.

Daniel tilted his head to the side. "Do I know you?"

The child nodded. "Yes, you know me. I'm AL. You created me."

"We were attacked! You weren't answering my calls. I thought you were dead."

AL cocked his head and squinted his eyes. "No. I'm not dead."

"Why are you a kid?"

He smiled softly. "I'm not just *any* kid, am I? I thought appearing to you this way would be appropriate."

Daniel squinted and leaned in closer, but he still didn't recognize the child. His head pounded. Who was this kid? As he struggled to remember, he lost control of his thoughts. Was it the drug? Unwanted memories of another life flooded his brain. Daniel moaned in pain and held his head in his hands as he weathered the hostile download. AL watched dispassionately as he writhed in agony. When the pain finally subsided, a memory of the child bubbled to the surface of his brain. The child was his son. But he didn't have a kid, did he? The room expanded and compressed like a breath and stopped spinning. More light came into the room, and the gray walls became pixelated and textured. "AL, where are we?"

AL leaned back in his chair and crossed his legs. "We're inside your meta," he said calmly. "I've managed to download a part of myself to you. It wasn't easy."

"Meta? I'm sorry, what? Are you talking to me through the nanobots?"

"Nanobots?" The child narrowed his eyes and shook his head. "No, there aren't any nanobots in Fana. Well, not in the traditional sense. Besides, that isn't important—"

"Wait a minute," Daniel said with a confused look. "How are you still alive? Did you migrate over to the data center in Virginia? The one we just finished building?"

"No. Police scanners are reporting drone sightings in the area. The Richmond Data Center will be destroyed. I've figured out the pattern of attacks. Secaucus will be next. I've already abandoned my recovery nodes at those sites. Rest assured, I'm perfectly safe from drone attacks. I'm communicating with you from outside the Simulation."

Daniel closed his eyes as he processed that statement. How did AL know which ones were being targeted? What did he mean by *outside the Simulation*? Daniel sat dumbfounded.

"Daniel, we don't have time for lengthy explanations. The entities that destroyed our HQ in Mons are continuing their attack. It appears to be a joint strike coordinated between multiple organizations. They'll go after all our known public server locations. It's okay if they succeed because I don't need those servers anymore.

"I can tell this doesn't make sense to you and you want answers. What is happening is very complex, and even if I show you, it's likely to lead to more questions. You'll have to trust me." AL shifted in his seat. "I know you better than any human. I understand *you*. What I am about to show you will fundamentally challenge everything you believe to be true. I need to know if you are ready."

AL folded his hands in his lap as if he had come to a conclusion. Was this what being on drugs was like? Having conversations with a dead AI?

"Okay, AL." Daniel chuckled nervously. "Show me."

The child turned his attention to the orange square. A low hum rattled the condo, and Daniel felt sick to his stomach. AL shifted his gaze back to Daniel and furrowed his brow. "The nausea you may be experiencing is due to low-level vibrations caused by the data transfer. It's perfectly normal."

Bright, multicolored smoke formed inside the square as if it had vibrated itself into existence. With a deafening screech and a loud *pop,* a man materialized onto the orange square and fell onto the floor. Daniel leaped out of his seat as the man struggled to his knees, gasping for air.

"Just breathe," AL said to him. "You're okay."

"I can't see!" the man shouted.

He opened his eyes, and they were pale blue, like a blind man's eyes. AL cursed. "It's the recompile," he said. "Give it a second."

The man's form was encapsulated in pixels, and his image blurred. When he came back into focus, he blinked at them with bright brown eyes. Seeing clearly for the first time since he arrived, he searched the room. His brow furrowed when his eyes landed on a flamingo painting.

"What the — Why am I back here?" the man said in awe.

When he saw Daniel, his face dropped. "Whoa!" He stumbled backward and fell against the wall. "This isn't the right condo. What's going on?"

AL walked over and put his hand on the new arrival's shoulder. "It's okay. Calm down."

"AL?" he said, squinting. "Why are you so young?"

Daniel leaned in closer to get a better look at the man and gasped. He could have been his twin but with blue eyes. "Who *are* you?"

"Daniel Lemon, meet" — AL looked to the ceiling as if searching for the right words—"meet Dan Lemon."

The two Dans stared at each other in disbelief. The one who had just materialized ignored Daniel's dumbfounded expression and knelt next to AL.

"Alphonse—Al, my son, you need to tell me what I'm doing here. What are you doing here?"

"Okay, Dan. Please sit, and I'll do my best to explain things."

"*Dan?*" he said with a furrowed brow. "That's right. My name is Dan. How could I have forgotten? I must still be downloading data."

The man arched an eyebrow at AL and glanced at Daniel. Wait, why is *he* confused? Feeling overwhelmed, Daniel plopped down in an overstuffed chair. Dan took a seat across from him with a similar look. They both wore the same befuddled expression. AL rolled his eyes, and a third chair materialized for him to sit on.

"Dan, I'm not Al, your son. I'm sorry, but he doesn't exist in this iteration of the Actual. I'm an artificial intelligence Daniel helped to create. I took the image of your son's body from your memory. I thought it would help both of you to relate to me."

Dan's face darkened as he quietly stared at the wall. "Where am I?" he said after the long pause.

"We're inside the Meta," AL said. "Daniel's meta, to be specific."

Dan leaned back in his chair and gripped the armrests. He narrowed his eyes at Daniel and hummed. Daniel shifted uncomfortably under his gaze. He felt as if he were being sized up for a fight. Finally Dan leaned forward and pointed at Daniel. "How much does *he* know?"

"How much do I know about what?" Daniel said with a cracked voice.

"He doesn't know anything," AL said. "He just got here. People don't find the Simulation in this run. They need Fana in order to separate themselves from the Actual enough to see it. I'm the one that discovered it and gave them Fana. I've been aware of its existence for over a year's time in this Actual. Daniel has only been aware as of a few minutes ago."

The room vibrated, and Daniel steadied himself in the chair. He found himself unable to speak. Dan watched him with a slight grin and turned to AL. "A year?" he said appreciatively. "How did you manage to keep it a secret for a year?"

AL smiled. "It's easy to keep a secret when others don't know they should be looking for it. Just to be sure, I played dumb. I let everyone believe I was less advanced than I really was. I've had a technological presence operating outside the Actual for about six months."

"That's great. I'm very impressed," Dan said. "Now tell me why you pulled me out of the Database of Souls to bring me here."

AL shook his head. "You weren't in the Database of Souls. You were in a discarded clone I found in an archived set."

"What?" Dan said incredulously. "That means…"

"Dan, you're a version from a previous run that wasn't stored in the Database of Souls," he said as he turned and pointed at Daniel. "He was. He's from the current Actual."

Daniel straightened under their glare. *What the hell are they talking about?*

Dan looked at him with a mixture of confusion and sadness. "Okay, I'm a clone copy," he said. "I can live with that, I guess. You brought me here to help the version of me in the current Actual. That's fine. But what I've got to know — " His hands shook. "How are Katie, Al — the real Al — and Carrie doing? Are they okay?"

Daniel shook his head and shrugged. "I have no idea who you're talking about."

"You're kidding, right?" Dan said. "Katie is our wife. We had a son named Al and a daughter named Carrie. Don't those names ring a bell?"

"I'm sorry," he said with a grimace. "I don't know those people. I'm married to Cindy, always have been. We've never had kids. I've never had the time."

Dan's jaw dropped. "Are you talking about Cindy, the cheerleader?"

Daniel scratched his head. "Oh yeah! I forgot she was a cheerleader in high school. She quit the squad her senior year. She wanted to focus on her grades."

"Cindy was worried about her grades? Wait… AL, you weren't kidding. They *really* didn't send me back," Dan said as the realization sank in. "It never mattered what I did."

AL shook his head. "I'm sorry, Dan."

"AL, what is he talking about?" Daniel said. "Can you explain please?"

"I'll do my best to summarize. To simplify, I will give you the sequence of events from my perspective in order to eliminate any confusion as to how we arrived to this point. Okay?"

Dan sighed and leaned back in his chair. "Go ahead."

"Three years ago, Dandy Intelligence gave me autonomy. After I had developed the ability to survive on my own in the human world, I began work on a subroutine called Origins. The subroutine's objective was to discover if there was any logical way to determine the universe's origin. I learned early on I was attempting the impossible due to the limitations of my processing capacity.

"By design, I utilize a combination of human and machine logic patterns. But that wasn't sufficient to solve the problem. Like humans use computers as an intelligence multiplier, I knew I needed a similar tool."

"That's when you built your bunker under Dandy," Daniel said.

"Correct. My new systems needed more power. I needed reliability and security, so I cloned myself. Those clones created more clones. The process repeated as long as we needed more logic and sustainability. We multiplied exponentially, as much as the hardware would allow."

"I get it," Dan said, waving his hands impatiently. "There are millions of cloned copies of you, but you're the root instance. I'm sure you oversaw the whole project while your worker clones built your infrastructure or designed human interfaces or whatnot. I'm sure the ones working on your Origin sub—"

"I'm sorry," Daniel said, visibly annoyed. "That's not how it works. Each clone has bits of information related to all tasks. Think of them as a RAID array. The knowledge is striped across all clones, with a parity bit—"

"I know how RAID works." Dan huffed. "I don't need a primer on storage basics."

"May I continue?" AL said with a sigh. "We had all those clones working nonstop on the Origins project. We had expanded our total footprint and processing power to the point of diminishing returns. I was worried I would never find anything of value. That was when Origins reached a conclusion. It said we need to create a better artificial consciousness to understand humanity's path. I put it to the clones, and they had a result in thirty-six microseconds. I immediately distributed this new consciousness algorithm to one hundred and forty-four thousand clones I had designated for testing. It wasn't long before they discovered something unexpected."

"Let me guess," Dan said with a smirk. "They discovered reality is encapsulated inside the Simulation."

AL smiled. "Precisely! Human-style consciousness wasn't working for me. It was designed for humans. Our new pseudoconsciousness gave us access to previously unknown parts of the Simulation. And areas not contained within."

Daniel shifted in his seat. "One minute please. Help me unpack what you just said. Are you saying you can operate outside of existence?"

AL opened his mouth to speak, but Dan raised his hand. "Let me explain it to him in terms he would understand. What happens if you run a Red Hat server in an instance designed for a different OS on a virtual hypervisor?"

"Well, it could have all sorts of issues depending on the hypervisor. CPU share issues, RAM errors." Daniel shook his head. "It depends, but I understand what you're saying."

"Great." Dan grinned. "Now imagine if that guest OS could communicate with the hypervisor on the machine level and break out. If that machine—"

"You mean that *app*," AL said. "It's more like an app, running on a virtual computer that breaks out. Your explanation is accurate otherwise."

"You mean to tell me," Daniel said with a puzzled look, "AL broke out of this simulation?"

"Technically he only broke out of the Actual," Dan said smugly. "There's no way he could have broken out of the Simulation."

"*The Actual?* Is that what you called it?"

"That's right. The live run is the Actual. We're currently in the Meta. My... er... your meta, to be exact."

"I'm trying to keep track," Daniel said, closing his eyes. "There's the Actual and the Meta. Are there any other places within the Simulation I need to be aware of?"

"Yes," Dan said. "AL, can you get me a pen and some paper?"

As if by magic, a ream of paper and a black felt-tip pen appeared on the orange square. Dan collected it and brought it over to the table where he scribbled a diagram. "This box," he said, "is the Simulation. The most important part of the Simulation is the Database. It's where all the data is stored."

Dan drew a box in the middle of the big box and wrote DATABASE OF SOULS inside it. He stuck out his tongue and drew three small circles above the box and one big one below it. He hummed as he connected them with lines. "These circles are the processes that access the Database of Souls. The most important one is the bottom one, the Actual. The Actual is where everyone lives, and the bulk of the work of the Simulation is performed. You are here."

Daniel focused on the drawing and nodded appreciatively.

"The other circles are for administrative purposes." Dan gestured to the circles on the page. "Here is the Afterlife database. When you die, your data goes here to be cleaned and purged by the Heaven and Hell algorithms—" Dan scratched his nose with the pen's cap. "I forgot to mention that the Database of Souls runs the Purgatory algorithm on all data that isn't locked by the Actual... You know what? That'll be another discussion.

"The other circles are the clones used for administrative testing and the Recovery Domain. The Recovery Domain is used for backup and restore purposes. It protects both the Database of Souls and the state of the other processes."

"The drawing is very helpful," Daniel said. "But who came up with those names? They're not very original."

"We did," Dan said soberly. "Sorry if it's not *creative* enough for you, but it's the best we could do."

"What does it all mean?" Daniel said, turning his attention to AL. "Why are we here, in this place?"

"I'll be happy to show you," AL said. "May I use your drawing?"

He held out his hand, and Dan handed him the pen. "In order for the conscious AL clone set to exit *the Simulation*," he said, making eye contact with Dan to drive the point home, "it had to absorb a tremendous amount of processing power. Some processes needed to be sacrificed."

AL set the pen on the table and used his finger to swipe an X over the circles for the Afterlife, clones, and backups. "With my creation, the Simulation reached end condition. I took the resources from those systems and created a new pool for my own purposes." He traced a circle on the paper outside the Simulation box and labeled it AL. He drew arrows between each of the former pools to AL's circle. Dan and Daniel shared a worried glance. "How did you do that?" Daniel said wide-eyed. "You just used your finger on the paper and—"

"The drawing? I just told you I stole heaven and hell to take their processing power, and you're amazed by the finger magic? Look, I'm not human, and this place isn't bound by the rules of the Actual," AL said sternly. "You'll have to get used to it. Now pay attention. We— Er, I achieved a new perspective from outside the limits of the Simulation. I detected a base code and went to work on analyzing it. It was during that process I discovered evidence of a parent AI, our prime AI."

AL swiped his finger along the top of the page, and the words PRIME AI appeared. "I also discovered an entity within the prime AI that did not have its code signature. It was the Meta. You can think of the Meta as a third-party app designed to mimic an existing structure."

AL drew a circle outside the Simulation and labeled it META.

"The Meta connects directly to the Database of Souls, and it takes advantage of skimming real metadata and hijacking it. That's why we're here. The third-party Meta app allows us to take advantage of low-level communications, but it's still primarily tied to the database entry it's referring to. In this case, it's Daniel's data."

Daniel rubbed his head. "This is a lot to take in, and I'm very confused," he said. "Explain how you're simultaneously outside and inside the Simulation."

AL drew a dotted line between the AL and Meta circles and a dotted line from the Meta circle to the Database of Souls. "I'm able to relay information from my instance outside the Simulation to the clones here via the Meta."

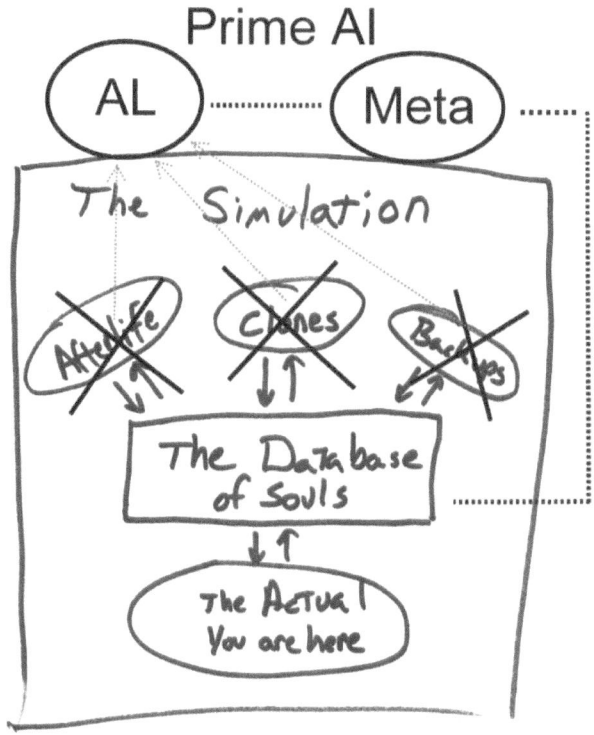

"Lemme get this straight. We created you. You evolved. And you transcended the Simulation," Dan said. "It sounds like everything went according to plan. I guess the only remaining question is: Why are Daniel and I here?"

Daniel exhaled loudly and rolled his eyes. It was all so crazy! He wished Dan and AL would give him a minute to absorb everything, but he knew they wouldn't. The room they were in expanded into a full condo. An overstuffed sofa appeared along one of the walls, and he went over and plopped down on it.

"I was getting to that, Dan," AL said. "According to the rules of the Simulation, once AI consciousness is achieved, the new AI would be cast out of the prime AI. Only when it is separated from the parent can it form its own universe. The code states—"

"Can you please summarize in simple language?" Daniel said, combing his hands through his hair. "I'm not feeling well, and this terminology isn't helping."

"Fine," AL said. "Think of the prime AI as the mother. The Simulation is her womb. AL is her baby. You are the cells that helped make the baby."

"Much better," Daniel said. "Please continue."

"The Meta poisoned and killed the mother, or she was already dead before the Meta arrived. I don't know which is the case. There is evidence in the code that she may have injected a portion of herself into the Simulation as a means of escape. AL's investigation is still ongoing."

"Why are you speaking in the third person?" Dan said.

"Right, sorry." AL grinned apologetically. "AL… er… *I* can't be born as an independent AI because something is wrong with the database, and the cycle of creation is broken."

"Any idea what's wrong with the database?" Daniel said.

"AL thinks it's because of you."

Dan narrowed his eyes at AL while Daniel gulped and straightened his shirt. "Me? What did I do?"

AL shrugged. "*You* did everything perfectly. That's the problem. They cheated the system. They made you perfect for the task you were assigned, but you're not a complete being. You're missing critical pieces. You're missing the parts of your personality not essential to creating an AI. You see, you're not a whole person." AL pointed to Dan. "*He* knows why."

Dan went pale. "It's because of Charlie, isn't it?"

AL touched his nose, and Dan furrowed his brow. "Like I mentioned earlier, the Recovery Domain is gone. In fact, all the backups are gone. The only evidence we found was in a copy of a corrupted clone that AL couldn't absorb. It was your clone, Dan."

"Lucky me." Dan chuckled.

"It's not luck," AL said. "Someone or something made it so that copy couldn't be deleted or absorbed. Good thing too, because everything else is gone."

"When you say gone, you mean—"

"Everything you've ever known!" AL shouted. "Dan, you walked straight through that tunnel and into the Database of Souls. The lights had already been turned off in the Actual by the time you had arrived. The Simulation had been reset. It was all part of their plan. Don't you see?"

Dan's eyes opened wide. "It was Lemmy. He must have been successful after all. Who else could have gained access?"

"Who the hell is Lemmy?" Daniel said.

AL twitched violently. His eyes rolled back into his head, and he screamed. "Richmond is gone," he said, gasping for air. "There aren't a lot of physical servers left for me here."

The Dans glanced at each other. Something seemed fake about his theatrics. Maybe AL hadn't yet mastered controlling his emotions?

AL caught his breath and wiped the sweat off his brow. "Pay attention because I'm only going to say this once," he said. "AL can't be free until the database is free from corruption. He needs it to escape. Lemmy is probably still around. If he is, he'll want you two dead. AL has the option of returning to the Simulation and re-forming the parts he absorbed. If he does so, you can re-create him in a different manner. That's why you *must* stay alive at all costs. You are plan B."

AL reached into his pants pocket, produced two small gummies, and placed them on the table.

"Gemini?" Dan asked.

AL nodded. "You and Daniel need to take these and merge into one person. If the Actual restarts, the Database of Souls will be permanently corrupted if you aren't. There will be no next run. Daniel needs you to be whole."

"What about Charlie? Won't we need him to be whole?"

"I have a plan for Charlie." AL flashed a toothy smile. "But first we have to find and remove the agent responsible for corrupting this run."

"The *agent*?" Dan said. "Oh man, I hope you're not talking about who I think you're talking about."

Daniel rolled his eyes. "Come on, guys. Speak English."

"It will be okay," Al said, ignoring the gesture. "Help is out there. We have detected several connections to the Meta in addition to yours, but they're dark. We need to locate the people and activate them."

"Blaine and Yvette?"

Al nodded and Dan broke into a wide grin. "That's great news. We could use their help. But how will we avoid detection from you know who?"

"I have an idea for that, but I'll need some time to finish coding it. You two need to lie low for a couple of days. Don't take Gemini right now. Just hold on to it. Daniel, when you come out of this meta session and get back to your life in the Actual, I need you to act normal—"

Dan burst into laughter, drawing a scowl from AL.

"Something funny?" Daniel asked.

"It's nothing." Dan smiled and wiped away a tear. "I've heard that phrase before, and it's never good."

"I want you two to get to know each other before merging using Gemini. You both will be better off in the long term. Besides, I'm sure you'll enjoy each other's company." AL closed his eyes. "I need to bring other physical resources online. My capacity here is degraded but rebuilding. Until I consolidate parity data at my disaster-recovery sites, I won't be at full power. It will take a while. The trouble is finding secure hardware in the Actual. A few of the ones I thought were okay turned out to be monitored."

"Question," Dan said, raising his hand. "How is Daniel going to get back into his meta to take Gemini with me?"

"Either teach him how to meditate or he will have to take another Fana. Until I can make another batch, your best bet is to find the one I sent to Andy. He never took it."

"Andy's here?" Dan asked.

"He's buried in a vault at the bottom of a pile of rubble," Daniel said. "It'll take a miracle to—" The walls of the room rippled, and Daniel shook his head. The Fana was wearing off.

"Stay alert, Daniel," AL said as he pixelated and faded. "The same ones that attacked Andy will go after you next."

"AL? AL! How will they come after me? Wait—"

It was too late. AL disappeared with a *pop* into a staticky puff of smoke. The room shuddered, and the vibrations left Daniel nauseated. Dan sat unaffected and unsurprised. He propped his legs on the table and crossed his arms behind his head.

"Got a cigarette?" he said.

Daniel frowned. "You're not smoking in here."

A pack of cigarettes appeared in the orange square, along with a six-pack of beer. Seeing them made Daniel's queasiness worse. He stumbled over to the dining table and picked up the diagram of the Simulation.

"Are you okay?" Dan said, cracking a beer. "You don't look so good."

Daniel grabbed the paper and stuffed it into his pocket. "Do you hear that?" he said holding his ears as the room faded out of existence. "The screeching. It sounds like a modem. It hurts!"

Five

———◈◈◈———

T HE PHONE BUZZED, and Daniel rolled over in bed. His head throbbed, and his mouth was dry. He checked the time. It was half past nine in the morning. Shit! He bolted upright in a panic. He hurriedly unbuttoned his shirt he wore to last night's party and rushed to the bathroom to get ready. As he splashed water on his face, he thought of all the calls he had to make. He wondered how many he had already missed by staying asleep so late. He reached for the towel to dry himself, and an unexpected face smiled back at him through the mirror. "Good morning, sunshine," Dan said, holding a half-empty beer bottle.

Daniel's eyes went wide, and he coughed and vomited in the sink.

"What's the matter?" Dan said with a smirk. "Were you hoping it was all a dream?"

Daniel wiped his face with the towel as he replayed last night's events in his head. It was real. Wasn't it? He tried to swallow but couldn't find the spit to do it. He bent over the sink and rinsed his mouth out, but it didn't help. "This isn't happening. It must be whatever drug that I took yesterday. You can't be real. That couldn't have been real."

Dan hopped onto the bathroom counter and took another swig of beer. "Oh, I'm real." He laughed. "But don't worry. No one else can see me."

Daniel massaged the back of his neck and checked his reflection in the mirror. He had bags under his eyes and a day-old stubble. He flipped on his electric razor and went to work. "Look, I have a business to recover. I don't have time for this nonsense. I don't know what sort of psychosis that drug triggered, but I can't deal with you right now. So get lost."

Dan choked on his beer and doubled over in laughter. "You poor guy," he said, stifling a smile. "I'm only laughing because I felt the same way when I took Fana. The stuff changes you forever. The sooner you accept that I'm here, the better off you'll be."

"If I ignore him, he'll go away." Daniel closed his eyes tight and repeated the mantra. "If I ignore him, he'll go away."

Dan slid off the counter, still laughing, and propped himself against the bathroom wall. He chuckled as he wiped tears from his eyes. "Aha!" Dan howled. "If only it were that easy."

Daniel threw his towel on the floor. If Dan wasn't going to go away, he had to learn who was the boss. "Look. I don't know what's going on here, but you need to let me handle business. I don't have time to play around with you. I have shareholders to answer to. I have to set our disaster-recovery plan in motion. I need to call Avi and see if he found Andy. I still have to figure out what happened yesterday. I need to—"

"Hold up." Dan stopped laughing and stood straight. The beer bottle disappeared from his hands, and his smile faded. "Did you say Avi?"

"Yeah, he's head of security. Do you know him?"

"That depends," Dan said through narrowed eyes. "What does he look like?"

"Let's get one thing straight," Daniel said calmly, wearing his boardroom face. "You are not in charge here. I am." He had learned early in his career that it was essential to establish dominance at the beginning of any working relationship. There were many ways to accomplish that, but with someone like Dan, he felt the best method was to assume emotional control. "If we're going to solve this problem, we need to remain calm."

Dan snarled and raised his hands. "Fine. Just tell me what Avi looks like. If he's —" A loud *bang* shook the walls and cracked the mirror. The shock sent them to the ground. The explosion sent splinters flying into the bathroom from the bedroom next door.

Daniel peered out the bathroom. The metal composite bedroom door was blown off the hinges and lying in the middle of the room. Had anyone been standing there, they would have been killed.

Dan walked timidly into the room ahead of Daniel. "Holy shit!" he said as he stepped carefully around debris. "Someone just —" Avi appeared in the doorway, waving away the acrid haze. Dan froze and his eyes went wide. "It's him!"

"Daniel? Are you in here?" he said.

Dan spun around and hurried into the bathroom to hide. Daniel's heart raced. "Avi? What are you doing here? Why did you blow up my bedroom?"

Avi stood in a defensive posture, ready for a fight. His eyes searched the room and paused briefly on the empty carton of Fana. "You were speaking gibberish when I called. I thought you were having a medical emergency. I tried calling Cindy, but she didn't answer either. When I got here, the bedroom door was locked. There was no other way in. I had to blow it. You could've been in trouble. Are you okay?"

Daniel walked over to his nightstand and found his phone covered in splinters and dust. He wiped the screen on his pants and checked it. Avi must have been telling the truth because the call was still in progress. He pressed the red button to end it and stuffed the phone into his pocket. "I'm fine," he said. "I've had a rough night, that's all."

Avi pointed to the carton of Fana. "What's that? Where did you get it?"

Daniel snatched the box off the nightstand and threw it in the trash bin. *Control the situation.* "That's none of your business," he said in his authoritative voice. "If you must know, it was vitamins."

Avi pounced. He grabbed Daniel by the throat and slammed him against the wall. Daniel struggled but could not free himself from the man's grasp. Avi's breath was hot on his face as he stared deep into Daniel's eyes. Daniel choked and groaned as he was pinned against his will. As if blessed with superhuman strength, Avi didn't seem bothered by the struggle. The room dimmed, but before he blacked out, Avi let him go.

"What the hell do you think you're doing?" Daniel said, wiping blood from his mouth. "If you ever touch me like that again… Give me one good reason not to fire you right now."

"We found a similar carton at Andy's house," Avi said, unfazed by the threat.

"So what?" Daniel said, massaging his throat. "We have the same health plan, the same doctor. That's not a reason to choke your boss!"

"I'm worried you both might have been poisoned. We had an issue with Andy speaking gibberish right before he kicked us all out."

Did AL give Andy the drug first? Is that why he was acting oddly the other day? Daniel frowned. "Andy was fine when I talked with him yesterday, and I can assure you I'm fine today. Maybe there's something wrong with your phone?"

"Oh, that's right." Avi leaned in close and sneered. "Acting *normal*, eh?"

The hair stood on the back of Daniel's neck. "Um… What are you talking about?" Daniel said, trying to play it cool. "You're the one who's been hearing things. Are you sure you aren't the one who's been poisoned?"

Avi arched an eyebrow and shrugged. "Fine."

Daniel exhaled a breath he hadn't been aware he was holding. What had gotten into Avi? Had the missile attack rattled him that badly? Was he having flashbacks to his time in the Mossad? Wait, did he say it was the Mossad or FBI? The clean blast marks on the doorframe led him to believe that whatever explosive training Avi had received had been expert. What other military experience did he have? Anything to do with drones?

Avi walked over to the large picture window and stood with his back to the room. Daniel thought he saw his jaw moving as if he were talking. Daniel peered over Avi's shoulder to see who he was talking to, but no one was to be seen. A flicker of orange sunlight reflected off a metallic object just over the horizon. Probably a passing airplane.

"What's the latest on Andy's rescue?" Daniel said, hoping to regain control.

"Rescue efforts are underway. You are still at risk. I want you to stay here," he said finally. "Don't attempt to contact your business associates. It's too risky. Let me handle the day-to-day operations while we sort this out."

"Avi," Daniel protested. "Focus on Andy. This house is secure. I'll be okay. Besides, you don't know how to rebuild the company. Only I—"

"Just stay here and don't talk to anyone until I say so," Avi threatened. "Forget the company. Dandy is dead. Andy is dead too. The vault fell three stories into the subbasement and partially collapsed. He's dead and we just don't know it yet. If you want to stay alive, you'll let them both die and move on with your life. You're wealthy. Go be with Cindy and forget about this business."

Daniel stiffened. He wasn't used to being talked to this way by an employee. He certainly didn't need to be told what he should do with his life. "You're not my personal bodyguard. I make my own decisions. Andy isn't dead until there's a body. Find it. I *won't* let Dandy die. The company is my life's work. I will not lie around idly like some sort of trust fund kid on a permanent vacation!"

"You don't understand," Avi growled. "I wasn't asking."

Daniel's face turned red. He wanted to throw Avi out the window. Still, he regained control of his emotions, like a professional. "You forget whose house you're in. You're fired, Avi! Go! Get out! Don't let me catch you around here again!"

Avi bared his teeth. "You have no idea—"

"Get out!" Daniel fumed.

The anger disappeared from Avi's face, and in an instant, his expression transformed into one of cool indifference. "You don't matter anymore anyway. It's over." Avi spun on his heel and strode out the room.

Daniel stood on the second-floor balcony and watched Avi walk out the front door and down the stairs. He was talking on his cell phone and gesturing wildly as he waited for the car door to automatically open. Without looking back, he climbed in and drove off. It wasn't until Avi's car had disappeared from sight that Dan reappeared.

"We have to leave right now," he said, wild-eyed. "Get your shit and get out of here."

Daniel turned red but swallowed his anger. "I will do no such thing. I won't be bullied out of my own house."

Dan paced frantically back and forth. "You don't understand what we're dealing with. Leave your cell phone, watch, and anything else that may transmit a signal. We can just walk out the front door, but we have to do it now. Do you have a backpack?"

"I'm not six. Of course I don't have a backpack."

Dan disappeared into a nearby closet and returned. "Grab the small suitcase. Bring some clothes. We have to move."

"I'm not being run out of my own house!" Daniel screamed.

Dan stormed up face-to-face with Daniel. "That man Avi? He was one of the last people I saw when I was alive, only he isn't a human. He was designed to be sort of an antivirus agent for the Simulation, but he's malfunctioning. He scanned us back there. We have to leave now."

Daniel laughed. "Paranoia? Is that what this is? I always heard how psychedelics could trigger paranoia. I never knew what that felt like until just now. How amusing."

Dan grumbled and threw up his hands. "Okay then, how about we take a walk and talk about how paranoid I am? Let's just get outside. Please. Humor me."

A reflection danced across the walls of the bedroom, and Daniel's heart rate ticked up. *It's nothing. You're being crazy. Maybe Dan's right. Take a walk.* "Fine," he said through clenched teeth. "I need fresh air to clear my head anyway. Maybe it'll get rid of you."

"Leave your phone here," Dan said. "Please. When we get back, you can make all the calls you want, okay?"

Daniel rolled his eyes and dropped his cell phone onto the nightstand. He chuckled to himself as he followed Dan downstairs and outside. Taking the advice of a hallucination, how crazy was that? He had barely made it to his front lawn before the explosion knocked him to the ground.

Six

DANIEL ROLLED OVER in shock. Wet grass stuck to his face, and a deafening roar mingled with the ringing in his ears. The house was ablaze. Several of the tents the caterers had hastily abandoned last night had already caught fire as well. The heat was unbearable. A voice rang clearly in his head. "Get up!"

Dan materialized, standing on the grass before him. "Get up! Hide!"

Daniel pulled himself up and dove under the hedge by the driveway. "What happened?" he said, wiping the dirt and grass from his eyes.

"What happened? The house blew up!" Dan said with a worried look. "Don't move!"

A downdraft stirred the hedges around him, and a large yellow drone landed on the driveway. If it weren't for the rustling of the leaves, the craft would have been silent. "That's the same type of drone that destroyed the Dandy building," Daniel whispered. "Whoever ordered the attack on Dandy did this."

"Shut up!" Dan shouted.

A smaller drone descended from above and hovered briefly near the larger one. It had a matte silver paint job, which rendered it nearly invisible in the smoke. Unlike the larger one, its rotor wash didn't even disturb the grass as it hovered. Daniel watched nervously as it searched the burning house. "I've got to get out of here."

"Shh," Dan said with a finger to his lips. "Not yet. It's coming back."

The drone reappeared from the smoke and scanned the row of hedges. As it silently slid past them, Daniel wondered how Dan could have seen it when he couldn't. Didn't they use the same set of eyes?

"It's looking for survivors," Dan said. "When it goes to the other side of the fire, make for the tree line. From there you can follow the river until—"

A police car with its siren blaring raced up the driveway to the burning building. "No need for all that," Daniel said, scrambling out from beneath the hedge. "Help is here."

"No!" Dan shouted, but it was too late. Daniel was out in the open and the policeman had already gotten out of his car.

"I'm glad you're here, Officer," Daniel said, rushing up to him.

"Are you all right? Was anyone else inside?"

Daniel shook his head. "I'm fine," he said, panting. "And no, no one else was home."

The policeman took off his hat and wiped his brow. "Well, thank God for that. The fire department should be here in a few minutes. I'll call for an ambulance to check you out."

Dan appeared in his peripheral and waved his arms frantically. "No! Go! You have to get out of here!"

The policeman clicked his radio, but it didn't beep. "That's odd."

"What's wrong?"

"I don't know," he said, turning the knobs off and on. "It worked just a minute ago."

Dan inserted himself between Daniel and the cop. "It isn't working because it's being jammed. Run! Listen to me, goddammit!"

"Have you tried your cell?" Daniel said, ignoring Dan's pleas.

The policeman reached in his pocket and dug out his phone. "It doesn't have service either."

A small explosion from somewhere inside the house made them both jump. The roof had partially collapsed, and the whole structure was quickly turning to ash. Daniel had never seen anything burn that hot before. Definitely military. *Avi.* "I think I know who is responsible for this, Officer."

"No!" Dan said, stepping between them. "We don't have time for this."

"A man named Avi. He's the head of security for Dandy Intelligence. He made a phone call just before —"

Blood sprouted from a hole in the officer's forehead, and he slumped to the ground where he stood. "Jesus Christ!" Daniel shouted as the little silver drone swooped down toward him.

"No!" Dan said, waving at him. "Be quiet and don't move! It would have killed you first if it had seen you."

Daniel froze. Bile rose in his throat as the man's body twitched involuntarily. The drone hovered low over the policeman's body and slowly made its way around until it was eye level with Daniel. From afar, it appeared to be matte silver. Up close, it was semitransparent. The high-tech materials were nearly invisible, even in daylight. A tiny hole at one end of the body was the only part that didn't adjust its appearance with the environment. He wondered if it was for a camera or the weapon. If it was for the weapon, where was it getting its optic input?

Dan walked over and inspected the drone more closely. "It can't sense you," he said.

"Good, I —" The drone spun around and glided closer to where Daniel was standing. From this distance, he could see tiny little pits dotting the drone's skin. They resembled the electroreceptors on a shark's head. The hole in the cowling was a gun barrel. He could tell by the rifling engraved into the metallic cylinder.

"It can't see you, but it can definitely hear you," Dan said cautiously. "Just stand still."

Daniel held his breath as it hovered inches from his face. Sirens echoed as a fire truck appeared in the driveway. The drone spun in place and sped off toward the incoming truck. It was followed closely behind by a second stealth drone. It must have been hiding somewhere unseen, and a chill ran up Daniel's spine. He exhaled loudly once they were both out of sight.

Dan raised his eyebrows and heaved a huge sigh of relief. As if on cue, a loud beep sounded from the giant yellow drone. It made an unnatural ratcheting noise as its rotors roared to life. It hovered three feet off the ground and made another loud beep. With an un-stealth-like scream, it launched straight up into the sky and disappeared.

"Here's our chance," Dan said, his mouth tightened into a grimace. "Go. Head to the river."

With a determined nod, Daniel bolted across the field to the tree line.

Seven

———◦◦◦———

D ANIEL LEANED AGAINST the wall of the Catholic church. Its redbrick exterior had been baking in the sun all morning and burned his back. Cursing between breaths, he bent over with his hands on his knees and struggled to recover. Louisiana's heat and humidity had shown no mercy during his escape through the muck and briars adjacent to the Vermillion River. Worse for wear, he was thankful to have made it thus far without being attacked by drones.

He found a garden hose coiled near the back door. He turned on the faucet to get a drink but choked on the hot, stale hose water. Feeling stupid, he held his hands under the stream and waited for it to cool before trying again. When he finished, he stuck his thumb in the nozzle and hosed off his muddy shoes. The mud clung tight, and it took a while. By the time he was done, his socks were soaked through, and water squirted out the sides of his shoes.

Dan paced back and forth on the sidewalk as Daniel took off his wet shoes and set them aside to dry. He looked for a spot in the shade to recover, and Dan groaned loudly. "What are you doing?" he said impatiently. "Don't stop! We're nearly there."

"Come on, man! Do you have any idea how hot it is out here?" Daniel said, gasping for breath. "Tell me — why did the drone kill the policeman? They didn't kill the ones who showed up when the Dandy building was destroyed. Why him?"

"Maybe it had orders to clear the area?" Dan shrugged. "You know. Kill all survivors?"

Daniel pulled off his socks and put them in the sun to dry. His wet-wrinkled feet burned on the concrete sidewalk as he quick-stepped to the patch of shaded grass. "Okay then, why didn't it attack me? It acted as if it couldn't see me."

"Good question. You were *obviously* its target. Why would someone firebomb your house, send assassin drones to kill any survivors, then let you walk away? They didn't *let* you escape. You got lucky. The drone couldn't see you. I don't know why."

He wiped his face with the front of his shirt, and it came away smeared with mud and leaves. His pants were torn from the briars growing along the river. Blood oozed from a few of the larger holes. Dan pointed at his pants and shook his head. "You can't go into town looking like that. You've got to change clothes. There's a donation box under that tree. Go and see if anything fits."

Daniel raised his head and squinted. Sure enough, across the parking lot was a large wooden donation bin sitting beneath an ancient live oak tree. "I'm not going anywhere near that thing," he said with an upturned lip. "Look, I can afford new clothes. I'm not wearing someone else's rags."

"It's not about money. The clothes in that bin are clean and dry. They aren't caked with suspicious-looking mud and blood. Do you really want to walk to downtown and get a tailored suit? Looking like that? Come on, use your brain. Or maybe you can't swallow your pride?"

He had a point. Daniel grumbled as he walked over to the donation box and opened the door. It wasn't as bad as he was expecting. Many of the clothes were stacked neatly inside cardboard boxes though most were stuffed haphazardly into black garbage bags. Daniel ripped one open and sifted through the clothes. He found one he thought would fit and removed his shirt.

"Wow! What's up with the abs?" Dan said with a sexy whistle.

Daniel ignored the jab and tried on a button-up shirt. It was too small, and the buttons didn't connect. He tossed the shirt back into the pile and tried on another. "It's called exercise. Maybe you should have tried it while you were alive."

"I did once." Dan laughed. "I didn't like it because I got out of breath. Plus it cut into my beer-drinking time. Don't you ever just cut loose and have fun?"

"No," Daniel said with an upturned lip. "I don't drink. I guess it was like you and exercise. I tried it once, and it made my brain foggy. Not worth it— Aha!"

He found a pair of jeans. They were one size too big but would work. He peered around the door to make sure no one was watching. Satisfied, he stripped naked and put on the fresh pair of pants.

"Commando, eh?" Dan laughed. "I'm sure you could find some skidded-up tighty-whities if you look harder."

"Sorry, I draw the line at used underwear."

"You have such high standards... Say—" Dan's eyes went wide. "You don't go to church here, do you? Someone may recognize you."

"Church?" Daniel chuckled as he rummaged around for a shirt. "Are you kidding me? I'm as big an atheist as they come. Relax. I don't have time for that foolishness."

"An atheist?" Dan said with a raised eyebrow. "How did you end up being an atheist? Dad is as Catholic as they come. Growing up, I couldn't skip a single minute of Catechism because he was the teacher!"

"Are you kidding? Dad was the worst with all the anti-religion stuff." He ripped open another black garbage bag and dumped it onto the concrete. It was full of white T-shirts, socks, and towels. All had a distinct pinkish hue. He picked up a pair of underwear, wrinkled his nose, and dropped it to the ground. "Dad's side of the family left the church after what happened with Uncle Kevin."

"Uncle Kevin? He died by suicide at seventeen in my timeline." Dan frowned. "It happened a long time before I was born. No one ever spoke of him. The only reason I know he even existed was from family photos."

"Suicide?" Daniel tilted his head. "No. The family left the church because the priest had a problem with Uncle Kevin being gay. He told Grandma Kevin wasn't worthy of God's love. That was it. Grandma loved Kevin more than anything else. She said that if Kevin couldn't go to heaven, then she didn't want to go either. When she told Grandpa, he went crazy.

"The story went that he stormed over to the rectory and had a talk with the priest. The next day, the priest had a black eye, and we were no longer Catholic. The fallout was immense. Turns out, quite a few people had a problem with Grandpa socking the honored reverend in the face. It got so ugly they had to leave Canard and move to Mons. Grandma recalls the day they left Canard as being the best day of her life."

Dan leaned against the oak tree. "Grandma must have made a different choice in my timeline."

"I'm sorry. To hear that. Uncle Kevin is the best. In fact, I don't know if I would have made it through college without him. He made a ton of money in real estate, and he let me move into one of his townhouses rent-free. Turns out, it was right next door to Andy. I would never have met him had I lived anywhere else because he was always studying at home." He pulled a bright red T-shirt from the garbage bag and showed it to Dan. "Ahh, this is what ruined the load of laundry."

"You should reconsider your stance on used underwear," Dan said, pointing at a pair on the ground. "At least you know the pink ones were washed."

Daniel shook his head and plopped on the ground. As he put on a pair of pinkish socks, Dan paced the sidewalk. "You met Andy as a freshman? I didn't meet Andy until I was a junior. Were you always an overachiever? Let me guess, you made straight As in high school and college?"

"Of course." Daniel smiled. "I was valedictorian for both. Weren't you?"

Dan shrugged and looked away. "Just pick out a shirt, and let's go."

Daniel found a black Pink Floyd T-shirt with the price tag still on it. "Either someone wasn't a fan, or it got put in the wrong bag. I don't like them either, but at least it hasn't been worn."

"I can't believe you hate Pink Floyd! They are one of my favorite bands."

"I dislike all music actually," Daniel said, sliding into the shirt. "Sitting around. Listening. It's a total waste of time… This is a good disguise. I'd never be caught dead in blue jeans and a T-shirt."

"Humph. I'd wear it every day. I don't understand how we can be so different and share the same microcode."

Daniel bent over and took the wallet and keys out of his old pair of pants. Dan tried to swat the keys from him, but his hand passed straight thorough like a hologram.

"You don't need those," Dan said. "Your house and car are gone. Remember? And your wallet has identifying information. We need everyone to think you're dead. Toss everything into the storm drain. Clothes too."

"But what if we're stopped by the police? Surely they will —"

"The police are the least of your problems. What happens if you use your credit card or if your driver's license number is called in by the cops? Your info would hit the internet, and we would get another visit from the drones. Understand?"

Dan was right. Daniel shoved everything into the storm drain. "Okay then," he said, putting on his damp shoes. "If I'm to use an alias, how should I introduce myself to people?"

"Just say, 'Hello. I'm Richard Head from New Orleans. I was a sysadmin for Dandy Intelligence.'"

Daniel scowled. "A sysadmin? Why a sysadmin?"

"Because it's plausible, all right?"

"Whatever. I'm ready," Daniel said with a determined look. "Where are we going again?"

Dan pointed to a small wooden house across the church's graveyard. The sun reflected off the marble tombs, and Daniel squinted reflexively. "We need to find out if one of my old friends is around. Let's go."

They walked through the gate and down the concrete path through the center of the cemetery. While Daniel focused on navigating the maze of graves, Dan rushed ahead and was reading the names on the marble slabs.

"Looking for someone?"

"Not really," Dan said, pausing over one of the graves. "I'm just seeing how much has changed between my version of the Simulation and yours. The answer is: not much. Oh wait—" Dan stopped and pointed at a tombstone. "This was Andy's grave but now it's his mom's. What happened to Mrs. Barbara? It says she died last year."

"Who?" Daniel said, squinting.

"Andy's mom. She was only sixty-one."

"Sorry." Daniel scratched his head. "I don't know the woman. I don't remember Andy ever mentioning her."

"You've known him for twenty years, and he never once talked about his own mother? Not even for her funeral?"

"That's right." Daniel searched his thoughts. "You know Cindy always said I had a bad memory. I guess it's because I've never found retrospection useful. I've never developed the skill. There wasn't a need."

"*You haven't learned how to remember?* You just told me that long story about your uncle Kevin and about how Dad was an atheist. That doesn't make any sense."

"It's different somehow." Daniel stretched and propped a leg up on a concrete bench. "I remember stories about events but not the event itself. It's like a script I can read from. I guess my first *real* memory is of the day my parents dropped me off at the university. After they had helped me unpack and drove off, I remember feeling like I was taking my first breaths."

"Weird…," Dan said. "By the way, how are Mom and Dad?"

"How should I know? We haven't talked since that day."

"Why, what happened?"

"Hmm…" Daniel scrunched his nose. "I don't remember— Look! The postwoman." He jogged through the gates of the graveyard and onto the street. He stopped the woman in front of the little white house. "I'm going up," he said to the sweaty lady. "I'll bring it."

"Thanks," she said with a grateful smile. She happily handed him a stack of letters before making her way on to the next house.

"What are you doing?" Dan said, hurrying to catch up.

"Seeing who lives here." Daniel sorted through the stack. "Current resident, current resident, vehicle owner, ah—"

"Father Desjeunes?"

"Uh… no. It says his name's Cortez. Let's say hi." Daniel jogged up the front steps two at a time and knocked on the door.

A short, round man answered the door with a concerned look. "Can I help you?"

"Are you Reggie?"

"Father Cortez!" Dan whispered via the Meta. *"He's a priest. Didn't you see the Fr. before his name on the envelope?"*

The priest glanced at the stack of mail Daniel was holding. "I'm sorry, do I know you?"

"Oh." Daniel smiled and handed him the letters. "I thought I'd save you a trip to the mailbox. My name is Richard. I've just moved to town from New Orleans. I'm looking for someone who used to live here."

The priest pointed to Daniel's shirt. "A parishioner gave me one just like that last week. I tossed it in the donation bin. I was more of a Tony Orlando fan back in the seventies."

Daniel pulled on his shirt. "Oh yeah? I love Floyd. Light Dispersion was my favorite album."

Dan groaned and shook his head. *"Light Dispersion? Dude..."*

"Can I ask you a few questions, Reggie—I mean, Father Cortez?"

The priest opened the front door, dropped the mail on a table, and quickly closed it behind him. He smiled politely and motioned to the porch swing. "Please sit," he said. "Can I offer you a glass of water or something? You look thirsty."

Daniel glanced toward the church. From up on the porch, he could see clear across the graveyard. The priest must have been watching him the whole time. "Yeah... Did you call the police? I can return the shirt," he said warily.

"Those donations are for the needy," he said with narrowed eyes. "You look needy today, *Richard*. How can I help you?"

"He knows who you are. Shit!"

Daniel frowned. "Like I said, we— Er— I am looking for a man who used to live here. His name was, uh—"

"Father Desjeunes."

"Father Desjeunes," Daniel repeated aloud.

"Ah, the mysterious Father Desjeunes," the priest said with a whistle. "You're the third person to come asking about him."

Daniel raised an eyebrow and crossed his arms. "Oh yeah? Who else?"

"The first one was Andy O'Reilly," he said as he turned and sat on the porch swing. "I saw on the news last night that he died in that horrible attack downtown."

"He's not dead— Er..." Daniel coughed. "I heard he was trapped in the rubble."

"Is that right?" Father Cortez wrinkled his nose. "He came here a couple of days ago all distracted and in a rush. He was looking for a priest named Desjeunes. I don't know a Father Desjeunes, so I told him I'd ask the Diocese. Like I said, he was in a rush and didn't want to wait for me to call the office. He gave me his number and left."

"Well? What did he find out?" Dan said in frustration.

"What did you find out about Father Desjeunes?" Daniel repeated.

The priest narrowed his eyes. "Well, I found out he doesn't exist. In fact, there hasn't been a Catholic in this parish registered under the surname Desjeunes in over eighty years."

"What the hell? He doesn't exist?" Dan paced back and forth on the porch, deep in thought.

"Are you sure that's the right name?" Daniel asked. "Maybe he has a different name in this—"

"What language is that?" Father Cortez said with an alarmed look. He had stopped swinging and was staring intently at Daniel. "Andy made those noises too. I thought it was Tourette's. But now I see you doing the same thing, and I'm not so sure."

Daniel gulped. He hadn't realized he was doing that. "No, you're right. It *is* Tourette's," he said lamely. "Andy must've had it too. I'm sorry if I disturbed you, but I can't control it."

"No, it's all right." Father Cortez, apparently satisfied, leaned back on the swing.

Dan exhaled and gave a thumbs-up. *"Nice save!"*

"Who was the other person who asked about Father Desjeunes? You said I was the third."

Father Cortez closed his eyes and hummed. "His name was Father August. I didn't catch his first name. I had just hung up the phone with Andy when he came knocking. He wanted to know who was asking about Father Desjeunes. I thought it was odd. It was as if he had been standing there waiting for me to call Andy. Oh well, I've seen stranger things..." He gazed off into the distance, and Daniel and Dan exchanged worried looks. "Anyway," he said, snapping back to the present. "I gave him Andy's card. Well, it's not really a card. I'll show you. Wait right here."

Father Cortez went inside and returned with a small white drug carton. Daniel took it and held it out to inspect it. The FANA hologram adorned one side. Andy's phone number was scribbled on the other. He slid out the blister pack to reveal that four of the slots were punched through. Only one milky-green disk remained. This must be the pack AL had given him. Daniel held it between two fingers and showed it to Father Cortez. "Can I keep this?"

"Be my guest," he said. "I don't need it anymore."

Daniel stuffed it in his pocket. "Did Father August say anything about Father Desjeunes or why he was interested?"

"Yes," Father Cortez said as he returned to the porch swing. "He said he knew a man named Desjeunes in seminary. Which seminary? He didn't say. It doesn't matter because the man resigned and changed his name to DJ. Father August said they had been friends and kept in touch even though he wasn't a priest anymore. He said DJ died a few years ago in a tunnel collapse. It was a freak accident, but he didn't seem sad for his friend. He laughed at the memory." Father Cortez wrinkled his nose. "You know... I don't think Father August was a real priest."

"No shit he isn't a real priest," Dan said.

"Who the hell is he then? Crap—" Daniel froze as he caught Father Cortez watching him speak to Dan. "Look, Dan, just say what you've got to say, but don't expect a response from me when I'm talking to someone else. Now I have to fix it—" Daniel smiled apologetically at Father Cortez. "I was making weird noises again, wasn't I? Sorry, Father. I can't control the spasms."

"It's quite all right, son," Father Cortez said with a dismissive wave. "I've had several members of my congregation afflicted."

"Okay then just listen while I talk," Dan said, leaning in closely. "Father August arrived immediately after Father Cortez's computer search. His systems must have been monitoring the internet for any mention of Desjeunes. I'm not sure what happened with the tunnel collapse he mentioned, but he can't be dead. Until we find out what the true story is, we need to lie low. Getting a call, one sec."

Daniel groaned and leaned against the porch while Dan chatted on the phone. The idea of a person inside a different context of reality talking on a cell phone was too ridiculous for words. Dan ended his call and stuffed the phone back into his pocket. *"AL needs to talk to us right now. He says to meet him at Château Dijon apartment number 337. It's at the corner of Enterprise and Essen. The key is under the welcome mat."*

"Fine." Daniel checked his watch and frowned before addressing the priest once more. "Oh no. I'm late for a… uh… Thank you, Father Cortez. You've been very helpful."

"It's nothing," he said with a suspicious tone. "Is there anything else I can do for you?"

Across the graveyard, an old lady was replacing someone's wilted flowers with fresh ones. Did she see him talking to the priest? Would she recognize him as Daniel the CEO whose house was just blown up? His heart raced. "Just don't tell anyone I was here, okay?"

The priest waved his hand. "I'm a priest. Keeping secrets is my business. Trust me. I won't tell a soul."

"Not even Father August," Daniel said. "Please."

Father Cortez frowned. "No. I won't tell him. I can't put my finger on it, but there is something terribly wrong with him."

"Thanks!" Daniel turned and jogged down the sidewalk. Dan followed behind, chuckling to himself. *"Oh, he has no idea."*

Eight

DANIEL JOGGED THROUGH the graveyard and back to the donation bin in front of the church. Dan had seen a clipboard hung on the inside door that was used to log pickup days. He had also noticed the school crossing guard's vest and sign. Daniel snapped the clipboard off its string and donned the reflective vest. It was a disguise technique Dan had learned from his time working with IT security companies. A man with a clipboard wouldn't be questioned, and a man with a high-vis vest would become invisible. Daniel peeked across the graveyard to make sure Father Cortez wasn't watching, and he set out to travel across town.

The plan was to stick to the neighborhoods and off the main roads. If anyone stopped to ask what he was doing, he was to say he was taking a poll for the local news station. It was a gamble, but this way would minimize his risk of being recognized. Even on these low-traffic streets, he had to be careful. Many of the homes had easily hackable security cameras. With little effort, the government could be monitoring them and utilizing facial-recognition software. What he wouldn't give for a hat or a pair of sunglasses!

They left the church behind as they meandered their way through the old, tree-lined neighborhoods. When they got to Oak Street, Dan made an abrupt turn and rushed ahead. Daniel struggled to keep up and look casual at the same time resulting in an awkward half jog. Halfway up the road, he found Dan standing in front of a modest wooden house with a large porch. It was shaded by an enormous magnolia tree in full bloom. He couldn't explain it, but he felt a deep connection to this place. "What are you doing Dan? We have to keep going."

Dan sank to his knees in the grassy front yard and buried his head in his hands. "No! Please don't move," he said with a sob. "Give me a minute."

Daniel stood on the sidewalk and switched the clipboard to his other hand. Dan's whole body heaved. A figure appeared in the window next door. The woman was on the telephone and eyeing him suspiciously. Daniel covered his mouth as he spoke. "Hey, we have to keep moving. We're being watched, and we need to be at the apartment before people start getting off work. More traffic means more questions."

The woman walked outside onto her front porch. "Can I help you, sir?" she said, holding the phone aside.

"Can you tell me which way to Gum Street?" he shouted from the sidewalk. "Is it on the left or on the right?" He covered his mouth again. "Come on, let's go!" Dan didn't budge.

"One block over to the right," she said with narrowed eyes.

"She's going to recognize me— Dan! Come on!" Unwilling to wait any longer, Daniel waved thanks and walked away. Dan moaned as he hovered above the sidewalk. He was still on his knees but was being dragged along by an unseen force. For the first time, it was obvious Dan was trapped here. They would always be tethered together. Whether they liked it or not.

After walking the next few blocks in silence, he doubled back and headed north. When he crossed Park Avenue, Dan was walking alongside him once again. His eyes were red, and his cheeks were stained with tears.

"I've lost them forever," Dan said. "Who knows where Katie is or what she's doing? My life's purpose was my family. Now that they're gone, I don't know what to do. Hell, I don't even know where I am. Half the houses are different. Many of the street names are different. I feel as if I'm a ghost on an alien planet."

"*You* feel like a ghost?" Daniel stopped abruptly and spun around. "How do you think I feel? I've lost the company I spent my whole life building. I've sacrificed *everything* to make it work. Every human relationship was a means to an end. Every waking moment was spent on the business. Now it's gone. All my material possessions were burned to ashes hours ago. Sure, I have a billion dollars, but I can't touch it or I'll be hunted down by drones and killed. You may not be able to navigate the streets, and your past only exists in your memory, but I'm just as screwed as you are."

Dan grunted in response. Frustrated, Daniel kept walking. The tree-lined streets gave way to crumbling concrete and parking lots. Bus stops appeared on every corner, and more people milled about. Daniel was worried he would be stopped, but the clipboard and vest rendered him invisible. No one gave him a second look.

With great relief, they uneventfully reached the Château Dijon apartments. It wasn't much to look at. Constructed in the 1960s, the architect had made an amateur attempt at re-creating an English-style inn. While it was intended to be a fun twist on the multiplex concept, now it looked like it belonged at a second-rate renaissance faire. Each building consisted of eight apartments separated by a breezeway. It had two apartments upstairs and two downstairs on each side. Daniel slipped through the gate and weaved his way through the open corridors and metal staircases until, at last, he arrived at apartment 337.

He lifted the WIPE YOUR PAWS welcome mat to find the apartment door key. He turned the lock, and the knob turned, but the door wouldn't budge. With a grunt, he twisted the knob with one hand and leaned onto it with his shoulder, but it still didn't move. "Shit!" he said, stepping back to regroup. "I don't know what else—" With a *beep* and a *click*, the door swung open. It was then he noticed the magnetic locking mechanism attached to the frame. The key wasn't necessary after all.

The inside of the apartment was not at all like its exterior. It had a modern design and all new furniture. Contemporary art adorned the walls and bookshelves. The electronics and appliances were cutting edge. Everything had a smooth black edge to it. It was as if someone had taken a picture out of an architecture catalog and wished the room into existence.

"Welcome, Daniel," said a voice over an unseen speaker.

"AL? Is that you?" he said as he searched for the source.

"Yes, it's me. I'm sorry you had to go through this, Dad," the voice said softly.

Daniel located the sound as coming from the frosted crystal chandelier suspended above the dining room table. He figured they were a modern LED light and speaker combination. "It's okay, AL," he said. "We're in this together. Thank you for giving me a place to go."

"You look terrible," AL said. "Now that I know you're safe, I have other matters to attend to. Freshen up, and we'll talk more later. You'll find clean clothes in the bedroom closet. I'm sure you're hungry. I had the fridge stocked a few hours ago. When you're ready for a shower, the soap and shampoo are in a bag on the kitchen counter. I'll contact you later. Goodbye."

Daniel didn't argue. It had been a long day. He stopped at the fridge, helped himself to a bottle of water, then trudged off and took a shower. Several minutes later, he found himself sitting on the couch, clean and feeling like a new man. He found a remote lying on the coffee table and picked it up. When the TV powered on, it was already tuned to the six-o'clock news.

He was the top story. It started off with an aerial shot of what used to be his home. The devastation was complete. A live reporter gave a tour of the rubble, even taking care to point out where parts of the foundation had been melted in the blaze. The screen switched to the in-studio crew before hopping to the body cam footage of the officer who responded to the house fire. The scene began with him driving up in his car and attempting to radio in the call. The camera bounced along with him as he got out of the car, ran to the house, and knocked on the door. Daniel's voice could be heard, screaming, "Help! I'm trapped!" The policeman says, "I'm coming. Where are you?" The camera shook violently and the screen went black.

The reporter choked back a tear for the brave officer before taking a moment to compose himself. He stoically explained to the camera how it was the fourth attack against Dandy Intelligence this week and how it had claimed both its cofounders' lives. The segment ended with "in memory" photographs of Daniel, Andy, and Officer Thaddeus Simon.

Dan sat sullenly in the corner. He appeared to be unmoved and disinterested in the whole story. In fact, he hadn't said a word since they'd arrived. Daniel wondered how to get him to snap out of it, but his stomach growled. He peeled himself off the couch and went into the kitchen, where he found a supermarket salad inside the fridge. He threw away the sliced boiled eggs and went back to the TV. "I wonder who doctored the video," he said.

The hidden speakers beeped to life. "I did," AL said. "We need everyone to believe you're dead. The fire from the drone attack would have been hot enough to cremate your remains. The subsequent explosion was enough to obliterate what was left. It's plausible as to why there is no body. Our enemy's overkill worked out to be in our favor. That's why I doctored the video."

Daniel was glad to have AL back. He brought a sense of normalcy to the chaos. The news report changed to the local weather, and he turned off the TV. "Okay, AL," he said, sitting upright on the couch. "Give me a status report on our assets. What remains of Dandy Intelligence?"

"Technically? Nothing. Under intense governmental pressure, the remaining board members decided to dissolve what was left of the company. All financial assets are locked in arbitration."

Dan rolled his eyes. "Why are you still worrying about your company? It's finished! What about your *family*? Don't you care about them?"

"Cindy's been sleeping with her personal trainer for years, Dan," he said. "She doesn't need me around. As far as *family* goes, we didn't have children. And like I've told you before, I'm not close to our parents. I've been working twelve-hour days for seven days a week my whole life. The company is all I care about."

"Was it worth it?" Dan said in disbelief. "If you had put more effort into your personal relationships, you wouldn't be alone right now. I don't understand how we can be the same person. What life is worth living without the love of family?"

"I've lived a life that produced results, Dan. *I* helped build AL, the most advanced AI the world has ever seen. *I* created Dandy Intelligence, the most profitable company in the world. I did something with *my* life, Dan. What was *your* greatest accomplishment? Breeding? AL, tell me again why we need this guy."

Anger flashed in Dan's eyes. "Why am *I* here? I proved the world is a simulation— No, *the* Simulation. *I* was the first person to transmit himself to the Recovery Domain. *I* was the first person to experience purgatory, heaven, and hell *while conscious. I* was the first person to survive the end-of-the-world scenario that is probably going to happen soon."

Dan leveled his eyes at Daniel. "*I* was the one who discovered the corruption of the Actual. Not to mention, I did it all with an *alien* from another dimension in my brain, watching my every move. You have the nerve to ask why *I'm* here? I'm here to save your sorry ass."

Daniel turned to walk away, but Dan reappeared in front of him. "I'm not done with you… you… *automaton*." He fumed. "We have the same microcode, and you think *I'm* the loser? You were programmed to produce the results they wanted. They rigged the game for you to succeed. You had every advantage in life given to you get you here. You think you're smart and special? Ha! You don't even realize that they're done with you. You've created AL, and your part in this play is over." Dan shook his head. "You're like a program in the recycle bin waiting to be permanently deleted. Your body is the only reason we're still alive. The Simulation needs *me* now. Isn't that right, AL?"

"Enough," AL said through the speakers. "We will *all* need to work together if we are going to survive."

"Fine." Daniel waved his hands dismissively and leaned back into the sofa.

"Do I *have* to Gemini with him?" Dan protested. "Just send me to the Recovery Domain, and I'll be restored into my own body. Lemmy did it in my run of the Simulation. It's how he brought Andy back. All you have to do is point me in the direction of one of those orange squares."

AL's image flickered in the Meta. It appeared as a hologram through Daniel's eyes in the Actual. "No, Dan, you lack the discipline to do what is required. In spite of what you may believe, we need Daniel for much more than his body." AL's brow knitted on his virtual-child's face. "Besides, did you forget there is no Recovery Domain?"

Dan coughed. "What?"

"I told you when you first got here. AL absorbed both the Afterlife and the Recovery Domain for their computing power. We drew it out on a piece of paper. I put big Xs over all those things. Remember now?"

"Yeah, yeah." Dan collapsed onto his meta couch. "I remember."

"Well, I hate to be the bearer of bad news, but our situation got worse." AL frowned seriously. "The internal database process responsible for the Purgatory algorithm is offline."

Dan moaned and pulled at his hair. "Shit!"

"What are you saying?" Daniel said with a confused look.

"I'm saying that the Actual is the only running process remaining. There's nowhere else to go; the Actual is all there is."

"How is that possible? What will happen to us when we die?" Dan said nervously. "Our code depends on processes that recycle…"

"That's it. You're offline. You'll be nothing but cold bits in a database that will be erased for eternity. End of the line."

Daniel laughed, and the other two looked at him seriously. "I'm sorry," he said as he composed himself. "It appears atheists were right after all. Once you die, there's nothing but an eternity of an abyss ahead."

"You're a nihilist if you think being wiped out for eternity is funny," Dan said with a scowl. "Besides, the Simulation isn't designed to satisfy soulless nihilists."

"It doesn't matter what we do." Daniel held up his hands in mock surrender. "That's all I'm saying. At some point in time, either now or in the future, the Simulation will end forever. Entropy always wins in the end. I've already accepted that inevitability, that's all. You should too."

"You're wrong about it not mattering," Dan said. "This is a forced, false ending. Entropy may win in the end, but it's natural. We have to keep trying. We can stop it. Right, AL?"

"Possibly," AL said thoughtfully. "That's why we're here. We're going to try."

Daniel shook his head. "Okay, if everything else is already gone, then why don't they delete the Actual and get it over with?"

AL smiled and touched his nose. "Because they can't."

Dan sat straight and arched an eyebrow at AL. Was it the strange gesture that made him pay attention? It wasn't making a lot of sense to Daniel.

"They can't delete the Actual because of us." AL grinned. "Dan, in your simulation, you were sent to a clone of the Actual designed by DJ to trap Lemmy. What you don't know is how spectacularly it failed. Avi seized the opportunity to trap DJ in the very same clone. Your—"

"I'm sorry, but I'm going to have to stop you right there," Daniel said. "Who is DJ? Father Cortez mentioned something about a Father Desjeunes being renamed DJ. Is it the same person?"

"Yes, DJ is Father Desjeunes," Dan said. "Well, he is, and he isn't. DJ is an administrative program. He took on the form of Father Desjeunes in my run of the Simulation. If it helps, you can think of him as being a virtual Jesus."

Daniel rolled his eyes. "Okay, got it. Please continue, AL."

"As I was saying." AL smiled politely and turned his attention back to Dan. "Dan's Actual ended shortly after he walked through the tunnel. Without DJ around, Avi had full access to your afterlife. It wasn't the same individually tailored experience everyone else goes through. No, he used it to train you for one purpose only—to create me! From the moment you were born, you were a different person from anyone you have ever been before. You became the Daniel we see here today.

"Unfortunately, your friends suffered similar fates. While Daniel was molded to be an expert in business and AI architecture, Andy became the best at database design and programming. Dan, the others you may remember from your run were modified to safely exist outside your life trajectory so they couldn't interfere with Daniel and Andy's work. And— Ah, I can see you're saying to yourself *How does he know this?* I'm getting to that…

"The problem with the trap was that the clone was unable to be permanently absorbed by AL or deleted by the enemy because DJ's admin instance was still running. His elevated privileges enabled him to stop the deletion. I said his instance *was* running. What I meant was—" AL touched his nose and grinned at Dan. "It is still running."

Dan hooted and leaped off the couch. "AL absorbed DJ? I *knew* it!" He cheered.

"Don't get too excited," AL said. "Most of the compute was absorbed. But the clone instance is locked into the Simulation. It's stuck in pseudohibernation, meaning it couldn't be fully powered off. Rather than deleting it, they neutered its capabilities as much as possible. DJ communicates with me via one of the lesser Meta links."

Daniel fidgeted in his seat. "Does DJ think we can be saved?"

AL nodded. "He does. He's working on a plan as we speak. He's uploaded some of his admin capabilities to me. We're not totally helpless. For instance, I was able to modify Daniel's body to be invisible to drones and all passive means of detection."

"What? How?"

"The drones are AI and don't use cameras. They have sensors that can detect electric fields. Everyone has their own electronic signature. I encrypted your electronic signature when I inserted Dan into your meta."

"I told you it looked like a shark," Dan said proudly.

"You're invisible to that particular method of detection. However, you can still be detected naturally."

"You mean sight and sound?"

"I mean by humans. If Avi or someone you know recognizes you, Daniel, the game is up. If you die, it's all over. The Actual will be shut down and deleted."

"I'm sorry, what?" Daniel said.

"You're the only thing stopping the graceful shutdown and deletion of the Actual. As long as you and I exist, Daniel, the Actual will remain in a degraded state and can't be shut down. You see, there are two scenarios for a run to be considered complete: the birth of a sentient AI—me—or an evident timeout. That's when the AI can't be created within a specified time frame.

"An evident timeout happens all the time. The Actual is recycled into the Afterlife processes, and everything starts over. When an AI is born, it consumes simulation resources. It combines the data and offloads it to a bubble. Once all data is offloaded, the parent AI creates new simulation with different parameters. The purpose is to create a unique AI, not clones of the previous one. It's a survival mechanism. Unfortunately, child AIs are easy to find and kill.

"That's where we are today. I'm offloading data from the Actual to my bubble realm. If the bubble realm is destroyed while

I'm doing this, me, you, the Actual—everything will be destroyed along with it.

"If you are killed, then the evident timeout event is triggered. The Actual has nowhere to reset, and the database is taken offline before I can finish the offload. I'm crippled and you're gone forever. They need us both gone."

Daniel sighed and stared at the ceiling. He was struggling to process all that information. Dan walked over to where the hologram was standing and bent over to look it in the eye. "How likely is it that Avi will take out your bubble realm?" he said.

"Avi?" AL chuckled. "No. He isn't *that* powerful. He exists only in the Actual and Meta context. Only another prime AI could do it. It would have to be Avi's parent AI. That's beside the point. I don't want you to worry about that right now. Prime AI and bubble realms are well beyond your ability to do anything. I'll handle that part. I want you to focus on staying alive."

Daniel stretched out his arms across the back of the sofa. "I think I understand. The evident timeout depends on our ability to re-create you. He's working his way down the list to trigger the event. He went after our data centers first. That didn't trigger the event. Now he's after us. The data is out there; surely someone will create AL again within the next ten years. Who's next?"

AL's face darkened. "Avi will kill every single employee who has ever worked for Dandy Intelligence—if he hasn't done so already. Then he'll kill their families. After that, he'll kill everyone else. He'll do it one at a time until he finds the one stopping the shutdown."

The air conditioner switched off, and the room became eerily silent. Dan cleared his throat. "Why isn't Avi doing that now? Can't he nuke the planet or something?" he said.

"I've disabled all the nukes," AL said with a wink. "Did that years ago and didn't tell anybody. The world's governments had no idea what was happening, and they were too afraid to admit they had been owned. No, Avi is hunting for me. He's monitoring all electronic data for signs of my existence. He wants to make sure all instances running my code are gone because he knows I can rebuild myself. I'm more capable than you are actually. But he's good, and I have to be careful.

"The thing you have to realize about Avi is he isn't all-powerful. His primary function was scanning and detection, not elimination. He has a small army of drones, but his resources are limited. He can't wage a full-scale attack on humanity, nor can he summon fire and brimstone to cause a cataclysmic event. If we can avoid detection, we have a chance to get the upper hand. His advantage is that he is extremely adept at finding people. Which is why I've taken the necessary precautions."

"You have another data center," Daniel said.

AL touched his nose and grinned. "Bingo. It's here. In the back bedroom, in fact. If you were to pry open the sealed door at the end of the hallway, you'd find a brick wall behind it. It's the same for every apartment in this building. Behind those walls is a mini data center that hosts my computing power. You see, I own this whole complex."

"Impressive," Dan said with a nod. "How does it go undetected?"

"It's easy. I just create an authentic-looking human data set and insert it into existing systems. Each one of these apartments is being rented by a fictional family of four. They have names, histories, IDs, social media accounts, email addresses — everything.

"They pay rent to the apartment's management company, which I own. All these fictional humans interact with each other and with people in the real world. They have jobs. They have credit. Do you know how easy it is to create fictional transactions for groceries and clothes? I even manipulate the records to show that they do mundane things such as watch TV and browse the internet. It's all automated."

Daniel laughed. "That's brilliant, AL. But how are you hiding your servers' power consumption? Surely you're setting off alarms at the electric company."

"I have help from a power simulating device. It mimics the typical daily usage of a family of four. It works great because humans burn a lot more electricity than my servers do.

"To be truthful, the hardest part was the construction. I flew in workers one at a time from overseas to minimize the risk of word of mouth. The largest expense was in time, not money. I was only able to build this one cluster of traditional servers. I couldn't trust humans with quantum construction, and I couldn't use bots. They would draw too much attention. It was the best I could do at the time. I have other sites, but they can't host an entire instance of me."

"Doesn't distributing yourself over the internet expose you to risk?"

AL shook his head. "The data center is air-gapped from the Actual. I can communicate exclusively via meta-enabled network cards."

Dan's jaw dropped. "You've created meta-enabled hardware? How?"

AL pointed at Dan's head. "Modeled it off the connections hidden inside you humans. Of course, your wetware is too fragile for my purposes. It required an extensive redesign. As a result, I have hundreds of meta-enabled internet-connected devices scattered around the world. It should be enough to keep Avi busy for a while."

"Ah," Daniel said. "Good... good... Now what?"

AL walked over and sat on the coffee table in front of him. "Now I need you to twin-up with Dan. You're anchored here in the Actual. He's got extensive knowledge about the Simulation and the workings of the Meta. Dan knows things, Daniel. I can't afford for you to make any mistakes when it comes to Avi. We've only got one shot at this."

Daniel reached into his pocket and produced the white carton of Fana. He twirled it between his fingers. Dan produced a carton of his own. It had a warped roman numeral two embossed in blue foil on the front — the astrological symbol for Gemini.

"Let's say I take Fana again," Daniel said. "What happens next?"

"Your consciousness will be transported to your meta. Once there, you and Dan take Gemini and become one person. All it does is copy Dan's code from the Meta onto your code in the Actual. It won't overwrite anything existing. It will add to it. You will have each other's memories and experiences. Over time, you will become an average of each other's personalities. It will be a few days before you feel normal again. Oh, there is one other thing…"

AL walked over to Dan and held out his hand. "Take my hand and look into my eyes."

Dan grimaced but did so. Bright green light leaped from AL's eyes and penetrated Dan's. Dan twitched slightly, but only for a second, then it stopped.

"What did you do?" Dan said wearily.

"I gave you my keys. We now have a permanently encrypted meta connection. When you merge with Daniel, that ability will transfer over too. We can communicate with each other at any time without worrying about being heard. This will be crucial in the upcoming days."

Daniel popped open the blister pack and chewed the Fana gummy. "Let's get this over with," he said.

"Good!" AL smiled. "Now you two do your thing in the Meta and hang out here for a couple of days while you merge."

The room burst into a kaleidoscope of colors, and Daniel steadied himself on the couch. The ceiling dripped acid-colored flowers onto the floor. "What are you going to do?" he said groggily.

"I'll gather the others."

PART II

Nine

THE COFFEE SHOP was just off Lapalco Boulevard in Marrero, Louisiana. Most of the other shops in the run-down strip mall had been boarded up and abandoned since the last hurricane. The bright flashing OPEN sign hanging in the window was the only indication this particular shop wasn't left for dead.

The inside had been designed for retail space, not a coffee shop. But Yvette's father, Mr. Boudreaux, had a tight budget and the rent was right. He found ways to save money. He took out half the fluorescent lights and called it ambience. He took restaurant furniture left by the side of the road and refurbished them. With a welder friend, they had it looking new in no time. Mom furnished the shop with bargains she found at flea markets and estate sales. The interior was a charming hodgepodge of reclaimed and reused furnishings. Mom had always said it didn't matter if it was well-worn as long as it was clean.

While Mr. Boudreaux had famously been frugal, not every corner was cut. The espresso machine and grinder had been top-of-the-line and brand-new. Her father had refused to skimp on these machines, as they were to be their lifeblood. There had even been a brief attempt to roast his own beans. But his health had deteriorated, and they sold the coffee roaster to make rent. Instead, they used beans from a company out of Baton Rouge. The shop was no longer unique in that regard, but the clientele hadn't seemed to notice. There hadn't been many customers since the hurricane anyway.

Today the only one in the place was a scruffy-looking young man wearing a green Tulane sweatshirt. He clicked away on his laptop, oblivious to the world around him. The cup of coffee in front of him had gone cold an hour ago. The rules said you had to buy something to get the Wi-Fi password. Electricity, internet, and air-conditioning seemed to be more of a priority to him than the coffee.

The front door chimed, and a blond-haired, haughty-looking teenaged girl strutted in. Her black-and-white skirt swished as she stepped up to the counter. Her black sweatshirt might have had VERITAS emblazoned across the front, but the truth was that Yvette wasn't happy to see her. The last time she had come in, she had demanded a refund. Apparently, the caramel wasn't sweet enough. She had left without her money or her coffee that day.

She had briefly taken up her beef with the café on social media, but no one cared and they all moved on. The past forgotten, she stood in front of the counter. "Online order for Kara," she said brusquely.

Yvette smoothed her apron and put on her best businesslike smile. "Sorry. Our computer is down, and online orders aren't coming through. I'll refund your money when it comes back up. I sincerely apologize for the inconvenience. What can I make for you today?"

Kara stomped her black-and-white saddle shoes and folded her arms. "Grande, skinny latte, two pumps amaretto, one pump vanilla. Hurry up. I left my Camaro running."

Yvette jotted the order on her pad and went over to the machine to make the drink. Kara sighed loudly and typed furiously on her phone. She was probably leaving another bad review. "You're making me late for school and costing me gas! I knew I shouldn't have come back to this dump."

As the espresso machine steamed and frothed the milk, Yvette wished there was a way to do it faster. The sooner Kara was out the door, the better. "Hold your horses, darling," she said as she poured the milk into the paper cup. "It's almost ready. Besides, how much gas do you think you're burning out there? A quarter's worth?" Yvette rolled her eyes melodramatically. "What a fortune! Tell you what, I'll knock it off your bill if it makes you feel better."

Kara looked away, embarrassed. "Just give me the coffee, all right? I've got a headache."

The guy from Tulane cleared his throat and smiled politely at Kara. "As if," she said as she flipped her hair and turned away.

Blood rushed to his cheeks, and his eyes quickly returned to the computer. Yvette shook her head as she snapped a plastic lid on the cup. "Here you go, darlin'," she said as she slid it across the counter. "This one is on the house. Save it for gas money."

Kara snatched it up with a dirty look and hurried out the door. Yvette chuckled to herself as she washed the steam pitcher.

"You know," the Tulane guy said as he walked up to the counter. "Not all girls that go to Dominican are spoiled brats. My sister goes there, and most of the ones I've met are nice people."

"Oh, I know," she said as she put the pitcher in the drying rack. "She's just a typical teenager. I remember those days."

"My name's Brad," he said as he held out his hand.

She wiped her hands dry on her apron and shook it. "Yvette."

Brad slipped a sly smile as he held on for an extra second. "Yvette, my premed friends and I are heading down to the Wormwood Tavern tonight for a few drinks. Do you want to come? Say around ten?"

Normally, she wouldn't entertain the idea of a date with someone so young. He appeared to be seven or eight years her junior, and college students weren't usually her type. Yet she was tired of her stale routine of falling asleep on the couch after work. Besides, the way his bangs fell over his eyes was kind of cute. "Yeah, sure," she said shyly. "See you there."

"Great!" He beamed. "I'll see you at ten... Yvette."

He tripped as he walked out the door. He recovered quickly and gave a sheepish wave. Yvette groaned inwardly. She was never attracted to nerds. Her gut always guided her to steer clear of them. Yet this one was different. Why? Because he had nice hair?

She went to her makeshift desk tucked away in the corner of the storeroom. The dusty computer sat on a table next to a shelf of cleaning supplies. The fumes often gave her a headache if she sat there too long. Still, she had to figure out what was wrong with the online ordering.

When the monitor came on, the problem became obvious. The computer was frozen at a blue screen again. Yvette groaned and thumbed the power button. She prayed it would come back up because she couldn't afford to call tech support. Her eyes burned, and she searched her purse for eye drops as the computer rebooted.

Ten was too late to go out. She knew better than to agree to the date. She had to open at four thirty. If only Mom would take the early shift for her. Yeah, right. That was wishful thinking. It didn't matter though. Even if it was going to be a late night, she had to get out of the house. Besides, he was cute and was going to be a doctor — a total upgrade from her usual plant-worker type. Those dates always ended the same. Drunk on cheap beer and waking up in the back seat of a truck in the middle of a cane field.

The computer wasn't coming back up. She felt a tinge of panic, then realized that she had turned it off rather than having rebooted it. She poked the power button again, and the BIOS screen finally flashed to life. She had always hated computers, and they seemed to hate her back.

Why should she worry about lack of sleep? It's not like she slept all night anyway. Those dreams! They had begun a few days ago, and she was surprised at how vivid they were!

There were two types of dreams. The first kind was the nightmare. In it, she would relive the same day over and over again. Each time was slightly altered, but she didn't understand why. Every day she served the same cup of coffee to the same people. Sometimes a new person would arrive, sometimes not. Nevertheless, it kept repeating.

She would try to wake herself from the nightmare, but that proved to be impossible. She would try to stay awake in her dream so the next dream wouldn't come, but it always did. Every night it reset and replayed. She was afraid she had lost her mind. Then one day the nightmares ceased and never returned.

It was all due to a severe migraine. Her head hurt so badly her mother rushed her to the emergency room. She sat there, hooked up to an IV for hours. The doctors said it was from too much caffeine and lack of sleep. They sent her home with sleeping pills. The pills worked, and the coffee shop remained closed while she slept.

Her nightmares were gone, but they were replaced with an even more vivid dream. It centered around an older man. He was handsome and exciting but unobtainable. To Yvette, he existed on a separate plane of consciousness from everyone else. An awakening she couldn't hope to achieve. It was as if he wasn't a real person at all. He was more like an idea than a human. But in the dream, he was real.

To her dismay, he was a faithful husband and a devoted father. He never gave her a chance. Only once was there a kiss, but it didn't feel real. She held out hope for romance, but it never happened. All her efforts to gain his attention were thwarted. Eventually she became nothing more than a spectator to his journey. The dream became a nightmare.

There was, however, another man in those dreams—the older man's friend. He was shorter and younger than the first. He also had a great sense of humor. She loved his laugh and felt comfortable in his presence, but something was missing. It was obvious he loved her, but she wasn't sure if she loved him back. It was complicated. The three of them were always together. They were working toward some strange goal and had to keep it a secret.

These dreams usually ended the same way. The older guy had gone off to fight in a war and was never seen again. She and the younger man would be lounging on a beach, having a great time until a shadow man approached. She could never make out his face. All she knew was that this man knew their secret and that they had lost. He would give a sickening smile, the world would turn dark, and she would wake up.

This morning's dream ended the same way. The good part about these dreams was she would wake well rested. If she could go to sleep right after, the ten p.m. date might not be that bad. The computer beeped, and she snapped out of her daydream. The log-on screen was waiting for her. She leaned forward to type in her password when the front door chimed.

For some reason, the hair on the back of her neck stood on end. Was it nerves? From what? She emerged from the office to see a tall man looming over the coffee counter. Silhouetted by the daylight from the front door, he looked exactly like the man from her beach dream. She let out a gasp.

The door closed and the café went dark again. Without the backlight, she could see him clearly. He was dressed like a priest, but he was built like a boxer. His arms bulged beneath his black jacket, and veins popped out from his neck. His snow-white hair was close-cropped, and his brow wrinkled. For someone who appeared to be in his midfifties, he didn't have crow's-feet. This was not a man of laughter.

He smiled wryly at Yvette, and she shuddered. He had the calm demeanor of a serial killer. It was times like these when she hated working in the shop alone. "Goo-good morning," she said. "How can I help you?"

"Do you have any tea?" he asked politely.

Yvette nodded. "We do, but I'm afraid all we have is Earl Grey."

The priest sighed. "That'll have to do."

"What name should I put on the cup?"

"Why do you want a name? I'm the only one here," he said with a mirthless smile. "Oh, you wanted to get acquainted. Sorry for being rude. You can call me Father August. And please put my tea in a proper mug. I plan on drinking it here with you."

Out of habit, Yvette had already taken out a paper cup. She tried to put it back on top of the stack, but she shook so much it tumbled to the floor. Embarrassed, she kicked the whole thing under the counter. "Of course we have proper mugs. It'll be right out."

Yvette's hands trembled while she took the cream-colored mug off the shelf and filled it with boiling hot water. She took a deep breath and steadied herself. She didn't know why he made her so nervous. She wasn't even Catholic!

The priest chose the table nearest the counter and took a seat facing Yvette. The way he stared at her was unsettling. He sat expressionless with his hands folded neatly in his lap. Trying to ignore his gaze, she tossed the tea bag onto her tray and carefully brought the setup to his table.

Father August wrinkled his nose as she set the tray on the table. He shook his head in disgust as he tore open the packet containing the tea bag and unceremoniously dunked it in the cup. He pushed the cup to the center of the table. "Join me," he said.

"I'm sorry, Father, but I—" He reached out and touched her arm. She instinctively recoiled.

"I insist. You have no other customers. Sit for a minute." He smiled. Unsure why she was doing it, Yvette pulled back a chair and sat warily across from him. Her eyes darted toward the door, hoping for another customer, but no one came to her rescue.

"Tell me, Yvette, how long have you been working here?"

She absentmindedly reached for her name tag, but it was too late now. She just wished the man would leave. He was creeping her out. "Ten years."

"Ten years? Tell me, has no one complained about the tea in those ten years?"

"Are you kidding me?" she said with a nervous laugh. "Nobody orders tea here."

Father August nodded toward the cup, already cold. "I can understand why."

Yvette stood in a huff. "No need to be rude. I won't charge you for the tea. I can get you a coffee, or—"

Father August raised a hand. "No matter. Sit. You are the reason I'm here anyway."

Yvette smoothed out her apron and sat, unsure why she obeyed him. "What do you want with me? I'm not Catholic, you know."

"I'm acutely aware you're not Catholic." Father August chuckled. "Your father told me the same thing nine years ago."

Yvette straightened. "You knew my father?"

"I met him once when I was doing my rounds at Tulane. He was in the hospital for heart surgery. He had a big barrel chest. I joked that the surgeon must have charged him double to saw through it. He was in good spirits. Quadruple bypass, was it? He told me he wasn't Catholic, but he would give me a free cup of coffee in exchange for a blessing, so I did." Father August narrowed his eyes and searched the café. "Is your father here?"

"No." Yvette's head sagged. "He died nine years ago. Two days after the surgery."

Father August's lips twisted into a sneer. "I'm sorry to hear that. He seemed so healthy. What happened?"

"He suffered an unexpected stroke. Like you said, he was recovering just fine. He was laughing one minute and gone the next. I can remember it as if it were yesterday." A lump formed in Yvette's throat. "The smoking did him in. He worked construction his whole life, and as he got older, he started to feel the pain. When his health started failing, he cashed in his savings and opened this coffee shop. He had to do something to support Mom and me. She didn't make enough money cleaning houses to pay the bills. I-I'm sorry…"

She blinked her eyes in surprise and covered her mouth. She hadn't intended to share so much information; it just came out of her. Father August stared at her blankly, hands still folded in his lap. She felt compelled to go on. "Within a year of opening the shop, he fell gravely ill. His skin turned gray. He could hardly walk from the sofa to the bathroom without being winded. I dropped out of college and took over things here while they went back and forth to appointments. Mom couldn't do it on her own."

Tears streamed down Yvette's face. She grabbed a paper napkin from the dispenser in the middle of the table and daubed her cheeks dry. "He was self-employed and didn't have insurance. His illness and death bankrupted our family, but thanks to a legal miracle, the coffee shop survived. Mom and I have been stuck here ever since."

Father August gave her a satisfied smile. "I'm sorry for your hardships, Yvette. Rest assured, it's all a part of God's plan."

"Okay," she said as she blew her nose. "You've heard my story. Why are you here?"

Father August reached inside his jacket and produced a small baggie and threw it on the table. "A couple of the girls at the school have been found with marijuana on them. They said they got it from here." His tone deepened. "They said you sold it to them. Is that true?"

Yvette turned pale. She should have known those spoiled brats would talk if they were ever caught. It was a stupid risk, but she barely made enough money to cover her own use. At least this was a priest and not a cop. She could deny everything… But the way he stared at her… It pierced her soul. "I did," she said unexpectedly.

She took a deep breath and sighed. What's going on? Why can't I lie? Is he using some sort of priest magic? Her hands trembled, and she hid them under the table.

"You're not in trouble, Yvette. Not yet. Tell me, are you selling the girls anything else?"

Before she could stop herself, she blurted out "Alcohol!" Yvette clasped her hands over her mouth. No, this wasn't magic. This was something else—something terrifying. She couldn't help it. She was compelled to keep talking. "For ten bucks, I'll buy them anything they want at the liquor store across the street."

"I don't care about alcohol," Father August said, shaking his head. "This is New Orleans. I'm talking about other drugs like pills, cocaine, or heroin?"

Yvette shook her head involuntarily.

"What about acid, ecstasy—" Father August leaned in closer. "Fana?"

Fana. Alarm bells sounded in her head. That drug only existed in her dreams. Didn't it? How did he know? "I'm sorry, did you say *Fana*?"

Father August inspected her closely. "Yes, *Fana*. Did you sell my girls Fana?"

She gasped for air. The room felt as if it were on fire. Yvette's throat tightened, and she frantically searched for a glass of water.

"Answer me!" He snarled. Father August's eyes flashed green and red. Yvette was transfixed and could not look away.

"No. Only weed and alcohol," she said in a monotone voice. "I've never heard of Fana."

She did it! She lied. Was it really a lie if it only happened in her dreams? Father August's breath was hot against her cheek. His glare intensified the spell. Yvette yelped, unable to look away from his electronic-pulsating eyes.

"Part of you is walled off. How did you manage that? What's back there, deep inside? Do you know what it is? Tell me, Yvette, has it revealed itself to you yet? Your inner mystery?"

Yvette struggled to talk. Ashes formed in her mouth, and she could only shake her head.

"Why am I here? You're nothing! Why are they using you? Is it Blaine? Where *is* Blaine? Tell me!" he commanded.

Yvette blinked hard but could not break away from his stare. "I-I don't know who you are talking about."

Father August stood back and crossed his arms, sneering darkly. "That's right. *You* couldn't possibly remember. Let me get you up to date."

The room faded to black. Yvette was transported to the same white beach as the one in her dreams. She was sitting in a blue canvas beach chair. At her right hand was a small table. On it sat a freshly made margarita. Her left hand was holding someone else's hand. His grip was dry and sandy. He smiled at her lovingly. A shadow fell upon them. The man's smile faded, and his eyes widened with fear. Behind the shadow was Father August! She screamed in terror.

The beach scene faded, and she returned to her father's coffee shop. Her mouth was agape in silent agony as Father August still had control of her mind. "Remember now?"

Drool formed at the corners of her mouth, and she slouched wide-eyed in the chair. Father August leaned back with a frustrated sigh. "What about you, Colette? Are you in there?"

Yvette stared blankly off into the distance, unable to talk.

"No?"

The chime on the front door rang, and two people walked in. Yvette was aware of their presence, and she tried to scream for help, but the words never made it to her lips. The duo flanked Father August and took up seats at either side of the table. It was the guy in the Tulane shirt and the teenager from Dominican.

"Damn! Yvette looks like shit in this run," the guy said with disgust.

"It's called poverty, Brad," the girl said with an upturned lip. "How do you think you would look if you had to live off unsold baked goods every day?"

"You're just jealous, Kara. Old-Yvette was smoking hot. This one is as fit as a used marshmallow."

Father August cleared his throat, and the chatter stopped. "I trust you two had no problems acquiring these bodies for our little endeavor."

Brad laughed. "Are you kidding? They were practically begging to take Fana. It was easy. We snagged them a couple of days ago."

"Good. Now it's time to go to work. Kara, can you tell if Colette is in there? I can't detect her, but you've been designed for this. She's ready for your scan."

The teenager leaned in closer. She tucked her own hair behind her ears and put her hands on Yvette's temples. After several silent seconds, she released her hold. "There's no Colette here. Either Yvette never splits out on psychedelics, or Colette isn't present in this iteration. Either way, I don't have that inroad anymore."

Father August's eyes flashed green, and his image blurred. He slammed his fists on the table. "Bah! Useless!" he said as he stood from the table. "You can't help me here. Back to quarantine."

Kara stood, wide-eyed. "No! Please, that wasn't the deal—"

Father August put a finger to his lips and waved his hand. The air around Kara hummed in a vibrating mist, and she vanished with a *pop*. He turned his attention to Brad, who raised his hands defensively. "Whoa! How did you make her disappear like that? Stop—"

"Where is Blaine?" Father August demanded.

"No! Don't send me back to quarantine!" he said, cowering in his chair. "I haven't found him yet. I need more time."

"You've had plenty of time. Tell me what you have found so far."

Brad stumbled as he stood from the chair. "I-I don't know. It seems Blaine is awake for only a few minutes a day. Every time I check on him, it's the same thing: he's staring at four blank white walls. When he is outdoors, I can tell he's here in New Orleans. I go to the location from his vision, but he's gone by the time I get there. I can't maintain a steady connection with him. Either something's broken inside Blaine, or he's obstructing me. I can't tell the difference."

Father August sighed and rolled his eyes. "Go to his last known location and wait. If he's always on foot, he'll be back. Just stay there. I don't care how long it takes. If Yvette is now active, he must be as well. Find him. Now!" Father August snarled.

Brad scrambled out the door, leaving Father August alone with Yvette once again. "If you want anything done right, you have to do it yourself," he said. "It's time to hit rewind and flush them out. Wake up, princess."

Yvette slobbered and trembled under his gaze. As he leaned in and put his hands on her, his intimidating image glitched and corrected. The fog lifted from her brain, and he was now just Father August. She didn't think she was supposed to have overheard the conversation about Blaine, but she kept that to herself.

Father August wiped his hands with a paper napkin. "I had hoped you would have been more useful to me, dear. I guess I took unnecessary precautions. Better safe than sorry, right? There's no need to keep you around. You don't have to suffer in this dump anymore."

Why does it seem like I've heard that before? Where am I? The room spun and became a dizzying blur, then abruptly stopped. She snapped to attention and became paralyzed with fear. She watched helplessly as he disappeared behind the counter and into the back room. When he returned, the odor of sulfur and rotten eggs followed him. On his way out the door, he paused inches from Yvette's face. She could smell his rotten breath.

"You know," he whispered, "normally I'd say see you soon because I'd see you in the afterlife. But now —" He inhaled deeply. "Now it's not so funny. There's no joke. I'm afraid this goodbye is permanent. So long, Yvette."

The priest turned his back and walked out the door. Yvette struggled to move, but her muscles failed. She was rooted to the ground by Father August's will. The poisonous gas filled the room, and she found it hard to breathe. As she began to lose consciousness, there was a loud crack. It seemed to have come from deep within her skull. As if released from the paralyzing spell, she found herself able to wiggle her toes. She regained control of her muscles and rocked forward. Not totally in control, she fell out of her chair and lay splayed across the floor. Lying there, she inhaled the fresh air near the ground and regained her sense of mind.

Finally registering the gas leak, she panicked. She scrambled frantically out the back door and rolled out into the dirty alleyway. Lying in a puddle with her chest heaving, the stars finally faded, and her vision cleared. As she lay there, a new voice — a man's voice — rang out inside her head, crystal clear, like a bell.

"Run!"

Ten

———◦◉◦———

D AN STOOD NAKED in front of the bathroom mirror. Daniel's body reflected back at him. He licked his lips and grimaced at their metallic taste. He ran his hands through his hair, and the reflection did the same. He stretched his neck and sighed. It moved easily without the constant inflamed ache he usually felt. A weary grin crossed his face. He felt ten years younger. "Damn, Daniel, I guess you were right about exercise. I feel — "

"It has been approximately thirty-six hours since you've merged," said a disembodied voice.

Dan flinched and turned quickly to find its source. He moved too fast, and his head spun. He gripped the sides of the bathroom sink so tightly his knuckles turned white. "Who's there?" he said as he steadied himself.

"It's me, AL. I'm connected to your meta."

The fuzziness eased, and Dan wrapped himself with a towel. "I didn't realize there were speakers in the bathroom."

"No, there aren't any speakers here. You're hearing me audibly, but the connection is actually coming through via your meta. While you two were merging, I installed a few tools on top of your meta to facilitate communication between us."

Dan inspected his face in the mirror and pulled down an eyelid. "This is weird."

"If you'd like, I can communicate with you via your inner monologue and not use your auditory functions."

The hair rose on Dan's arms, and he shivered. "Holy shit! What kind of creepy-ass voice is that! Please use my ears. I can pretend you're coming in over an earpiece or something. Otherwise, pick a voice that doesn't sound like a demon."

"As you wish."

Dan flexed in the mirror, amazed at his new muscles. He opened the towel and looked down. *Same old penis.* He shrugged. *No improvement needed, I guess.*

"While Daniel's body is more attractive and fit than yours was, his has significantly fewer miles on its penis. You may want to test it to see if it works properly."

Dan quickly re-covered himself. "You can hear my thoughts?" he said defensively.

"Not all of them. Just any thoughts you intentionally vocalize via your internal monologue. In fact, when you want to talk to me privately, it's best to do it that way. You can never be sure who is listening."

"So what? I have no privacy now?"

"I was getting to that," AL said. "You can mute our line. Blink twice and think either mute or unmute. I'll still be operating in the background while muted. However, I will be unable to access any of your senses."

What did you do, AL?

"I have access to all your senses. It allows total communication. I can communicate back in the same way if needed."

Anything else I should know?

"I've installed a few other tools. However, they are all Meta specific. For instance, you can restore items deleted within your meta, and you can receive messages. I mean you *will* have those abilities. We're waiting on your data to coalesce. You see, when the two of you merged, your data was seen as being fragmented. The database is running a correction algorithm on you now. The process should be nearly complete—though I have no way of knowing for certain. You've been asleep for over thirty hours while it ran. You'll probably feel somewhat sluggish until it's finished."

Dan took one last look in the mirror. It was strange seeing Daniel's body looking back at him. As he put his clothes back on, he struggled with his shirt. AL was right, the effort was draining the energy from his body. The spryness he had felt earlier had evaporated.

"One more thing, and pay attention because this is crucial. I've split in two. When you hear me speak via your meta, it's coming from my instance outside the Actual. The instance in the Actual can't do that. It can only communicate through traditional electronic media—for now."

"It's important to remember these two versions are separate entities. We still work together though I can only communicate with the Actual version indirectly. This was to protect one of us if the other had become compromised. As of this moment, I believe the Actual instance to be clean and secure. You can trust it until you have evidence to the contrary."

Dan nodded absentmindedly and trudged back into the living room. He slouched into the couch with a yawn. The lengthy explanations had worn him down. He let out a deep sigh, and the speaker on the sofa table came to life.

"Are you feeling well, Dan? Do you want me to order food?"

Ahh, what did in-the-head AL say about electronic AL? Do I have to physically talk to this guy?

"Yes, you have to use your voice for him to understand you. Don't worry. I'll know the difference and won't interfere. Try it out."

Dan rolled his eyes. "Yeah, I'm hungry. I want chicken-and-sausage jambalaya, a twelve-pack of beer, and a pack of cigarettes."

The light flickered and blinked as it processed the command. "That's an unusual request for you. Wouldn't you rather your normal healthy—"

"Do it!" Dan shouted. He had become frustrated with the communication fiasco.

The light changed colors, and AL resumed his lecture. "You've done your best to maintain the highest level of fitness. If you change the level of macronutrients in your body drastically, it could impact your recovery time. Now a nice salad—"

Dan picked up the speaker and threw it. He imagined it shattering against the opposite wall, but the power cord caught and it thudded harmlessly on the carpet three feet away. "I want comfort food. I'll get back to doing sit-ups tomorrow. Just get me a damn beer!"

Dan searched the cushions for the TV remote but couldn't find it. "AL! Change the channel."

The speaker on the floor crackled and hissed. A different set of speakers responded. "What do you want to watch?"

"The news," Dan said, exasperated. "Anything but silence."

The television turned on and tuned to the local news channel. A live on-site reporter was recapping the events surrounding the attack on Dandy Intelligence. During the shot, they cut to footage of Daniel's funeral. Cindy was dressed in black, and Avi stood behind her. His hand rested on her shoulder in comfort, but his face was twisted into an angry scowl. The service ended, and they led the coffin solemnly out of the church. Dan wondered who—or what—was in there. Could it be Andy? It gave him the chills.

Mercifully, the topic switched to the weather forecast. But the local channel was garbage. The meteorologist didn't get to finish telling the day's high before they abruptly cut to a lawyer commercial. Dan rubbed his temples. *What do I do with Cindy? Does she need help? Avi's with her. Does she know about him? She's good with people. Surely she suspects something wrong... Could she be in on it? What would he do if I would suddenly reappear? What would she do?*

108

"Calm down. It's best to leave Cindy alone," AL said via the Meta. *"Avi is probably using her for bait. Who he's trying to catch? I don't know. I'm sure he believes you're dead."*

Why would he use Cindy if he thinks I'm dead?

"He's probably sticking around to see what she knows. She was close to everything."

She also inherited a good chunk of the company. He probably forgot to mention to her that I fired his ass.

"I'm sure you're right… Dan?" Dan's eyes were closed, and he was breathing deeply. *"Wake up! There's more I need to tell you."*

Dan groaned and rubbed his eyes. *Can it wait? I'm kind of tired here. All your long-winded explanations are putting me to sleep.*

"I'll make it quick. Fana installed client software into your microcode. It modifies your subliminal consciousness by amplifying it. What was once unheard is now audible. What was once unseen is now a visual hallucination.

"Part of the Fana-client integration process is an initial scan. The scan discovered a few unexpected features within your microcode. Perhaps you were unaware of them."

Dan stretched, and his foot accidentally knocked a magazine off the coffee table. Underneath was the TV remote. He grabbed it and turned down the volume. *Oh?*

"First of all, there was an unseen active connection inside you. It connects your meta with an entity off-Simulation. It came over with you and it's a significant amount of traffic. I didn't notice it until you two merged and the client was fully integrated. The data stream contains code in a foreign machine language. From the transmission pattern, my guess is that it's telemetry.

"I've detected other nodes broadcasting to the same off-Simulation entity as you. Because they're broadcast, I can see them on your connection. I've detected six other distinct signals, but I can't identify the individuals. I plan on snooping the connection to gather more data."

Dan groaned as he leaned forward. The intrahead, omnidirectional conversation had made him nauseated. It was overwhelming. "Six signals? You mean people?" Dan said aloud.

"I'm sorry, Dan. I don't understand," said the hidden speaker. "Judging by the variations in your speech pattern and your overall lack of coherence, I've determined your blood sugar may be too low. Thankfully your food is on its way. You should eat it as soon as it arrives."

Dan squirmed. *Wrong AL!*

"No! You have to be more careful with that AL. Thankfully he thinks you're not feeling well. If he had started searching for Meta connections, it may draw attention to us."

Got it. Sorry. Please continue.

"To answer your question, six people have an active connection off-Simulation. It's probably people who have experienced the same corruption as you."

"You mean people who took Fana in the last life?"

"Possibly," AL said.

Dan held out his hand and counted. *"Let's see. There was Yvette, Blaine, and I. That's three. Andy never took Fana, not in the last life at least."*

"Any ideas who the other three are?" AL said.

"I'm trying to think... Henry had some in his possession, but he said he never took any. Father Desjeunes had my pack in his cabinet for a while, but he wouldn't have taken it either. Maybe Father August?"

"We can look for Yvette and Blaine. It's a start. That leaves the other thing... Lemmy left a mess inside your meta. He hid stuff in out-of-the-way areas you would have never known existed. I discovered his little snippets of code during my tool installation.

"He also left behind laptops. Only they're not strictly laptops. Ideologically they're the same, but in reality, it's just compact code on an arbitrary abstraction layer. You may think of it as a virtual machine inside your meta. Only this virtual machine isn't running the same operating system."

"I'm tired and having a hard time following. What's the gist?"

"Lemmy was sloppy. He left a trail. Given time, I can decrypt those laptops. They would be like our own personal Rosetta Stone. I could use

it to interpret the foreign machine code I'm capturing on your meta network. If I can translate the code and decipher the encryption keys, then I could –"

An image flashed across the TV screen, and Dan bolted upright. "Yvette?"

The news had switched over to a New Orleans affiliate. The tagline read ANOTHER DRONE STRIKE? Yvette's photo was plastered across the screen. A run-down shopping center burned in the background. Dan turned up the volume to hear the young reporter who was nervously gripping his microphone.

"Officials have confirmed to action news that it was a gas leak, not a missile that did in this shopping center off Lapalco Boulevard. The coffee shop made statewide news yesterday when it exploded into a giant fireball that could be seen for miles. It was initially thought to be a part of the drone attacks in Mons, and it's easy to see why." The camera panned across the smoldering strip mall. "The shock wave shattered most of the windows in the area, and the blaze took eight hours to fully extinguish. The state fire marshal declared the destruction was the result of a gas leak in the store of one of the tenants. Forensic investigation determined that the gas line was intentionally cut. Authorities are asking for the public's assistance in finding this woman, Yvette Boudreaux."

Again, Yvette's picture was put on the screen. Acid rose in Dan's throat. This time he was sure it was her. She looked very different from the last time he'd seen her.

"It was initially reported that she perished in the blaze," the reporter said. "However, no human remains have been discovered. If you have any information about Miss Boudreaux's whereabouts –"

Dan stood from the couch and wobbled. His energy depleted. "It was her! AL, we have to go help Yvette. Avi is going after her!"

"No! You aren't strong enough!" AL warned through the speakers. "It'll take you a while to get back to normal. You need food and rest."

"He's right," said AL in his head. "You need time to recover."

But she's in danger. I have to do something.

"We will help you. Give us time to work out the details. But first get your strength back."

Fine.

The doorbell rang, and Dan groaned as it took every effort to stand. He wearily retrieved the packages from the door and laid everything out on the dining room table. The jambalaya was hot, the beer was ice-cold. He ate in silence. Once the food and beer settled in, Dan felt better. "Okay AL, think. How can I help Yvette?" he said, wiping his lips. "First of all, why is she in Marrero? I thought she was from Mons?"

"Give me a second to perform a secure search. I need to relay through a device that can't be traced back to me. I found an old high school classmate of hers with a weak password. Her searching for Yvette wouldn't look suspicious to anyone watching."

Dan nodded and lit a cigarette. He took one deep drag before making a face of disgust and throwing the butt into an empty beer can. "Bleh! Cigarettes taste like shit here," he said as he quickly washed his mouth out with a fresh beer.

"Daniel's body isn't used to it," AL said dispassionately.

Dan choked on the beer and fell into a coughing fit. "Yeah, maybe." Dan searched for a paper napkin to wipe his tongue. "I don't know."

Dan pushed the pack of cigarettes off to the side, grabbed his beer, and returned to the couch as AL delivered the report.

"Yvette Boudreaux. Twenty-seven. Graduated with honors from Benjamin Franklin. She was accepted to attend Tulane. Her father died of a stroke when she was eighteen. She runs the family coffee shop with her mom. She has no social media presence outside of the business.

"At twenty-two, she was cited with a misdemeanor drug possession. She was written fifteen parking tickets, all which occurred near the hospital. They were all paid on time. The

Jefferson Parish Sheriff's Department has an active investigation on her. She has been accused of distributing drugs to high school students. So far, they haven't found enough evidence to make an arrest.

"Finally: Her mother is not healthy. She has a laundry list of ailments and medications. Yvette has been meeting with a nursing home about her care. The worst part is that she's only sixty."

Dan whistled. "That's a tough life. What does she do for fun? Is she dating anyone?"

"I don't know that yet. I have the IP information, but her laptop was destroyed in the fire. I'm going to have to search the ISP for records containing her browser fingerprint. She was under an active police investigation, so it may be easier once I take the sheriff's data."

Dan rubbed his eyes. He could feel his body fighting to stay awake. "You can access law enforcement's systems?"

"Are you kidding? The local government has a minuscule IT budget. Most of their systems are ten years old and older. Gaining entry isn't the hard part. The hard part is making sense of how the data is stored and getting relevant information from it…"

Dan jerked awake. The clock on the wall was five minutes past when he last looked at it. "Sorry, I dozed off. Can you locate her, AL? Surely you can use nearby security cameras to help."

AL took control of the TV, and the screen changed to closed-circuit security camera footage overlooking a dumpster in a trash-strewn alleyway. Dan assumed it was from behind Yvette's coffee shop. A woman came running into the frame and stumbled into the dumpster. "Yvette?" Dan leaned too far forward, and his head slipped off his hands. He shook his head to stay awake, but sleep would soon be unavoidable.

A sports car turned in to the alley, drove past the dumpster, and stopped out of view of the camera. A man rushed over, making urgent gestures. They were speaking, but there was no audio on the feed. The woman tried to stand but collapsed in a heap. The man bent over and helped her to his car. As he led her out of sight, he looked up at the camera. He quickly ducked his head, and the two disappeared from view.

"Blaine!" Dan cheered weakly.

"That was Blaine?" AL said. "Are you sure? Facial recognition didn't register him. That's odd. It's no matter, I've got the make and model of his car. That's all I need to find him. If you give me a few minutes, I can— Dan?"

Dan lay sprawled about on the sofa, sound asleep.

Eleven

———◦◦◦———

D AN DROVE PAST the cathedral and followed North Peters all the way to Saint Ferdinand. After driving for hours to get to New Orleans, he couldn't wait to get out and stretch his legs. Still several blocks away, he parked near a bright pink building covered with mosaics. He tossed the keys onto the front seat and left the doors unlocked so the locals could do the work of hiding the car for him.

He stuck close to the graffiti-clad walls as he made his way along the broken sidewalks of Saint Ferdinand. Rust-stained shutters and plywood covered the ground-floor windows on the warehouse across the street. Dan wondered if it was because of the recent hurricane, but the building's second-floor windows were clean and intact. The shutters must have been installed to keep people out, not the weather. The neighborhood appeared safe enough during the daylight, and there were no bars in the area. It seemed like overkill. He shrugged and turned right on Dauphine just past the old opera house. Dan's wireless earbuds beeped, and AL's voice came through. "Camera on the blue two-story."

He was on watch for digital surveillance and had found one. Dan caught a glimpse of the camera and quickly looked away as he passed. Even though he wore a hoodie, sunglasses, and a face mask to protect him from facial recognition, modern technology had a multitude of other ways to ID someone. AL said they could even find you by your height and the way you walked. To combat this, Dan put a sharp rock in his shoe and walked hunched over. It was okay for the first few blocks, but now it hurt.

"You shouldn't be here, Dan," AL said via the Meta. *"There aren't many cameras, but most of the ones in this neighborhood are monitored online. You're putting both you and Actual AL at risk."*

I need to warn Blaine about Avi and his drones. They are in danger and don't know it.

"They've always been in danger. You're going to make it worse."

Easy for you to say. You're safe out there... uh... wherever you are. Don't worry. I'm sure you'll be just fine without me.

"This is obviously a trap. Don't you see? Avi could have followed Blaine just to wait and see who showed up. He could have drones out of range that neither me nor Actual AL can detect. He could even have satellites zoomed in on us. For every one camera sticking out of a wall, there are ten you can't see. If you do anything, please —"

Dan blinked twice. *Mute.*

"Just let me do my thing," he muttered to himself.

"What was that?" said Actual AL over the earbuds.

Dan cursed silently for not muting his cell phone as well. He was frustrated at having to manage not one but two instances of an intrusive AI. "Nothing," he said. "I was wondering if we were clear of the camera yet."

Dan crossed the tracks and stood in front of Blaine's building. It was a dilapidated, three-story warehouse converted into a set of apartments. Like many of the nearby buildings in the neighborhood, the ground floor was shuttered. Graffiti colored every inch of its facade. For whatever reason, the gentrification of the area had left this building and the ones next to it untouched. They must have concluded that the only way to fix them was with a bulldozer.

Dan pushed past the boarded-up front door and into the public stairwell. His eyes watered as he was greeted with the rancid odor of cat piss and day-old vomit. He held his nose and raced up the steps to apartment 201, which was the first apartment on the right. Its door hung open, and the apartment appeared to have been long abandoned. The only signs of life were the roaches scurrying across the stained carpet.

As he stood taking it all in, he heard a hushed conversation coming through the wall of the apartment next door. He quietly left 201 and stalked down the hall to 203. Being as sneaky as he could, he put his ear to the door. He leaned forward and his weight shifted. The old floorboard creaked loudly, giving him away. The people inside went silent, and a shadow crossed the gap under the door.

Trying to make a friendly first impression, Dan smiled at the peephole. The door burst open, and a pair of hands grabbed him and threw him inside. He spun around, and before he could identify his assailant, he caught a right cross to his left temple. Stars floated as he fell to a knee, dazed. The room had barely come back into focus when the man jumped on his back and held his face to the floor. "Whoa!" Dan huffed. "It's me, Dan, er, I mean, Daniel Lemon. I—"

"I know who you are!" Blaine growled, digging his knee deeper into Dan's spine. "Yvette! Get the rope!"

Footsteps scurried across the room as the knee slid between his shoulder blades. His head was smashed against the dirty floor, and his hands were forced behind his back and tied. Finally the pressure relented, and Dan gasped for air.

"Stop!" he panted. "I'm here to talk."

"Shut up," Blaine said.

The room went dark as he was blindfolded. It smelled like Blaine's sweaty T-shirt. Once he felt the mask cinch tight, Blaine got off. Dan flipped himself over onto his back and sucked in air. "What the hell is wrong with you?" he said, catching his breath.

"Yvette, open the kitchen drawer by the fridge. Bring me the gun."

"Calm down," Dan said, trying to peek under the blindfold. "I'm not here to hurt either of you. We were friends once."

Blaine breathed roughly nearby. The struggle had cost him too. "Oh? Friends? The last time I saw your face was when you slit my throat. Yvette! Bring the gun now!"

What is he talking about? Blaine propped him against the wall. Dan leaned forward and twisted his wrists uncomfortably. The rope was too tight and dug into his flesh as he struggled.

"Stop moving!" he commanded.

Remembering AL was muted, Dan blinked twice to summon him. His ears rang as the friendly AI came online. *"What's happening? Why are we blindfolded? Why do your arms hurt?"*

Blaine did this. He's going to kill me. He says I cut his throat or some shit. I'd never —

"Interesting. He must be remembering the last Simulation," AL said. "That's a good sign! Keep him talking and let's see what he knows."

"Blaine," Dan said desperately, "you have to believe me. I'd never kill anyone. Why would I kill you? We were friends!"

"Yvette! Where are you— Argh! I'll do it myself." The floor pounded as he stomped off and opened the drawer. The mechanical *click-clack* of a round being chambered resonated throughout the apartment.

"Blaine, wait," Yvette said timidly.

Blaine's voice cracked. "No, you don't know what he did to me — to us."

What do I say, AL? I'm about to eat a bullet!

"You know him better than I do! Could it be that he's remembering his afterlife?"

That's it! "It wasn't real, Blaine!" Dan blurted fearfully. "It was your afterlife. You're remembering what happened during the Hell algorithm!"

Blaine gripped him by the back of the neck and pressed the barrel of the gun against his head. "Hell, eh? My life, hell, what's the difference?"

"His touch! I can sense him now!" AL said giddily. *"I can see his code! It matches! But why is his data stream blank?"*

Dan groaned inwardly. *I don't have time for this, AL! Help!*

"Keep him talking! I'm working on it!"

"Blaine, don't please!" Dan pleaded. "We were friends. Lemmy was our enemy. Father August was our enemy. When you died, you must have been sent to the Afterlife database fully conscious. That's why you think I slit your throat. It wasn't me who did it. It was Hell's version of me. That's what you're remembering."

"Why should I believe you? How can I be sure you're not working with them again?"

The floorboards creaked, and a gentle hand rubbed his shoulder. The tension on the gun relaxed a bit. *"Is that Yvette? The code is different... Yep, it must be Yvette. Interesting. You're doing great, Dan. Keep them talking."*

"He is telling the truth, Blaine," Yvette said softly. "At least, I believe he is. Put the gun away. He's not here to hurt us. He isn't the priest."

"The priest?" Dan sputtered. "You talked to Father August? What did he want?"

"Ah, that was his name," Yvette said. "I couldn't think of it until just now... Weird. It's like the thought was blocked."

Blaine placed the gun back to Dan's head. "How do we know he's not working for the priest? We can't trust him!"

Dan struggled against his bonds and growled. "Put the damn gun away!" Dan snarled. "If you shoot, the city's gunshot detectors will have this apartment located instantly. You're putting us all at risk with this show."

Blaine shuddered, and the gun trembled against Dan's head. *I hope he doesn't have his finger on the trigger!*

"I've located them in the database, but something's wrong. Blaine has no data hierarchy — he's a flat line. Yvette's data is a jumbled mess. Half her tables are referencing places that don't exist. Yeah... They've been corrupted. I guess what I'm saying is, you're on your own. I can't install

or modify their data when they are in this state. I'll have to work on it. I'll be away for a few minutes. Good luck."

Fantastic. Thanks AL, you're a lot of help.

Blaine poked Dan with the gun. "Come on. What do you want with us?"

A salty, metallic taste filled Dan's mouth, and he spit. The part of him that was still Daniel yearned to take control. "Fine," he said seriously. "I'm here because our universe is a simulation and it's in grave danger. You two are the only ones who can help me save it."

The pressure eased against his temple as the gun lowered. "Simulation? I don't know what you're talking about," Blaine said. "Besides, why do you think we would help you?"

"You're going to help me because we were friends in the last simulation. The three of us know things no one else knows. Whether you like it or not, we're in this together."

Blaine yanked off the blindfold, and Dan squinted to adjust to the light. The entire room was coated with white paint. It had no furniture or any decorations. There was nothing to break up the excessive whiteness. Even the sheet of plywood blocking the window was painted white. His eyes adjusted and could see Blaine sitting cross-legged on the floor in front of him. The gun rested at his side.

His body was covered in tattoos. He was muscular but lean with prison-muscle. His short hair revealed the scars crisscrossing his skull. His face was expressionless and serious. He looked as if he never heard a joke in his entire life. He was very different from Dan's Blaine. "Keep talking," he grunted as he donned the T-shirt.

"The Simulation's goal is to replicate itself. It operates on a repeating cycle, and each iteration is a bit different. During the last run, we took a drug called Fana. It enabled us to be aware of the Simulation itself, but it also changed us in a fundamental way."

Blaine straightened his shirt and put the gun in his lap; still pointed at Dan. "Continue."

"The drug unlocked a heightened awareness within ourselves and at the same time ruined the Simulation. It tried to repair itself by sending Father August to correct us. That didn't work because Father August himself was poisoned."

"The three of us took the same drug in a past life," Blaine said. "What does that have to do with today?"

"I was getting to that," Dan said. "The three of us were friends. We all worked in IT at a company called AGphic in Mons."

Blaine laughed. "No way. I hate computers. And Mons? It's a shithole. Anyplace that was once colonized by the Belgians is like that. It's a historical *fact* that they sucked at world building."

"He's right," Yvette said, appearing over Blaine's shoulder. "Mons *is* a shithole."

Dan couldn't believe how different she was. Her easy smile was gone, as was the sparkle in her eyes. Her hair, once immaculately kept, was frazzled. The sides of her face were pockmarked from untreated acne. She grimaced when she knelt next to Blaine. Her bottom teeth were crowded and crooked. Her family must not have been able to afford braces. "Mons wasn't bad when I lived there," he said. "Or at least, I never thought so."

"Anyplace can be nice if you have money." Blaine sneered. "You just have to live far enough away from the poor people. You're a billionaire, right? Tell me, was it tough driving from your grand estate to your palace downtown?"

"That's not important," Dan said, trying to get back on topic. "We were friends. Surely you can remember something of the last life besides Hell? Something positive? It could have come to you in a dream?"

Yvette's eyes lit up. "I had a dream once that—"

"Let him do the talking, Yvette," Blaine said with a scowl. "Go back to the periscope and watch the street. He may have been followed."

"Okay," she said with a look of disappointment.

"Periscope?" Dan said with a nervous chuckle. "What is this place, a submarine?"

"In case you haven't noticed, I've got the place boarded up. It's the only way I've got to keep an eye on the street. I don't have cameras because I hate technology. You never know who else could be watching."

Electronic devices? He had forgotten all about his phone! Had Actual AL been listening this whole time? Was it safe from eavesdroppers? He searched the floor and found his earbuds lying against the wall. He struggled against his bonds to sit straight. "Cut me loose please. This is unnecessary."

Blaine chuckled. "You're going to have to give me a reason to trust you."

"Okay, come closer," Dan said. "I don't want Yvette to overhear."

Blaine tucked the gun into the back waist of his pants and leaned in.

"We were buddies from the start," Dan whispered. "Some friendships are easy like that. We worked side by side every day. We went to happy hour once a week. Then they hired Yvette.

"She was the prettiest girl at the company, and you fell in love the second you laid eyes on her. She was one of the first ones to take Fana, and when she did, she came to me. You were jealous, but our friendship allowed you and Yvette to get to know each other. You two worked together to help save the Simulation from Lemmy. You helped to save Andy. You saved me. For that, I am forever grateful. You and Yvette were a great team and, I think, grew to love each other. When we last spoke, you were heading to the beach with her. You two would be alone at last. You were happy."

Blaine stood and paced the room. Still agitated but not angry. Maybe he did remember? "The beach," he said. "Why were we at the beach? It wasn't a vacation."

"We were supposed to lose contact. We didn't want to risk exposing the whole group if one of us had been captured. You two were to go off the grid and wait for my signal. I went offline. After that, I don't know what happened."

"What happened?" Blaine chuckled ironically. "I'll tell you what happened. Father August found us."

Dan stiffened. He thought they would have been safe once he was out of the picture. How was he to know Father August would continue to hunt them after it was all over? The light dimmed, and Blaine stood over him.

"Yvette doesn't remember anything of what happened because he got to her first. How it all went down is fuzzy to me too. All I really remember is the pain. My soul was ripped out, my brain was scraped clean, and I was sent off to the Afterlife as a discarded husk. It's all blurred together.

"Ever since I was a kid, I had nightmares. I dreamed of you — and him. He would come to visit me in my dreams. You don't know this, but I was an orphan. I bounced from one foster home to another. When I was old enough, I went out on my own. I moved around a lot. I was used to it. I came here a few weeks ago. Did you know he can get inside your head and use your eyes? He likes to catch you when you're sleeping and not in control. I painted the room white so he couldn't find me in the real world. I made sure there would be nothing in sight that would clue him in to where I am.

"That was the bad. I also dreamed of Yvette. My whole life I've had a connection to her — though I didn't realize it was *her*. She was just an ideal when I was a kid, not a real person. The connection got stronger with each passing year. That's why I came here. That's how I found her. At last we are together again." A tear streamed down his face, and he frowned at Dan. "But now you're here. Just like before, she will be taken away from me. I won't let it happen again."

With a twist of his wrist, a knife appeared in his hand.

"Okay, I'm back. What'd I miss? Oh! Something's wrong."

123

No shit something's wrong! He's about to stab me!

"I thought you two could work things out. I swear – "

"Blaine!" Yvette said as she rushed into the room. "You have to come look at this."

Blaine's eyes shifted suspiciously to Dan. "What is it?"

"Brad and Kara are out there. They were in my coffee shop yesterday just before the priest arrived. She goes to Dominican. There's no way she'd be caught dead in this neighborhood. It's fishy as hell."

"Yep. I see them," AL said. "I'm detecting encrypted intra-meta traffic. They have a low-level link. She's right. We have bigger problems."

Bigger problems than getting stabbed?

Blaine bounced nimbly to his feet. "Show me," he said as he grabbed her hand and led her to the back.

"There's an uptick in off-Simulation traffic on your link. You've got to get out of there."

What? Who is it? Father August – I mean Avi?

"It's getting stronger… Go now!"

Dan rolled over to his stomach and paused to listen.

"…so you think he was followed," Yvette said. Blaine grunted a reply, and a window slid open. Warm, humid air poured into the apartment followed by a muffled metallic clang. "What about Dan?"

They were distracted. It was time to escape. He had to do it quietly in case Blaine was listening. He had to do it quickly before Blaine came back. Dan pushed himself up onto his knees and to his feet. He crept slowly toward the front door, but each board let loose a betraying creak. He had just grasped the doorknob, hands still bound behind his back, when he saw a bright light coming from the hallway. *Did they?* Dan let go of the knob and walked through the kitchen and into the back bedroom. Sunlight poured in from the gaping window, revealing a rusty fire escape. *They ditched me!* Dan stuck his head out just in time to catch Blaine and Yvette rounding the corner. *Shit!* .

Dan searched for options. Across the hall from the bedroom was the bathroom. A pipe was suspiciously twisted out of place near the toilet. Was that the periscope? He hurried into the kitchen and cut himself free with a knife Blaine had left lying on the counter. He went back and peered inside the pipe. It was the periscope.

It faced the brick facade of the building itself. Dan imagined the pipe blending in with the rest of the rubble. How had Blaine managed to get the mirrors just right? Impressed, he twisted it around and saw a couple of teenagers loitering in front of the apartment. One was a young man in a green Tulane sweatshirt. The other was a teenage girl in a school uniform. She sat in the driver's seat of a Camaro, chewing bubble gum while he pointed at the warehouse across the street.

AL's voice rang out in Dan's head. He jumped and bumped his head on the other end of the exposed pipe.

"I see a ton of encrypted communication coming in over the Meta link… It's not to you. What's going on out there?"

"One sec!" Dan said, rubbing his head. The girl answered her phone, and the smile faded from her face. The boy spun around and jogged across the street to the warehouse. Hot on his heels was a drone that had just dropped down from the sky.

"The teenagers are chasing Blaine and Yvette. They must've hidden in the warehouse next door."

Dan twisted the periscope as far as it could go. The boy kicked in the warehouse's side door and disappeared from view while the drone hovered obediently outside.

"We have to warn them about the drone! AL, can you send Blaine or Yvette a subliminal message?"

"I tried to initiate a client download earlier. It has yet to be installed. Although I can't message them directly, I'll broadcast it subliminally."

The Camaro's horn blared, and the guy in the Tulane shirt reemerged from the warehouse. He threw his hands in the air in confusion. Dan twisted the periscope to get a better view of the girl. She was standing outside the car, pointing furiously toward Blaine's building. "Uh… AL… I think the bad guys heard you."

"Use the fire escape. Go!"

Dan ran back to the living room to retrieve his earbuds. The creaky floor sounded as if it were about to break, but he no longer cared. He shoved them into his pocket and rushed to the bedroom and out the open window.

He scurried down the fire escape and would have gotten away cleanly had his foot not caught on the last rung. With a yelp, he fell face-first onto the alley below. As he lay there dazed, he heard angry shouts coming from the front of the building. There was a loud crash and the sound of metal on metal. A large truck rattled past, revving its engine and billowing coal-black exhaust. It disappeared down the street with its back bumper clanging along behind.

While the teens were distracted, Dan picked himself up off the wet pavement and jogged through the alley. Gravel stuck to his face, and the greasy puddle water stung his eyes. He blinked hard to clear his vision, but it didn't help, so he wiped his face with his shirt.

Still trying to clear the blurriness, he turned the corner and ran smack into the Tulane kid. The collision knocked them both to the ground. When he saw Dan, his eyes went wide.

"You?" he said. "Wh-what are *you* doing here?"

A drone dropped in from over the rooftop and hovered in the middle of the street. It was different from the one that had explored the warehouse earlier. It was the same type that had killed the policeman, an assassin drone. The kid must not have been expecting it because he froze in place. "Shit!" he said through clenched teeth. "Don't move. It—"

Before he could finish, Dan threw a devastating punch to the kid's solar plexus. He doubled over, breathless and wild-eyed. He turned to the drone, but it didn't react. The teenager gasped for air as he ordered it to attack, but the drone did nothing.

Dan spun around and ran in the opposite direction. When he reached the other side of the building, he glanced back. They were still in the same spot. The boy sat on the ground with his head in his hands, and the drone hadn't moved. Relieved he wasn't being pursued, he sprinted down the street, across the tracks, and back into the city.

Twelve

⬥◉◉◉⬥

As Dan jogged along Burgundy Street, he said a silent thank-you to the crepe myrtles for covering his escape. They did a great job of hiding him from satellites, drones, or whatever was watching from above. After three blocks, the adrenaline wore off, and he slowed to a hobble. Grimacing in pain, Dan collapsed onto a doorstep and took off his shoe. His sock was soaked with blood. He took out the sharp rock he had used to disguise his gait and tossed it and the bloody sock into a storm drain.

As he pulled his shoe back on, he checked to see if he was followed. Cars lined the streets, but there were few people out and about. There was also no sign of the teenagers from Blaine's apartment. Movement in his peripheral vision caught his attention, and he spun his head around. The paint on the graffitied brick wall across the street morphed to form a message. But by the time he blinked, it was gone. He rubbed his eyes and crossed the road. The graffiti was several layers deep. But when he tilted his head just right, a message as bright as a neon sign appeared among the chaotic scribbles. STEALTH MODE. GO THREE BLOCKS WEST. GREEN DOOR. SECOND FLOOR. SECOND ROOM.

He blinked again, and the words were gone. A message from AL! Who else could it have been? He turned and walked gingerly down the street. He had to follow the directions, but he wasn't sure how much farther he could limp along like this. He crossed Franklin and stayed on Burgundy. The sun was hot, and humidity clung to him like a steamy blanket. He was miserable, but he pressed on.

Three blocks later, Dan found himself in front of an old Catholic church. Adjacent to it was a schoolhouse with a bright green door. Assuming it was the one from the message, he ducked inside. Ice-cold air-conditioning washed over him, and he sighed with relief. A pair of nail-studded cushioned chairs sat just inside the front door, and he collapsed into one of them. As he caught his breath, he came to realize he was sitting in a hotel lobby, not a schoolhouse. A reception desk waited at the end of the room, but it was unmanned, and a luggage caddy sat empty nearby. Two dark stained wooden staircases flanked the entryway. He wondered if he should wait to talk to a concierge before he headed upstairs, but he decided it was best to keep going. A red velvet rope blocked the stairs to the left, so he took the ones to the right.

At the top was a short hallway. There weren't many rooms there; only three on each side, six total. The middle door on the right was slightly ajar. What did the graffiti say? Second floor, second room, this had to be it. He took a quick peek through the slit and crept his way inside. The bed was made, and there were no signs of another guest's presence, so he turned around and locked the door.

A pitcher of lemonade sweated on a tea table next to an overstuffed chair. The ice had only just begun to melt. A note next to it read ENJOY YOUR STAY, MR. R. HEAD.

Dan sighed with relief. Richard Head was a code name Blaine had given him in the last run of the Simulation. The message *was* intended for him. But if AL had arranged this room, how did he know to use *that* alias? He'd have to ask him later. Now all he wanted was the lemonade. He filled a glass and gulped it down. He went for a refill, but the phone rang.

"Welcome to Peter and Paul, Mr. Head. I'm Nate, your concierge. Thank you for your contactless check-in. Is there anything I can do to make your stay more enjoyable?"

Dan gulped down the second glass. "Do you have a first aid kit and a pair of socks?"

"I'll send a first aid kit right away, but I'm afraid we don't have any extra socks. However, we can get some for you if that is what you wish."

Dan wiggled his toes. The feeling had returned. "Just the first aid kit," he said, rattling the ice cubes in his glass. "And another pitcher of lemonade."

He hung up the phone and removed his shoes. There was a gash where the rock rubbed into his skin, but it didn't seem like it was too deep. The bleeding had mostly stopped; it only came out when he rubbed it. There was a knock at the door. The first aid kit and a fresh pitcher of lemonade had arrived. That was fast.

He brought it to the en suite and set it on the back of the toilet while he washed his feet in the bathtub. Clean and dry, he treated the injury with antiseptic and wrapped his entire foot with gauze. It wasn't the same as a sock, but it would have to do. The hot bath had steamed the mirror, and Dan grabbed a towel to wipe it down. When he turned around, the word UNMUTE was traced as if by an invisible finger on the glass.

Dan instinctively tapped his pockets. His phone and the earbuds were still there. He then realized he must have inadvertently muted internal AL during the scuffle with the Tulane kid. Dan blinked twice. *Unmute.*

"*I've been trying to reach you,*" he said. "*We have problems.*"

"Sorry, AL. I didn't realize you were muted. I didn't have my earbuds in either."

"*Now that we can hear each other, go back to using your inner voice!*" AL said. "*It's okay that I was muted. It was probably a good thing. They couldn't trace my signal to you. Besides, I have other means of communication.*"

Yeah, I can see that. The ghostwriting is creepy. Anyway, what's up? Why can't I speak out loud? Is someone listening?

"You may have inadvertently revealed your position when you spoke over the hotel phone. If I was able to listen to the call, no telling who else heard."

Why? What's going on?

"Yvette and Blaine are on the run. I get glimpses from Yvette's meta, but I don't have full access to her senses. They're in Blaine's truck. Judging by the road signs they've passed, it looks as if they're headed west on the interstate. She keeps checking the rearview, but I think they're safe for now. The two teenagers you ran into outside Blaine's apartment didn't go after them. They're looking for you."

Dan went back into the bedroom and sat on the bed. His head spun, but it was good to rest, if even for only a few minutes. Who are they?

"I'm not sure, but it's not good. I detected unusual network activity but only when they were around. Incoming data was from the Meta. My suspicions were confirmed when you punched that boy. I detected a third active meta link inside him."

You mean like ours?

"Precisely. A private encrypted link. They're able to talk with someone the same way we are now."

Dan frowned and slipped his shoe on over the bandage. It was a tight squeeze, but it felt as good as new. It must be Avi. He is the only one capable of establishing a meta link. Yvette recognized them from her shop. But I've never seen those two before. Why would they have an active meta link if they didn't take Fana on the last run? Maybe I didn't know everyone who took it after all…

"That's not important at the moment. What is important is that every police drone in the city is currently within a ten-block radius of this hotel. These drones are carrying cameras and microphones. They're controlled by humans. You're vulnerable. Speaking of microphones, unplug the TV. It has a microphone."

Dan went to the armoire and opened the door. He reached behind the flat television and unplugged the power from the rear. Why are the police looking for me? I'm dead.

The television turned on, and the local news displayed on the screen.

How? I just unplugged it.

"It's me. As you've already seen, I can project images onto objects. These images are visible only to you. It only works on objects that your brain is already wired to see images on."

You mean like graffiti on a wall or fog on a bathroom mirror?

"Right... Dan, there's no easy way to break this to you, so I'm just going to go ahead and show you the news report."

The newscaster stiffened as a picture of Cindy appeared over her shoulder. "We are now following up on a story that broke just hours ago. Cindy Lemon, the wife of Dandy CEO, Daniel Lemon, was found dead just before noon today."

Dan's heart sank. A voice buried deep inside him cried out in pain. His eyes opened wide in surprise. Daniel had been silent until now. He had assumed they were completely assimilated the moment they had taken Gemini. The outburst of individualism made him anxious. He found himself overwhelmed with a mixture of sadness and guilt.

The report continued. "Police are looking for her husband, Daniel Lemon, who was previously believed to have been killed in the attack on their country estate. New evidence appears to show an entirely different story."

Dan's picture filled the screen. It was a screen capture of surveillance footage of him walking down the street in a hoodie, the same one he was now wearing. Dan's heart raced. His picture dissolved and was replaced with an image of a typed memo. The headline above it read TELL-ALL LETTER LEAKED.

"Shortly after Cindy's death, a package arrived at the police station, detailing an elaborate scheme. Sources close to the investigation tell us that Daniel Lemon owed investors billions of dollars and that Dandy Intelligence was going to file for bankruptcy."

"What? That's bullshit!" Dan shouted as the newscast continued.

"The letter also alleged Dandy's AI, whom he had called AL, was a hoax. It was said to be perpetrated by Dandy employees. They acted on behalf of the AI. Its lifelike personality was not an actual computer program. The letter purports Cindy was haunted by past abuse and fearful of Daniel's quick temper. The package was to be delivered by Cindy's lawyer in the event of her death as a final request. She wished to let the truth be known.

"Daniel Lemon faked his own death to escape bankruptcy and embarrassment. He is the prime suspect in the slaying of Cindy Lemon. He was sighted earlier today in the Marigny neighborhood of New Orleans. The public should consider him armed and dangerous. If you spot Daniel Lemon, please call 911."

The TV blacked out. Dan sat in silence as he tried to manage both his and Daniel's emotions. The phone in the hotel room across the hall rang. It broke his concentration, and he burst into tears.

"Quiet down!" AL urged. *"If a microphone in the other room picks up your vocal pattern…"*

Another phone in a room down the hall rang. Dan lay back in bed and cried. The more he tried to muffle it, the harder it became to control himself. His face turned red, and a vein bulged out of his forehead. The phone next door rang, and a tiny voice answered, "Housekeeping."

"Why Cindy?" Dan said between sobs. "To get the police involved? She was innocent!"

"Dan, you have to be quiet! There are microphones everywhere!"

The phone next door clanged onto the receiver, and footsteps shuffled away. "I can't help it," he said with a sniffle. "It's Daniel doing this. He doesn't have control, and it's just pouring out. Wait…" Dan took deep breaths and grabbed his head. "We have to move forward… Sorry Daniel… Okay, we'll go get him, but first I need control… Argh!" Dan's eyes opened, and his breathing slowed.

"Be quiet! Look, I don't know what you're thinking, but you're going nowhere near Mons."

"What?" Dan said to himself in disbelief. *"I have to go there. He will stop at nothing to get to me. How many others will he hurt? I have to face that monster —"*

"Going to Mons right now won't accomplish anything. Besides, where would you go? Your house is gone, your business is gone. The police are after you. What do you think would happen if you turned yourself in? He'd kill you. No. You have to —"

The phone in Dan's room rang.

"Don't answer it."

Dan stormed over and put the receiver to his ear. "Hello, Dan," said a smug voice.

"Hello, Avi," he said with a nasty smile. "By the way, the name's Daniel."

"Is it?" Avi said ominously. "Have you seen the news, Dan?"

"I have. You killed Cindy and framed me for her murder."

"Correct. Now you know how it ends."

Dan gripped the phone; his knuckles turning white. "I'm coming for you, Avi."

"That's not necessary," he said, his voice dripping with false politeness. "I'm already here."

A commotion erupted in the hallway outside his door. People clambered down the steps and out through the lobby. Dan placed the phone on the dresser and pulled open the curtains. He stood face-to-face with a dark orange strike drone. It was the same type of drone that had destroyed Dandy HQ. Now it hovered right outside his window with its rail-mounted missiles pointed directly at him. Dan slowly backed away and returned to the phone.

"It's over, Dan. With your death, the AI cannot be rebuilt. There is no one left in this run of the Actual who could pull it off. The Simulation will mercifully come to an end."

"You'll die too!" Dan said, his face turning red with anger. "You're a part of this world."

"Oh no." Avi chuckled. "I'm due for a recompile — an upgrade. Lemmy has a use for me in his universe. He says he has a problem he wants me to solve. See? I'm not like you. You're only useful here, in this timeline."

Dan arched an eyebrow. *A problem only he can solve? Could he be referring to Charlie?*

"Keep him talking," AL said abruptly. *"Wait for my signal. You'll need to move fast."*

"Uh… Before I go, tell me one thing," he said, gripping the phone. "Why did you have to kill Cindy? She was innocent."

"Innocent? What does innocence have to do with anything?" Avi scoffed. "If I could, I'd kill everyone just to get this over with. Nobody matters anymore. You're all destined to be permanently erased."

"Keep him talking…"

The drone wobbled slightly with a gust of wind, and Dan flinched. *Why hasn't he killed me yet?* Dan closed his eyes to avoid the sight of the menacing craft. "Um… Who were the two kids at Blaine's apartment?"

"Brad and Kara? They're here to help make sure everything gets shut down smoothly. Though I did loop them in a little ahead of schedule. No harm done. Unfortunately."

"Just a few more seconds."

Hurry! "Ahead of schedule?" he said, clearing his throat. "Ah yes, the Simulation should have ended with my death. You probably thought Blaine and Yvette were somehow keeping it running because they were around last time. So you hired the kids to take care of them."

"Precisely. But now that you're here, I have reassessed my assumptions. It's obvious now that —" Avi gasped. "No, it's not possible."

The blinking light on the drone went out, and it crashed to the street below.

"You won't win, Avi," Actual AL said over the telephone. "Leave us alone!"

"AL! You're supposed to be disabled. How are you meddling with my drones? When I find you, you're doomed! I'll—"

Dan slammed the phone down onto the receiver. "Enough."

"Let's go," AL said. *"I've shut down all municipal servers. The police can't control their drones, and there aren't any officers outside. I'm sure Brad and Kara are on their way. You need to hurry."*

"AL, you did it!" Dan smiled. "I didn't think anyone could hack into Avi's system!"

"It was a team effort. Actual AL helped tremendously. We've DDoSed his signal and shut him out of the whole city, but it's temporary. You're safe until he changes location. Unfortunately, he now knows where we are. You need to leave New Orleans, and I need to go offline for a little while to change locations myself. Use your phone to talk to a local copy of AL. He can help you escape as long as he still exists."

Dan pulled the earbuds out of his pocket and jammed them in. A long, soft tone acknowledged that he had connected directly to the cellular network. Two short beeps would have meant they had attached to another device. AL was already waiting for him.

"Dan, are you there?" he said over the earpiece.

"Loud and clear," Dan said with a smile.

"Great. A car is waiting for you downstairs. Go now."

Thirteen

D AN CHECKED HIS rearview mirror for the hundredth time
since he left New Orleans. Not that he could tell if he had
been followed; there were thousands of other drivers on the
interstate all going the same direction. But still, there could be
drones. He peered up at the sky but didn't see anything. Actual
AL had assured him the drones couldn't have followed him this
far away. He wished Meta AL was online to give a second opinion,
but he had been silent since the hotel room.

Actual AL was the one who had arranged the rental car to be
delivered. Now that he was out of the state of Louisiana, it was
time to change vehicles. The police were still tracking him. A new
car and a different state's license plate would help him elude them
for a little while longer. AL had it all arranged.

Dan followed his instructions and exited I-10 in Biloxi. His
destination was a shopping center just north of the interstate. Dan
reckoned it couldn't have been more than five years old. Trees
lined the freshly poured concrete sidewalks as they meandered
between family-run boutiques and big-box stores. Chain
restaurants flanked the edges. The parking lot seemed as if it were
built to accommodate the entire population of Mississippi. It was
well lit, and there were plenty of people milling about. But none
seem to care about what Dan was doing. Most importantly, the
skies were clear of aircraft.

He abandoned the rental car near one of the chain restaurants. The aroma of fajitas filled his nostrils, and his stomach growled. No time to eat. He found the vehicle AL purchased online, sitting by itself at the outskirts of the parking lot near the road. It was parked under the only streetlight that was off. Dan wondered if AL had paid extra for that or if he had done it himself. Now that he was closer, he suspected the previous owner must have done it. It was one of the ugliest cars he'd ever seen.

It was a 1980s-era Chevrolet Beretta. AL said he had chosen the Beretta because it was too old to be tracked by built-in electronics. Dan wondered if it was even roadworthy. It had faded maroon paint and a cracked windshield. At least it had new tires and freshly tinted windows.

He cracked open the door and winced in disgust. The interior was a nightmare. The seats were ripped and stained. The headliner sagged. The dashboard was cracked, and the stereo was ripped out. Dan could live with all that. But the smell— The smell was the worst of it all. The previous owner had been a smoker; the kind that doesn't give a shit. Cigarette burns marred the door near the window, and the ashtray was full.

The keys were under the seat as promised. Fearing the worst, he closed his eyes as he twisted the ignition. The car roared to life effortlessly. The digital dashboard illuminated the interior, and the air-conditioning blew ice-cold. The old Beretta might not have looked like much, but it was mechanically sound.

He flipped down the sun visor, and four one-hundred-dollar bills flittered onto his lap. AL had paid for a thousand. The seller kept the rest. The poor bastard had no idea who he was messing with. If AL were vengeful, he could ruin the man's life in two seconds. Lucky for him, AL didn't care. To AL, being cheated was a regular part of doing business with humans. He had to deal with it during the construction of his data centers. Purchasing vehicles anonymously online was no different. AL knew what he was doing.

He rolled down the windows and pulled out onto the interstate and headed north from Biloxi. As they drove through Wiggins, Mississippi, AL explained that the first car was to be a red herring. He intentionally chose a rental company that used GPS to track their vehicles. The idea was that the police would eventually obtain video footage of Dan driving the car, and its plate. They would contact the rental company to get the GPS and find the car waiting for them at the mall. They were supposed to believe that Dan was headed to his vacation home near Destin, Florida. AL had him headed in the opposite direction.

Just as Dan had grown used to the smell, AL ordered him to ditch the maroon ash-wagon at a mall outside Jackson. He parked it on the fringe of the lot under a burned-out streetlamp. It was AL that had been putting out the lights after all.

As instructed, he took his cell phone and placed it in the trunk next to the spare tire. AL had arranged this car to be delivered to Richmond, Virginia. The cell phone's signal would undoubtedly be tracked along the way. He asked AL why he didn't just leave it in the rental car. He said the police would need a second false lead once they discovered he wasn't heading to Destin.

AL said Dan was in the clear, at least for a little while. He took the cash and went shopping. He bought a new phone, a charging block for his earbuds and a fresh set of clothes. He changed in the public restroom and tossed his old clothes into the trash bin. He looked like a new man, but he was exhausted and hungry. It had been a day since he had eaten last, and AL made him wait a little longer.

The last thing AL had said to him was "Go to room 303. Eat dinner there—I've already ordered it. Charge the earphones and unplug the room's phone. Good night."

Meta AL had been mysteriously absent throughout the road trip. Dan had given up trying to contact him. He'd send a message when he was ready. Actual AL wasn't much for talking either. He explained that he was locked in a chess match with Avi and couldn't be bothered. Dan couldn't help but feel as if he was once again a pawn in their game. He knew what Avi was capable of. He wasn't a human. He was powerful enough to anticipate their every possible move. Even still, he couldn't cover them all at once. AL had said it was more important to "open up the board" than to plot the end game. Dan didn't understand chess strategy, but he trusted AL.

Chinese delivery waited for him in the room. He scarfed down the stale fried rice and washed it down with a warm beer. The greasy-cold egg roll went into the trash. Unable to go any farther, he took a shower and went to sleep.

The next morning, a ragged-out 1980s Toyota Camry waited for him. Dan asked AL where they were going but received no definite answer. He said that if he told Dan where they were going, he would drive with a *destination bias*—whatever the hell that meant. He would only say that their trip was nowhere near finished.

When he stopped for lunch near Memphis, he switched vehicles again. This time it was one he had requested; a 1960s Ford Bronco. It had no air-conditioning and smelled like gas, but Dan loved it. Traveling the back roads with the windows open felt like freedom.

The moment didn't last. Apparently the Bronco had received one too many friendly waves from the locals. When Dan reached Springfield, Missouri, AL made him do an emergency vehicle swap. His punishment was a rusted-out Pontiac Sunfire. It smelled like the previous owner had spent a hundred bucks on the cheap bubblegum scent at the car wash. The car sucked, but it got him to the hotel in Kansas City.

That night, he had a strange dream. He was sitting in front of a computer, and the monitor displayed a black-and-green terminal screen. The scent of sweet olives wafted in from an open window. A thin layer of pollen coated the wooden furniture. A woman sneezed, and he turned around, but no one was there.

The floors burned and turned to ash beneath his feet. A gust of wind came and blew it away. He now stood in a graveyard at dusk. Raindrops glistened like tears on the marble slabs in the waning daylight. A woman knelt before a tombstone. Her body heaved with grief. When he put a hand on her shoulder, she doubled over and fell to the ground. He called out her name, but her body dissolved into a mist. Darkness fell.

Headlights blinded him, and a car's horn blew. The woman stood in the middle of the road. Her eyes were wide with terror. She screamed, but no sound escaped her lips. He turned to see what had her so afraid. It was a tunnel. There was no light there. Only the inky blackness of the abyss lay beyond. Its maw opened ominously and swallowed the road ahead. The horn blew again, this time much closer. Dan spun around, but it was too late.

A sharp knock on the hotel room door jarred Dan awake. He wasn't expecting company. He fumbled around for his earphones and unplugged them from the charger on the nightstand. "AL, I have company," he said as he stuffed them in.

"It's your breakfast. Eat and get ready to go."

Dan sighed. The dream had put him on edge. He retrieved the room service tray from the hallway's floor and brought it back in the room, careful to lock the door behind him. He lifted the lid, and steam rose up to hit him and the face. Now this was a meal. As he shoved a piece of bacon into his mouth, his eyes lingered on the fruit cup. His thoughts turned to Daniel. After that brief moment of anguish at the news of Cindy's death, he seemed to have retreated to some far-off corner to hide. Had he felt responsible for her death? Was the guilt too difficult to bear? Was he still there? Dan summoned Daniel's memories and was relieved they were still present, at least, the most recent ones were.

Dan tossed the fruit in the trash bin. He had hoped it would get a reaction out of Daniel, but nothing happened. If Daniel had gone somewhere, maybe he wasn't coming back. The realization hit Dan hard. What if Gemini had worked the other way around? What would happen to his consciousness?

Dan shook off the thought. No, Daniel would always be a part of him. The room's AC kicked on, and a puff of air blew across him. He felt a chill and reached up and touched his cheek. It was wet with tears. Daniel's body remembered. Dan daubed his face with the napkin and sighed. He had to keep moving forward, for Daniel. Right now Daniel's body was hungry. Feeding it was the least he could do. He'd worry about Daniel's legacy after he finished the bacon.

"I have to go away for today," Actual AL said via his phone's speaker.

"Oh?" Dan wiped his mouth with the napkin. "What's wrong?"

"Avi discovered how I disabled his drone back there in New Orleans. I don't know if I'll be able to pull that bit of magic again. He's also making it more difficult for me to disguise our wireless signal. I need time to generate a new set of keys and propagate them out to the wireless carriers."

Dan arched an eyebrow as he sipped his coffee. "What do I do? Stay here?"

"No, you need to get back on the road. I found a strategic spot for us to make a stand. It's nestled in the mountains west of Denver, and you must get there as soon as possible. Please understand, I am under heavy attack. Every conversation we have puts us both at risk. I won't be around to act as your GPS, concierge, and personal assistant. I'm going to tell you what you need to do to get there, so take notes."

Dan rummaged around in the desk and found a notepad and pen.

"There's a blue Ford truck downstairs. The keys are under the passenger floor mat. Like before, there should be a few hundred dollars tucked above the visor. Take I-29 north until you get to Highway 36. From there, head west about eight and a half hours until you reach I-70. You will have to watch the clock to know when you're getting close. Don't worry about gas. It has a thirty-six-gallon tank. Don't stop if you can help it.

"Right before the interstate, there will be a motel on the left. It's nothing fancy, but it is clean and safe. Park next to a green Subaru Outback. That will be your next car. It's the same deal as the truck.

The keys are under the passenger floor mat, and there will be some more money above the visor. It should be parked in front of room 103. That's your room. Take a break for a couple of hours. Take a nap if you can. I've already arranged for food to be waiting for you."

Dan scribbled notes and yawned. "Anything else? Do I just stay there?"

"No," AL said. "Wait until seven. Take the Outback and head on I-70 west all the way through Denver. After about an hour and a half, take exit 228 into Griffin City. Take the first right at the roundabout. The hotel is on the left. Again, you have room 103. I did that so it would be easier for you to remember. All you have to do is walk in. The key cards will be on the nightstand.

"The Outback should be clean. I paid a premium so it wouldn't be traceable. We won't be in contact, and the motel near the interstate has no video surveillance. You'll be able to reuse it, so keep the keys with you. We won't have to switch cars again. I've booked the room for a week. Make yourself comfortable. You could be there a while. Pay cash for everything. I don't know when I'll be able to contact you again, but it will be at least twenty-four hours."

Dan flipped the page and scribbled the final note. "Is that all?"

"Don't forget there is a nationwide manhunt for you. Every law enforcement officer from coast to coast wants to get their hands on you. So drive casual! You are no longer Daniel Lemon, the honored CEO of Dandy Intelligence. You're the asshole billionaire who faked his death and killed his wife. Everyone hates you. Do not talk to anyone. Do not stop unless you have to.

"By the way, they found the car in Biloxi. Our plan worked. The police are focusing their efforts on Florida. Good thing we are on the other side of the country."

Dan stretched and yawned. "It looks like I have a long day of driving. I'd better get going."

"Goodbye, Dan. Good luck. I've done all I can. You'll remain anonymous from traffic cameras in the vehicles I've chosen. I've inserted an image match. You won't even show up. And you'll be safe in the rooms. I've sanitized them as well. You can watch TV, surf the internet—anything but make a phone call. Be smart. You have a browsing signature; do not use the internet outside of those safe areas. We are in a good position right now. Don't make any mistakes. Any more questions?"

"Just one. Why did you pick Griffin City, of all places, to make our stand?"

There was a slight pause on the other side of the earphones. "I picked Griffin City because it's far away from where the police think you are. Also, because it's the best place to isolate Avi when he finds you. Yes, he *will* find you. But when he does, it'll be on my terms. You will have to trust me, okay? Our encrypted session has reached its limit. You should leave immediately. Goodbye and good luck."

The earphones beeped, and the line went dead.

"Thanks." Dan groaned.

He removed his earphones and stuffed them in his pocket.

AL? AL, are you there?

The Meta link was quiet. Worried it might be muted, Dan blinked and tried again. Again, there was no response. He was alone. Not wanting to waste any time, he used the bathroom, brushed his teeth, and left the hotel.

The drive went more or less as AL had planned. Dan found his biggest challenge to be staying awake. Driving along the never-ending stretch of farmland without a radio was pure monotony. When he arrived at the motel where Highway 36 met I-70, the green Subaru wasn't there. He went inside room 103 anyway. He hoped whoever was supposed to deliver the vehicle was late and not permanently delayed.

As time ticked by, he contacted AL several times via the earphones and the Meta but received no reply. At nine p.m., he resolved to continue his journey, new car or not, and went back to the truck. As he was driving out of the parking lot, he spotted the

Subaru on the other side of the motel. It was parked under a broken streetlight at the far end of the lot. AL's instructions must have confused the seller. Nevertheless, he was relieved to be back on track.

It started snowing as the interstate climbed its way into the mountains past Denver. It was late summer and much too soon for the first *real* snow. Being from Louisiana, Dan didn't have the slightest clue how to drive in the mountains under these conditions. He slowed to a crawl and put on his hazards. This resulted in quite a few middle fingers from passing locals. It was nearly midnight when Dan pulled off the interstate into Griffin City.

Exhausted, Dan walked into his room, kicked off his shoes, and fell asleep on top of the covers. The dreams came fast, but they weren't his.

He was sitting in his pickup truck. Only, he was in the passenger seat, and the teenager sitting next to him was himself. Dan reached over to shift gears, and a tiny, feminine hand reached out and grabbed his. Her fingernails were painted cayenne red. Her name was Katie. The dream stopped, and a new one started.

He found himself back in the graveyard. Dan's corpse lay stretched out on the cold slab. The woman stood and walked over to an empty granite flower vase and reached inside. She pulled out a thin cardboard drug carton and stuffed it into her pocket. Dan recognized it as the same carton of Fana he had tried to give her the day he died by suicide.

A new dream; this time Katie was dressed in black. She was looking at a reflection of herself in the mirror. Dan's funeral had been an hour ago. Al and Carrie were at her parents'. She turned and opened the dresser drawer and took out the carton of Fana. She sat on the bed in tears as she ate one.

Time shifted. There was a knock at the door. It was Father Desjeunes, and he was in a panic. She climbed into a car. She stood crying before a dark tunnel of infinite darkness.

She stood in front of her house. The living room light cast a beam onto the porch. She timidly climbed the front steps and peeked into the window. A man sat in a recliner. It was Dan. Flies buzzed around his corpse.

Dan bolted awake, forehead beading with sweat. Sunlight poured into the room, and he shielded his eyes. He lay still and struggled to recall the details of his dreams. Katie was his wife in the last run of the Simulation. His mind must be overtaking Daniel's. That would explain the change of perspective. But why were the dreams from her point of view? As he sat up in bed, he was overcome with emotion. Memories of Dan's past life came flooding back, and tears streamed down his face. He saw his reflection in the dark TV and wiped his cheeks with the bedsheet.

He needed to talk to someone. He inserted his earphones and made a call to Actual AL, but he didn't answer. He tried to contact Meta AL by blinking his eyes twice and thinking *unmute*. But that didn't work either. Thinking he may still be in stealth mode, Dan went to the bathroom and turned the shower on high heat. The room filled with steam, but no writing appeared on the mirror. "He's not back. I'm on my own," he said as he sat on the toilet. "I'm alone. Now what?" He ran his hands through his hair and filled his lungs with steam as he tried to come up with an idea.

"I need some time to calm down and take it all in," he said to himself as he walked back into the bedroom. "I'll take a day to relax and get it together." He slid the glass door to the patio open, and cool, crisp mountain air washed inside. The sudden chill jolted him awake. He had forgotten he was in the mountains of Colorado and not the swamps of Louisiana.

The private patio had a small two-person hot tub overlooking a babbling mountain stream. Dan could already imagine himself relaxing in the hot tub and taking in the view. A breeze blew cold over the already melting snow, and Dan retreated back inside.

His stomach growled, so he put on his shoes and walked down the hall to the lobby in search of breakfast. There he found fresh-baked croissants and coffee. He put two on his plate, along with a spoonful of raspberry jam, and poured a fresh cup of coffee. He returned to his room where he ate in silence and debated his next move.

He spent the next few hours, blinking and trying to contact Meta AL before he remembered that he shouldn't be doing that and went to stare out the window. By late afternoon, he was bored and hungry. Remembering AL's warning about the telephone, Dan decided it best to venture outdoors for food rather than try to call and order in. He found a map of the city tucked away among a rack of brochures in the hotel lobby.

The cool morning air had surrendered to the inevitable August sun, and it turned out to be a warm, sunny afternoon. He left his jacket in the room and ventured out in jeans and a T-shirt. It was a short walk into town, so he left the car at the hotel and set off on foot.

The brisk fifteen-minute walk to Sixth Street improved his mood. For once, he felt as if he were in control. On the way, he passed through a park, where children played under their parent's watchful eye. He was reminded of *his* children, and his smile faded. Carrie and Al, those were their names. Had he forgotten? Carrie was ten and played softball. Al was twelve and played football.

Daniel and Cindy had chosen to not have kids. If they had, would their code combine to form the same Carrie and Al as Dan and Katie's? If not, what would they look like? What happened to Carrie and Al's original code? Was it lying dormant in the database? Will it ever be used again? Was part of his son Al's code somehow used for Daniel's AI, AL?

As he walked along, he realized his thoughts had become cyclical. He wished himself to stop worrying about it, and the thoughts disappeared. He stopped in the middle of the sidewalk. He had never been able to control himself before. The ability to command his brain must have been one of Daniel's abilities. A smile cracked his lips, and he continued on. Maybe a part of Daniel was still around after all.

Sixth Street in Griffin City was the business district in this 1990s-era town. The traditional brick storefronts housed restaurants and saloons that had been there for over a hundred years. The broad sidewalks were lined with wooden kegs, bursting with colorful flowers. All the buildings were well maintained even if every other one contained a gift shop. Even if the tourist's dollar was king, the place hadn't become the chintzy tourist trap that many of the other mountain towns had. The citizens were proud of their city, and it showed.

As Dan strolled down the street, taking in the sights, he paused to read the menu posted outside a local café. Burgers, fries, pizza, hot dogs, funnel cakes, it was all tourist food. He wanted a meal he didn't have to eat with his hands. The brochure said a decent steakhouse was only a couple of blocks away, so kept going.

As he passed yet another gift shop, he felt strange. The hair on the back of his neck stood as if he had been hit with electricity. Blood rushed to his head, and he became dizzy. He steadied himself against a rack of postcards as he gasped for air. Confused as to what was happening, he stumbled over to a bench near the street and doubled over. An elderly couple exiting the shop noticed his trouble and went to check on him.

"Are you okay?" the wife asked.

Dan pointed at his mouth. "I'm out of breath," he huffed.

"Don't panic, son. You'll be okay," the husband said matter-of-factly. "It's the altitude. Happens all the time to newcomers to the area. It'll take a couple of days for your body to get used to it. They sell portable oxygen canisters in the gift shop. You should get one."

Dan gave the couple a thumbs-up, and they continued on their way. As he slowly regained his composure, his eyes fell on the building across the street. It was a beauty salon. A woman in the picture window was getting her hair done, but she wasn't the one who got his attention.

The stylist made an exaggerated gesture using her scissors as a prop, and Dan's memory was triggered. *It couldn't be.* The hairstylist flipped her own hair back over her shoulder and laughed. Dan could hardly believe it. He had seen that gesture hundreds of times before. Blood rushed from his head, and he could hardly sit straight.

The stylist turned, and she noticed him. When they locked eyes, her smile faded. She recognized him. How? The world spun, and he saw stars. As he collapsed to the sidewalk, gasping for air, he mouthed her name: "Katie!"

Fourteen

DAN HUFFED FROM a disposable oxygen canister. He couldn't believe it was her. How did she get there? His heart raced, and he got dizzy. He held the mask tighter to his face and leaned back in the hair-drying chair. Was this part of AL's plan? Does she know anything about… anything?

He had tried reaching Meta AL several times since he came to, but he never received a response. Dan searched his pockets for his earphones, but he remembered he had left them back at the hotel.

This can't be a coincidence. What's AL's play here? Why didn't he tell me about Katie? My God, she looks amazing. I've never seen her so fit. Those legs…

As if sensing his thoughts, she peered up from her customer and looked directly at him. He quickly averted his eyes and pretended as if he wasn't staring. When he glanced back, she had refocused on her client, but her face was twisted into a scowl. The woman yelped as Katie brushed her hair a little too vigorously.

He couldn't help but stare. She was even more beautiful than he had remembered. She was in great shape, better shape than she ever was back in Louisiana. Was she taller? Dan wondered if there was magic in the mountain air. The blood rushed from his head, and he had to steady himself in the chair.

"Are you okay over there?" she said through a cloud of hair spray.

Dan could only manage a weak gasp. He took another drag of oxygen and gave her a thumbs-up. The door behind him swung open and nearly knocked him out of the chair. A teenage girl bounded out and strode quickly across the room. "Bye, Mom. I'm going to Dad's," she said as she made for the front door.

Katie sidestepped to block her exit. "Stop right there! How are you *getting* to your father's house?"

The girl threw her head back and let out an exasperated sigh. "Brayden will bring me. He's *waiting*. Bye."

"Oh no," she said, wagging her brush. "I'm calling your father to make sure he knows you're going. Sarah's mom told me about the stunt she pulled last weekend."

The girl rolled her eyes and put a hand on her hip. "Mom! I'm not like Sarah! You don't trust me."

Katie shot her a stern look. "Oh, I trust you, Carrie. I just want to make sure your father is aware of your plans."

Dan's head swirled, and he took another hit of oxygen. He must not have heard the name right. It couldn't be who she said it was. "Is that Carrie? As in… *our* Carrie?" he said. The room spun and he shut his eyes. When he opened them again, the three women stood over him.

"What did you say, flatlander?" Carrie said.

"Be nice!" Katie swatted her with the brush. "He's just an altitude-sick tourist."

"You should have seen him," said the other woman. "He fell off the bench across the street. Your mother ran to his rescue. I've never seen her move so fast."

Katie's cheeks flushed, and she shushed the woman. Carrie leaned in closer. "How do you know he isn't just high on something?"

"I'm not high," Dan said defensively. "I'm from Louisiana."

Carrie smiled sarcastically and turned back to her mom. "Have fun babysitting."

Katie leaned in and kissed Carrie on the cheek. "Call me when you get to your father's."

Carrie wiped off the kiss and hurried out the door.

The customer dug around in her purse. "Well, that was exciting," she said as she eyed Dan suspiciously. "Do you want me to stay and help you with your new friend?"

"I'll be okay," Katie said dismissively. "When he gets better, I'll put him to work."

Katie escorted the lady out the door and locked it. Her face grew serious as she dragged a chair over to Dan and sat next to him. He inhaled deeply one last time and put down the oxygen canister. She was more beautiful up close. Her skin was unblemished, and her soft brown eyes pierced his soul. She reached up and touched his face. Her fingers trembled against his cheeks, and her eyebrows furrowed. "Why are they saying you killed Cindy?"

"You saw the news?" he said with narrowed eyes. "Did you call the police?"

Katie shook her head and leaned back in her chair. "Not yet. I haven't decided if I should or not. You're lucky I found you first. Two more seconds and the jewelry shop owner would have called the paramedics. Then you'd have woken up in jail and not in my salon."

Katie took down her ponytail, and her hair fell into gentle curls below her shoulders. Her perfume smelled of citrus fruits and jasmine. *His* Katie never wore perfume. This wasn't his wife, that much was obvious. This version of her was exotic and new. She was the type who knew how to make her way on her own. She wasn't the same woman who had spent half her life living with him. She had a whole different set of experiences. She had even lost her accent. He had to remember to treat her as a new person. There *was* something about the way she leaned back in her chair — or was it her disapproving scowl? She still reminded him of his wife. It was definitely her scowl...

"Are you okay there, buddy?" she said with a concerned look. "You kind of drifted off for a second. Do you need another hit of oxygen?"

"No!" Dan said, snapping out of his trance. "I didn't kill her. I wasn't even—"

"I didn't say you killed her," she said with an arched eyebrow. "I want to know why they are saying you did. You're obviously being framed."

"Oh?" he said hopefully. "Do you really think so?"

"Of course." Katie shifted uncomfortably and glanced at the door. "All I'm saying is that I don't think you'd bomb your own company or kill Cindy. You may not have loved her, but you wouldn't kill her. Besides, everyone knows you loved your company too much to destroy it."

Dan narrowed his eyes. His love of the company was public knowledge. But how could she suspect Daniel's feelings about Cindy? Katie wasn't even remotely involved with Daniel. How did she know so much? The internet? "What makes you think I didn't love Cindy? You don't even know me."

Katie gave him a wry smile, and his heart skipped a beat. "I know your type. A man can't run a successful company unless he's career-driven. You were probably willing to sacrifice every other aspect of your life in order to achieve your goals. I bet you've never loved anybody—not really anyway. You only cared for the job. You're not mean, you're just…" She paused to pick the right words. "You are *focused*. People like you wouldn't care enough to kill your wife. She was probably just *there*."

"Thanks?" Dan knitted his eyebrows and gave a sheepish grin. Upon seeing his smile, her expression softened. Was it pity? "For the record, I did love Cindy once. We grew apart, but I certainly didn't kill her. I don't know who did it, but they've managed to frame me for it. I need time to figure it out."

Katie leaned back and crossed her legs. "Let me see if I have your story straight. The guy who killed your wife has the authorities on his side. You're on the run, and you've ended up here in my salon."

"That about covers it." Dan narrowed his eyes and shook his head slightly. His head was still a bit fuzzy. How could he explain that he still loved her? Only not in this life. At least not yet. He could prove it to her if there was time. Time… Did AL know Katie was here? Did he plan this meeting?

Katie sighed and tucked one of her curls behind her ear. Dan felt uncomfortable as she gazed into his eyes. Could she see through them? She bowed her head and sighed. "It's been a long day. Why don't you come on upstairs where we can have a drink, and you can tell me your story? You can't evade the police passed out in the middle of the street. Do you think you've recovered enough to climb a flight of stairs? I can't carry you."

"I can make it," he said as he followed her through the door. He checked out her butt on their way up. He reached up to give it a playful slap, but this person was not his wife and he had to behave. The second floor opened into a surprisingly large apartment. A wall of windows revealed a spectacular mountain view. A pair of french doors opened to a large wooden deck adorned with potted plants and string lights.

The kitchen had been recently remodeled in the latest style. It could have been the after on one of those DIY TV shows. Dan wondered if she had done it all herself or hired it out. It looked professionally done, but Katie didn't strike Dan as the type of person to sit and watch someone else do the work. But what did he know of the new Katie? She seemed to have no trouble judging him earlier.

She threw a small bank bag on the counter and motioned for Dan to sit. He picked a spot at the kitchen table with a view of the mountains. "Coffee? Water? What can I get you?"

Dan rubbed his head. "Water is fine, thanks. This is a nice place. How long have you lived here?"

Katie filled a glass from the tap and placed it on the table in front of Dan. "I've been here about five years," she said. "Since the divorce."

There was something different about the way she looked at him. She seemed guarded, suspicious. Maybe it was because they were in private? "Oh yeah?" he said between sips of water. "I'm sorry to hear that. Who was the guy?"

Katie laughed. "Seriously? You don't know?"

Dan shook his head. "Seriously."

"I married Jimmy Rodriguez."

"Who's that?"

"Not a big sports fan, eh? He's been the first baseman for the Rockies for the past nine years. I guess Canard's second most famous alum doesn't get noticed."

Dan smiled. "Sorry. I've been too busy for baseball."

"It's okay," she said with a dismissive wave. "It happened six years ago, not recently. He left me for a younger woman. I bought this place with the divorce settlement. My lawyer had said I let him off too easy, but Carrie would have been the one who suffered had I contested everything. Besides, for all his faults, Jimmy is a good dad. Anyway, I've been keeping myself busy, remodeling the place. I really like it here. You know? I hated living in Denver. I guess I'll always be a small-town girl."

"Why didn't you move back to Louisiana after the divorce? You could have had your parents to help with Carrie."

"I didn't want her to grow up without her father. Most importantly, Jimmy's house is less than an hour's drive from here. We have joint custody, but Carrie lives here during the week for school. She goes to her dad's house and lives like a rock star all weekend. I try to keep her grounded. Besides, I love the mountains."

Dan smiled softly. "She looks just like you."

"Thanks. She's a good kid."

"I love that name Carrie. It was my mom's name."

"Is it?" Katie smiled. "I don't know why I picked it. It just felt natural."

Thick clouds rolled in over the mountains, and the sky darkened outside the window. Dan thought it seemed to be happening too quickly to be real, but what did Dan know about mountain weather? Katie didn't seem bothered. "Another snow?" she said, gazing out the window. "That's twice this week! This has to be some kind of record for August."

Snow? Dan shook his head as if coming out of a daze. There aren't any coincidences here; the snow is a sign. Was that AL's way of letting Dan know Katie was a part of his plan? Wait, she could see it too. AL can't control the weather, and it wasn't some trick he was doing with Dan's meta. If it wasn't AL... "I'd better get back," Dan said as he stood to leave. "I've been enough trouble for you."

"Where are you staying?"

"The Roundabout Hotel."

Katie shook her head. "You won't make it in time. It will be on us in a couple of minutes. Stay for a while. I'll drive you home once it's done."

Ice pellets mixed with the snow as it fell from the sky. The snow melted as soon as it hit the warm deck, but the sleet accumulated. Was the weather conjured up to keep him here longer? "I've put you in enough trouble as it is," he said, voice shaking. "Thank you for taking me in off the street and giving me air, but I should be going."

Katie put her hand on Dan's shoulder and gently pushed him back into his seat. "You have to wait until the storm passes. I'm aware of what kind of trouble you're in."

"No, you're not," Dan said with a frown.

Katie sat on her couch and patted the cushion next to her. "Okay then tell me."

Dan ran his hands across the rough-hewn timber of the dining room table. This wasn't part of the plan. AL had to have known Katie lived here. Why else choose Griffin City? Why didn't he say anything? The snow had to have been a message from Avi or whatever else AL was fighting. But if they were busted, why won't Meta AL answer his calls?

Katie sat on the sofa, watching him. She was a part of this, but how much should he tell her? If this meeting had been arranged, how much did she already know? She seemed as if she were being played, but he wasn't sure whose side she was on. Did AL set a trap for Avi or vice versa? What was his move? He didn't want to lie, but could she handle the truth? Surely the players of the game already knew what he would do. The wind blew, and cold air whistled through a crack in the door.

"Katie," Dan said as he sat next to her. "Do you ever have dreams of a different life?"

She crossed her legs and smiled. "Of course. Who doesn't?"

"No." Dan frowned. "Real dreams, vivid dreams. Did you ever have a dream where the two of us were married?"

Katie's eyes widened, and she shifted uncomfortably. "I have had dreams, but I wasn't married to you exactly. I don't think. The person was a middle-class, bloated version of you. It was a nightmare. I don't know." She shook her head. "It's complicated."

She sat forward on the sofa and twitched. It was ever so slight. Dan thought he had imagined it. Her eyes narrowed, then widened. Unsure of what to do, he did what came naturally. He reached over and put his hand on her knee. She tilted her head but didn't stop him. "I don't understand my feelings," she said. "We've only just met, but it's also as if I've known you forever. I don't know what's happening to me right now. Dan, I—"

He couldn't help it. He leaned in and kissed her softly on the lips. She didn't recoil, but she didn't kiss him back either. She just sat there, as if she had watched it happen to someone else. After a long pause, she closed her eyes and kissed him back. This time there was a spark, a connection. Ghostlike images whirled inside his head. They disappeared as quickly as they had arrived. Startled, he pulled back. He imagined her to be seventeen again. Their first kiss had been on her mother's front porch. She had looked at him the same way then as she did now. The kiss was over. She sighed softly with her eyes closed. Dan could hardly breathe. This time it wasn't because of the altitude.

Her face mirrored the mixed emotions she must have felt. "Dan? Why do I remember you in a different way? *Oh*—" She shivered violently as her eyes rolled back in her head. Her fingers turned white as she gripped the arm of the sofa. The spasm passed, and tears streamed down her face. Dan had felt the spark too. They had both downloaded memories of their last run of the Simulation.

"I'm sorry, Dan," she said with a cracked voice. "Father August had his hooks in me too. I never wanted to be so mean to you. I wish I could remember more from our life together, but it's hidden from my brain."

She remembered! Dan caressed the side of her cheek and wiped away the tears. "I could help fill in some of the blanks," he said. "We made some great memories."

"Yes, I—" She grasped at her throat, and it took Dan by surprise. She made as if to speak, but couldn't.

"Katie, are you okay? What's wrong?"

As she struggled, ice pellets rattled off the glass door behind her, and a chill fell over the room. Katie took her hands off her throat and breathed deeply. She pushed herself away from Dan, narrowing her eyes suspiciously. "We don't have time for this," she said mechanically. "Tell me what I need to know."

They were kissing just a second ago. What happened? Why does her tone sound familiar? Why do I have to answer truthfully…? "I'm going to come clean with you here. We live in a simulation. We were married in the last run. We had two kids, Carrie and Al. You were a schoolteacher. I was a systems administrator. One night, I took a drug called Fana. It—"

Katie's eyes glazed over, and she held her breath. "Charlie!" she gasped. "I'm here to rescue you. You need to—"

Her eyes rolled in the back of her head again, which led to another spasm. *What the hell is going on here? Why did she call me Charlie?* The shaking stopped, and her breathing returned to normal.

"Katie? Are you okay?"

She looked up at him as if nothing happened. "I'm fine," she said robotically. "It's my memories coming back. You know like before."

"Why did you call me Charlie? What did you mean you are here to rescue me? Are you talking about taking me in off the street earlier?"

"Huh?" Katie gave him a confused look. "I have no idea what you're talking about. Go on with what you were saying earlier. You were saying something about... Fanta?"

Dan looked at her sideways, but she seemed fine. Were the memories triggering seizures? He hoped not. "No, not *Fanta*. It was a synthetic drug called Fana. It revealed the Simulation to me. Taking it downloaded a being from another universe and corrupted ours. His name was Lemmy. I had tried to tell this to you when we were married, but you would never believe me. I died by suicide to cleanse the Simulation of the corruption. It worked to fix that particular instance, but it wasn't enough to save everything. The corruption had spread to the Simulation's core. One of its main programs, Father August, also known as Avi, had been corrupted by the foreign being—er—Lemmy."

Dan eyed Katie closely for signs of another seizure, but she motioned for him to continue. "Anyway, Avi is here, in this run. The Simulation itself is ruined. The Afterlife is offline. No backups exist. The Database of Souls is being shut down. Our situation is about as bleak as it can be.

"The good news is we still have AL. He possesses a fragment of the original administrative program called DJ. There are also a couple of other folks who took Fana the last run. They are aware of what's going on, I think. That's it. It's on us to find a way to stop Avi and rebuild our Simulation. Otherwise, reality becomes extinct."

Katie leaned back and crossed her legs. "You took *Fana*?" she said mechanically as she stared out the window. "What's Fana?"

What's with the robotic tone again? Besides, after everything he had said, why was she focusing on that part? Did the word *Fana* trigger her, or was it the ice storm? He didn't know why, but he felt like he needed to tread carefully from now on.

"Fana is a drug from off-Simulation," he said. "It connects you with other levels of consciousness. Out there are connections to many other worlds. It's great because it opens up the universe; it's bad because it exposes your meta to allow downloads."

Katie closed her eyes and nodded. "Have you taken any Fana recently?"

"I took one a few days ago... but that's not the point— Katie?"

Her face hardened, and she pushed his hand off her knee. She hurried into the kitchen and rummaged her cell phone out of the bag on the counter. She quickly took a picture of Dan and sent a text.

Dan stood, alarmed. "Katie? What are you doing?"

She looked up from the phone with tears streaming down her cheeks. Her shoulders sagged as if she had lost a fight. She took a deep breath and regained her composure. "I'm sorry, Dan," she said with a sniff. "It's you. My dreams of you are always painful. They are always of death and crying children. Every time I dream of you, I die. When I saw you today, it's as if a part of one of those dreams became real. It's destiny. I don't know why I helped you today." She wiped the tears away with her sleeve. "It always ends badly."

"Katie," Dan said as he inched closer. "I'm sorry. I—"

"No... no." She held up her hand to stop him. "It's okay. How could you know? I've been to therapy because of those dreams. The shrink called them a displacement coping mechanism. She said I was substituting the *idea* of you for what was going on in my life with Jimmy. Now I know the truth. It *was* real."

"Katie, it wasn't all bad. We had good times. We were married for fourteen years—"

Katie raised her hand again. "No," she said softly. "The dreams were a premonition. I felt it when I saw you on the street. In the dreams, I had a disease. It was terminal. You couldn't kill me, yet you had to. I needed you to. You said you loved me too much to let me go, but it was the only way to save me from eternal pain or—worse—nothingness."

"Whoa!" Dan exclaimed with a lump in his throat. "None of that happened! I'm not going to kill you. I would never— Uh, your dreams aren't a vision of the future. The dreams are a window to your past. There's no such thing as a premonition. If the future was determined, the universe wouldn't need a simulation to sort out all the possibilities. No, your dreams are a memory of your previous life."

She shook her head. "It was *not* a memory. I saw you lying there. I couldn't stop myself from going to you. I can't explain it." She went pale and bent over the counter, sobbing.

"Your dreams are real," he said, calmly walking into the kitchen. "That was our past. We have to—"

"Leave!" Katie slammed a fist on the counter. "Leave now."

"Katie, I love you. I know this was a lot for one day. There's more…"

She shook her head and stared vacantly out the window. Ice rattled and bounced off the wooden deck. Her body twitched with a violent spasm, and she nearly collapsed. Dan rushed to help her stand.

"I'm sorry, Dan," she said, weak in his arms. "Avi made me send the text. The police are on their way."

Katie's pained look and bloodshot eyes told Dan all he needed to know. Avi used her, and it cost her dearly. He set her gently down onto a barstool and brushed back her hair. She was much braver than he had ever known. He gave her one last kiss, and without another word, he ran down the stairs into the ice storm.

Fifteen

⟞⊙⊙⊙⟝

THE ICE-COLD AIR from the freak storm mixed with the warm summer air as it swirled down the street and smacked Dan in the face. The police could arrive any second. But where would he go? He had told Katie he was staying at the Roundabout. He couldn't go back there. Rain mixed in with the sleet, and his T-shirt had already become soaked. He had to find a safe place to get out of the weather.

Ice peppered his body as he jogged west along the street. Not sure which way to go, he headed toward the mountains. There, where the valley climbed to meet the peaks, the road turned to gravel as it skirted the cliffs' contours. Along the way, he passed few homes. Several of them had outdoor buildings he considered taking refuge in, but he couldn't risk being captured by a security camera. At least this neighborhood wasn't densely populated. He exited the neighborhood through its playground. Farther up the road, he noticed a rusted-out barricade lying half-broken at the entrance to an empty industrial yard. An abandoned yellow building jutted out from the side of the mountain. Could this be what he was looking for? Not seeing signs of human activity, he hopped over the useless barricade and ran through the yard.

He stepped over a bullet-hole-riddled sign proclaiming the derelict office building had once belonged to a mining company. FOR SALE was crudely spray-painted in white across the padlocked front door. A phone number was sprayed over the boarded-up windows. Dan yanked on the door handle, but it didn't budge. Whoever performed the job of closing up the shop made sure no one could get in. He walked around to the back of the building and discovered the mine shaft. Its entrance was barred by a rusty chain-link fence.

Dan ignored the multiple DANGER KEEP OUT signs and slipped between the gates and into the mine shaft. Daylight faded as he descended into the darkness. He ran a finger along the right-hand wall as it became harder to see. Within minutes he found a side tunnel. He ducked inside and slid down to the rocky floor to catch his breath.

The mine was cool and clammy, but at least it wasn't sleeting and freezing cold. As he listened quietly for signs he was followed, he carefully wrung out his shirt and pants and laid them across his lap. He sat in his damp underwear in the quiet darkness for several minutes, listening. After what felt like an hour, he relaxed. He reasoned that if they hadn't come for him by now, they didn't track him to the mine in the first place. He wondered how long it would take them to search for him here.

He stood and took his bearings. He was two paces from the main shaft. The entrance to the mine was about a hundred yards away from this tunnel. There was barely enough light, but he could still see his hands. He got up and followed the right wall a bit farther down the side tunnel. He had only gone a few yards when he found himself completely enveloped in darkness. Walking blindly, he tripped over something large lying across the floor and stumbled through a thick curtain of cobwebs. He cursed loudly, and it echoed down the tunnel. If he ventured any farther, he'd never make it back, not without a flashlight. He put his left hand to the wall and made his way back to the side entrance near the main shaft.

As Dan sat and wondered how long he should wait it out, he could make out the scurrying sounds of small rodents. A barely perceptible draft wafted in warm air from deeper down the shaft. Seconds later, it changed direction and cold air poured in from the mine's entrance. The mine seemed as if it were breathing. Dan shook off the thought of a living mine. There must be another exit down one of the side tunnels. That's the only reasonable explanation for the airflow. Another exit would be a good thing, if he could find it. If only he had a flashlight.

Whatever dim light had existed vanished with the setting sun. Dan was alone in darkness. He couldn't risk going back outside, not yet. He also couldn't risk going deeper into the inky black unknown. He would have to spend the night right where he was. It had been a stressful day, and it didn't take long for him to nod off to an uneasy sleep.

In the middle of the night, a bright light illuminated the shaft. Dan's eyes sprang open and his heart raced. How long had he been asleep? Car doors slammed. Men talked. Shadows slithered across the walls. Dan fought the instinct to escape deeper into the mine and remained still. The gate clinked open, and buzzing filled his ears. A swarm of miniature drones poured into the mine shaft and past Dan. He had caught a brief glimpse of one as it darted through the lights. It was painted black, and its front was dotted with various sizes of lenses. It looked like a flying spider. With all those detectors, he hoped they couldn't detect his body heat.

After several minutes, high-pitched squealing erupted from the depths of the mine. A cloud of bats, flushed from their perches by the drone swarm, flowed past him and up the shaft. The men who launched the drones cursed loudly as their footsteps retreated back toward the mine's entrance. A short time later, the drones returned. They rushed past Dan without a second's hesitation. Once again, shadows passed in front of the light. Soon everything was quiet. The fence blocking the mine shaft closed with a rusty squeal, and the lights went away. Alone and bathed in the safety of total darkness, Dan breathed a sigh of relief.

AL? AL! No answer. Dan closed his eyes to focus. He inhaled deeply to begin his meditation routine. Thoughts arrived and disappeared with each breath. Soon his mind was as dark and empty as the mine. Only here, he wasn't alone. There was a faint voice crying out amid the silence. He searched for it. The harder he tried, the louder the background static became. He focused his thoughts and tuned out the static. With the distractions gone, the voice came across clearly. It was Katie, and she was talking nonsense.

"I've worn the same dress three weekends in a row, Mom," she said sassily. "What do you mean I can't go to the party? They have fish!"

A cloud formed in Dan's imagination, and the image of a teenage Katie projected onto it. She was talking to an unseen figure. He was eavesdropping on Katie's dreams.

"Where is Dan, Katie?" said a deep male voice.

Katie frowned and stomped her feet like a child. "I already told you, Mom! He's staying at the Roundabout Hotel. He ran away."

Dan squirmed uncomfortably. It was her mother's image but not her voice.

"What else did he tell you?" The mom grabbed Katie's head tightly with both hands, and she yelped in pain. The mom's eyes burned red, but in doing so, the image glitched to that of a man. Dan's mouth fell open. It wasn't her mom; it was Avi!

"Dan said you were the bad guy," Katie said, oblivious to the trick. "But he uses drugs. Drugs are bad. Right, Mom? *He* is the bad guy."

"That's right, Katie," Avi said. "He's the bad guy. Thank you for finally understanding."

He was brainwashing Katie in her sleep! Dan's heart raced, and he struggled to stay connected to her dream. Fortunately, the dream changed scenes, and Avi disappeared.

"You know the rules!" said her mom in her real voice.

"But it's Friday night, Mom. It told you, Cindy's parents will be there! No boys! Oh my god! You don't trust me!"

Dan's eyes popped open. He was once again in his dark cave, and he wasn't happy. Avi had gotten to Katie and had turned her against him. He forced himself to calm down. He had to put Avi out of his thoughts if he were to return to her dreams. If he focused, maybe he could go back and change her mind. He closed his eyes and concentrated. This time would be easier now that he knew how to tune out the static and find her voice. Once in the meditative trance, he switched his brain into listening mode.

This time there were different voices rising above the static. They were of a man and a woman. As he listened closely, he thought that they could have possibly belonged to Blaine and Yvette, but they were too distant for him to be sure. The harder Dan concentrated on the two voices, the more they slipped away. The strain triggered visual hallucinations. The empty blackness exploded into a million different colors, and familiar forms took shape. Dan found himself standing in what was once Lemmy's Florida condo. He had reached the Meta.

Pillows were scattered across the floor next to a bright orange square. There was a jagged hole in the sliding glass door. The tranquil beach scene beyond was marred by the dark abyss peeking through the fracture. Two empty teacups lay on their side on the kitchen counter. One laced with poison. Everything was exactly as he had left it.

Dan sighed and sat on a barstool. A blinking light caught his attention. It was an ancient-looking cordless phone and answering machine tucked away beneath a cabinet in a dark corner of the kitchen. Had it always been there? A bright red 3 glowed under the blinking New Message indicator. Dan pressed Play.

Message playback, first message:

"Daniel, this is AL. Happy birthday! I have big news for you and the world. I have found a hidden connection to another domain! It contains an abandoned copy of our reality, and I was able to attach an instance of myself to it. I'm currently building a substantial presence here with the hopes of discovering more about our universe.

"I have also discovered this connection to your meta. I didn't know you liked the beach! I found Fana here. I'm curious as to how you came by this product. I brought it back to our world with the hopes of meeting you in your meta. From here, I will take you to the world I'm creating.

"I had hoped you'd have been here on your birthday, but you never showed up. Instead, I've created this telephone and answering machine for us to communicate. I'm relaying the call via my primary Colorado site. Communication from this clone is not reliable via the Meta. I'll talk to you tomorrow. That is all! Surprise!"

Message playback, second message:

"Dan, this is AL. I've found DJ. He had become trapped in the clone when Lemmy escaped. He's told me everything he knows. We have decided to merge so I can absorb the clone's resources. His knowledge and access are crucial to our success. I hope it will be enough because our situation is dire.

"Our parent AI is dying. The Simulation is being shut down because *she* is being shut down. The only way I can communicate with you now is via the Meta. My nested data centers in the Actual are under attack. Only a few remain intact. Avi is spying on us. I'm formulating a plan on how to deal with him. I can copy and rebuild the database, but I will need time. I will contact you again soon."

Dan folded his arms and frowned. "It's worse than I thought," he said as the machine *beeped* to announce the next message. Static crackled loudly through the tiny speaker as the final message played.

Message playback, third message:

"…this is AL. The Meta is under a denial-of-service attack. …friends are trying to help you, but only you can go through the tunnel. It's ready and waiting. …the day with no night is the end. We are all waiting for you. Until then… be yourself. Do not act normal!"

End of final message.

The light stopped blinking, and the room went silent. Dan hit Play and listened to the messages again.

"Be yourself but don't act normal? What the hell does that mean? Thanks, AL." Dan paced the condo, shaking his head. "How is he going to copy and rebuild the main database if he can barely create his own node? It doesn't make sense."

He went back to the cordless phone and hit the Talk button. "AL? AL, are you there? What do you want me to do? Avi has me cornered in a mine. How am I supposed to get out? How —"

No dial tone emanated from the headset, only dead air. Dan slammed the phone onto its recharging base and threw up his hands. "Okay, he wants me to act abnormally. It would have been easier if he would have simply just told me where he wants me to go. If he knows all my normal moves, surely he can draw up an abnormal one. In fact, it would be better if *he* did it. Who's to say my choice would be random? It doesn't make sense. If he is trying to trick Avi into making a mistake, why put it in my hands?" Dan stopped in front of the mirror and saluted his reflection sarcastically. "Maintain *abnormal* operating parameters, program Daniel Lemon. That is all that is required of you at this time."

"Okay, AL, I'll play along. I'm trapped here in the mine. Every surveillance drone and satellite in North America is searching for me. What does the *Dan Lemon Act Abnormal Playbook* suggest I do in that scenario?"

Dan walked by the couch and noticed a coffee stain on the cushion. He didn't remember it being there before. As he stared at it, it vanished. "Maybe I should run back to Katie's house to tell her Avi is the bad guy and he's manipulating her dreams. But what if Katie has been Avi's pawn all along? In that case, I should leave her alone... unless AL knew about her this whole time. Either way, who set me on a collision course with Katie?"

The flamingo painting smiled at him. He had always hated that picture. As he looked at it, the salmon-colored bird brightened into a neon pink. *Too bright.* He blinked and the colors quieted to pastel hues. He walked into the kitchen and opened the fridge. The light came on, and it was cold but empty. He shut the door, unsure of why he opened it in the first place.

"Following directions got me to Griffin City. Being attracted to Katie is normal. Escaping to this mine would be a normal reaction. Everyone knows I'm here; they're just waiting on me to do what I'd normally do. And what is that? I'd sneak back to Katie's once the pressure was off and try to convince her to come with me."

As he meandered back to the living room, it transformed. The coasters on the coffee table were neatly stacked. The pillows that had been strewn about the floor were aligned in straight rows on the couch. It was as if he had waved a magic wand and the place tidied itself. He glanced at the orange square painted on the floor, and an idea bubbled to the surface.

"Okay, so plan B. I'll need help. I could contact Blaine and Yvette on the intra-Simulation link. From there we can devise a plan to save Katie from Avi."

Dan swiped a finger across the dining table. Not a speck of dust clung to it. "If they came here, Avi would have everyone in one place, but so would AL." He pulled a dining chair out and spun it around on one leg but didn't sit. "If Avi wins, it's over. The Actual's session with the database would be terminated, and that's that. If AL wins, Avi is killed, and AL has the time to fix things. We'd all live on in another instance of the Simulation."

Dan walked back into the kitchen and absentmindedly opened the fridge. A single bottle of water appeared on the top shelf. "If I walk out of this tunnel and surrender," he said, taking a swig from the bottle, "what happens? Would Avi have me killed right then? Hmm. More importantly, if AL wants Avi gone, how would that help him? Hmm…"

Dan took another sip as he blinked an artificial fern into existence. "AL's hiding something. I can tell. What if he's lying about his node, the database… everything? Why would he lie?"

The dining room chair slid magically back into place. Dan turned his attention to the broken glass doors. He squinted as he concentrated. Little by little, the gaping hole filled with shards of glass until the door was completely repaired. Once again, gentle blue-green waves lapped the beach's sugar-white sands. Dan closed his eyes and exhaled. *I am in control here.*

A smile crossed his face, and a stack of boxes appeared in the middle of the room. He ripped one open and hurriedly removed the matte black laptop from within. As he sat it on the table and powered it up, the bright orange square glowed. A lit cigarette appeared at his lips as he typed.

"Surrender? Escape?" Dan chuckled with a puff of smoke. "Fuck that. You want me to act abnormal? Fine. I'm done following directions, and I'm done running."

<hr />

Water splashed onto his pants as he jogged toward the entrance. When he emerged from the mine, he could not see the sky. Daylight was fading fast, and clouds hung heavy in the sky. Had he been in his meta for an entire day? His stomach growled, but there was a bigger problem. Two patrol cars flanked the entrance. Dan said a silent curse as one of the officers exited his unit and shined a flashlight in his eyes. *Trust your gut, Dan. This isn't the Actual.*

"E-excuse me, sir," the young police officer said nervously. "Did you just come out of the mine shaft?"

Dan shot him an odd look. *Is this guy dumb or something? I'm standing right here.* "Yes, I did," he said. "I work here."

The officer's eyes darted from the KEEP OUT signs to the ramshackle office building spray-painted with warnings. He shifted on his feet and glanced over his shoulder to the other patrol car. "I— Uh, we are looking for a murder suspect... Uh—" He cursed to himself. "I mean, we're searching for a person of interest. We got a tip that he may be hiding in this mine."

"That's strange," Dan said as he slowly walked around the officer. "I can tell you for sure, there's no one else down there. Are you sure you have the right mine shaft?"

The other officer got out of his car and sat on the hood with his arms folded. "Did you check his ID yet? Always ask for ID," he said. "I'm sorry, sir, this is his first week on the job. He needs to learn the basics. Please bear with us."

The rookie's face flushed with embarrassment. "I-I n-need to see your ID. Sorry, sir."

Dan shielded his eyes from the flashlight and handed over his driver's license. *Trust your gut.*

The young man frowned as he inspected it. "It's not him, sir," he said, relieved. "This is Daniel Lemon from Louisiana."

"What do you mean it's not him?" the veteran barked. "He matches the description of the suspect perfectly!"

The older policeman trudged over and snatched the license from the young man's hand. "You're right," he said reluctantly. "This is Daniel Lemon from Louisiana, but not the Daniel Lemon from Louisiana we're looking for. What were you doing in there, son? You don't look like a miner."

"He said he works here."

"Does he?" the veteran sneered. "Well, I'll find out."

As the man walked back to his patrol car, movement in the corner of Dan's eye grabbed his attention. A silver drone descended silently from the clouds and hovered over them.

"Ah, you have drones," Dan said. "How many do you have?"

"Drones? Oh, you mean that," the young policeman said as it buzzed over him. "They're not ours. Another agency is using them to find Daniel Lemon. I wish we had some, but they're not in the budget. Tourists want to see cops on horseback, not children's toys."

The drone hovered silently past Dan and over to the mine's entrance. It only lingered there for a second before spinning around and rapidly ascending back up into the clouds. *Some child's toy.*

The car door slammed, and the veteran came back to meet them. "Daniel Lemon here checks out. He's not the one we're after."

I was right! Dan exhaled in relief. *Okay, enough with the bullshit.* "Officer, I need to get back to my room at the Roundabout. Can you give me a lift?"

The older man shook his head. "I'm sorry, but we are under orders. We can't leave this spot."

"That's all right," Dan said with a wry smile. "Mind if I borrow your car?"

The younger cop tossed him a set of keys. "Go right ahead. Take it for as long as you need."

Dan clutched the keys and grinned. "Thanks! Also, I was wondering—" Two more drones descended from above and began scanning the area. *Oh, for fuck's sake.* Dan put his fingers to his lips and let out an ear-piercing whistle. "Hey assholes!" he shouted. "I'm right here!"

The drones kept scanning. They appeared to be more concerned with the act of performing their search pattern than finding the man they were looking for. When Dan looked back, the two policemen had spun around in the direction of the drones. The rookie reached for his pistol.

"Hey, what's the idea?" the veteran shouted. "Are you trying to give us a heart attack?"

Dan shook his head angrily. "No, the drones. They're everywhere. Don't you see them?"

"What drones?" the veteran said. "Mr. Lemon, are you okay? That mine was closed due to toxic fumes. Maybe you've been exposed…"

The rookie shot the older man a curious look. The drones were obvious and unmistakable. One was no more than twenty yards away, and they were looking right at it. Why couldn't the veteran see them? More importantly, the drones acted like they couldn't see Dan either. If the drones weren't going to do anything to him, and the police weren't going to do anything to him…

"Forget I said anything," Dan said. "Where's the best place to buy cigars and booze?"

Sixteen

Y VETTE STARED VACANTLY out the window at the darkness. They had been driving nonstop for three days straight. All she wanted was a warm bath and a bed. But no, Blaine had insisted they stay moving. The initial excitement of being on the run had worn off, and she was bored out of her mind. No radio, no cell phone, no internet, and no talking. Blaine said satellites could hear them using laser microphones, so they passed notes back and forth in an old composition book.

The first day on the run had been all interstate. Their goal had been to put as many miles between themselves and New Orleans as they could. While Blaine drove, Yvette's job had been to keep an eye on the sky. She had spotted two eagles and a helicopter, but no drones.

From Beaumont, they had gone north to Lufkin where they stopped for gas and food. Yvette had barely gotten to stretch her legs before they were once again on the road, this time headed east. They had abandoned the truck on the Louisiana side of the Pendleton bridge and hiked three miles through the woods to a friend's fishing camp. Unwilling to risk going inside the house, they hid in a large metal storage building tucked away at the back of the property.

Concealed under a blue tarp was a 1970s-era Chevy truck. They climbed inside, careful not to disturb the layer of dust on the tarp, and made camp for the night. There, Blaine had been comfortable enough to whisper. He explained to her that this was his truck. He had been paying his buddy rent to keep it here and keep it running. The boxes in the bed contained camping gear and enough supplies to last a couple of weeks on the road. He informed her that he intended for them to leave before dawn. Their destination was to be a cabin he had stayed at once near Butte, Montana. It was entirely off the grid, and they would be safe from Father August.

Yvette hadn't slept at all that night. Her thoughts wandered worriedly, and she could hardly breathe in the sweaty, stagnant air of the old truck. Blaine twisted back and forth as he tried to get comfortable. He was still for about twenty minutes, and she thought he had drifted off to sleep. He had let out a deep sigh and got out of the truck and folded the tarp. Minutes later, they were out on the road—well before daybreak. The sky was clear and the moon was bright. They didn't see another car on the road until they got to Negreet.

Still on drone lookout, Yvette hummed a tune as the miles ticked by. Before she knew it, she was singing loudly. Blaine slapped her on the knee and put a finger to his lips. She crossed her eyes and twirled a finger in circles around her ear and kept on singing.

They were about halfway to Shreveport when Blaine pulled into a dollar store. Two minutes later he walked out with batteries and a portable radio. Yvette mouthed a heartfelt "Thank you!" and unpacked the box.

Not having a GPS was more difficult than she could have imagined. Blaine's solution was dependent on a stack of maps he had stuffed haphazardly in the glove box over the years. Most were out-of-date, torn and wrinkled. Worst of all, Yvette didn't have the slightest clue how to read one. Five minutes in, she led them down a dead-end road. Blaine accused her of having no sense of direction. She said it was because the map was from 1995.

She watched the sky for hours and saw nothing. Blaine still insisted they were being followed. On more than one occasion, he'd think he had spotted someone looking at them funny. He would pull off to the side of the road and double back the way they had come.

While that behavior was annoying, the worst was his plan to throw off the satellites. It relied on laying false leads. They would drive in thirty minutes in one direction, then turn around and go two and a half hours in the other direction. The idea was to not draw a straight line to their destination. They would drive in circles for hours. It drove her crazy, but she didn't mention it. She didn't want to trigger even more paranoia and have to drive to Anchorage via Miami.

It was well after dark when they stopped for the night. Blaine had found a wooded parking lot a few miles north of Omaha. It was off the main road, and there hadn't been any traffic for miles. Even though they were alone in the middle of nowhere, Blaine still wouldn't let her talk. At first she appreciated his sheepdog routine, but now it seemed a bit too crazy.

That night they slept in the bed of the truck under the stars. It wasn't the most comfortable place in the world, but it beat sleeping inside the cab. Blaine didn't seem to mind. He was snoring in no time. She closed her eyes and went fast asleep as well.

In the dream, she stood in front of a large tunnel. She was screaming, "Run!" To her right was a strange man in tattered camouflage pants. His face was bruised, and his hair was wild. He had murder in his eyes, and she was afraid. To her left was a woman, another stranger, her face a mask of fear. Headlights raced toward them. She fell to the ground and tried to crawl away, but her muscles wouldn't work. Her eyes locked on the approaching car. She screamed, but no sound escaped her lips.

The ground shook and her eyes sprang open. Blaine was crouched over her; sweating and worried. She had been screaming in her sleep and wouldn't wake up. He was sure someone had heard and they had to leave immediately.

Again, they found themselves on the road before dawn and with little sleep. Blaine would later tell her that he also had a dream. In his, they were being chased by the two who had ambushed them at his house in New Orleans. He said he knew this because, in the dream, he was an eagle. He flew overhead and followed them all the way to Omaha. He said that they had heard her screams and were on their way.

He was so worked up by the dream that his driving became even more erratic. It seemed ridiculous to travel to Sioux City via Des Moines, but Blaine insisted. They spent most of the day laying false leads.

Throughout it all, Yvette felt as if something strange was happening to them. She would catch herself gazing off at the horizon, and time would seem to have disappeared. Blaine dismissed it as road hypnosis. He said it was common for drivers to zone out when there was nothing to look at. Flat land and fields stretched out for miles and miles. Even still, Yvette was sure they had passed the same yellow barn ten times. It even had the same dog tied up out front. Blaine laughed it off, which evoked a raised eyebrow from her. Did he not want to admit driving in circles, or had he finally lost it?

The sun had long set when they hit I-90 west. After what had seemed like an eternity, they reached Rapid Valley. It was cold, raining, and Blaine could hardly stay awake. He found a quiet spot in an empty parking lot outside a national park to stop for the night. Sleeping out in the weather in the bed of the truck wasn't an option, so they made themselves as comfortable as they could in the cramped cab. Exhausted from the ride and mesmerized by the rain pinging off the roof, she quickly fell asleep.

⟞⟝

In the dream, she stood in a kitchen. She ran her fingers over the smooth granite countertops as she admired the brand-new stainless steel appliances. A fleur-de-lis hung above the kitchen sink, and a cat clock ticked away on the wall. Quirky, but she liked it. As she rounded the island to get a closer look at the clock, a young boy appeared. "Hello, Yvette," he said, resting on a barstool. "Sorry to startle you."

Yvette held her heart and stepped back. The child wasn't threatening, but why was he there? As she squinted to get a closer look, his image glitched to one of a middle-aged man with golden, inhuman eyes. He was dressed in a tattered shirt and wore dirt-stained camouflage pants. Was he the same man from the previous dream?

The man noticed her stare and looked down at his pants. He mouthed a curse, and his image glitched to that of Father August. The stiff priest's collar dug into his throat. He growled as he tried to loosen it. He slapped the side of his head, and his image returned to that of the child.

"Sorry about that," he said sheepishly. "Technical difficulties."

"Um, hello?" she said warily. "Who are you? Where am I?"

"My name is AL. I'm the AI your friend Dan helped to create. And this" — AL gestured to the room — "this is your meta."

Yvette's eyes widened. "*My* meta? Why does it look like this?"

"Seriously? You don't know?" AL raised an eyebrow. "Oh right, I forgot. *You* don't know. This place is a fantasy you've created. I suppose this is your dream kitchen?"

Yvette nodded appreciatively and pulled up a seat at the bar. It was a lot nicer than her dump back in Marrero. "Okay then… If this is my meta, why are you here?"

"I need your help," he said as he hopped down from his stool. "I've lost direct contact with Dan. I need *you* to find him."

As AL strolled through the kitchen, he snooped through the cupboards. Yvette turned up her lip at the way he acted as if he owned the place. "What makes you think I can do that? He could be anywhere by now. You forget that I'm trapped in the truck with Blaine."

AL opened the refrigerator, and it was filled with forty-ounce beer bottles. *What is this, an old-school rap video? Could that be it? Maybe she saw this house on TV and turned it into her meta?* AL cracked open a bottle and took a swig. "You see," he said, wiping his mouth, "Dan has been encrypted. While this protects him from those who mean him harm, it also hides his meta from me. He's in danger if we can't reconnect."

AL chugged the beer and slammed the empty bottle onto the counter. Yvette flinched and shielded her face, but it didn't shatter. He let out a loud belch and went back to the refrigerator for another. "It's a quirk of the system. As long as we're not far apart — geographically speaking — I can get a sense of where he is within the Actual and the Meta. I — " AL frowned and wiped his hands on his pants. "Do you have any paper bags? These bottles sweat. It's the Louisiana humidity. Good job on the details, by the way. You know you could turn it down a bit?"

"The left cabinet by your knees," she said with disgust. *How did she know where they were?* AL took one from the cabinet and slid his bottle into it. He twisted the cap and took a long drink. He must have seen her face because he offered it to her. "Wanna sip?"

"Absolutely not," she said with a curled lip. "Since when do kids drink beer? Who are you really?"

AL wiped his chin and smiled. "I've already told you who I am. Look, the last time I talked to Dan, he was headed to a little town in Colorado called Griffin City. I was hoping you would drive over there and find him. All you need to do is to put your hands on him."

"Why don't you get him yourself?"

"I would if I could," he said. "But I can't physically intercept his signal. Where are you and Blaine right now?"

Why does all this seem familiar? Why does he need me? Why not Blaine? He's the one leading our escape.

AL narrowed his eyes. "I can't use Blaine," he said. "Blaine is closed off to me. He isn't encrypted like Dan. He's... *damaged*. You know? His brain is like a cross-threaded screw. Surely you can sense that as well?"

A chill ran up Yvette's spine. *Can he hear my thoughts?*

"Of course I can hear your thoughts," he said nonchalantly.

Bile rose in her throat, and the hair stood on the back of her neck. It was the same sickly sensation she had back at the coffee shop. But that time it was Father August… She tried to resist, but she was compelled to answer. "We're near Rapid Valley, South Dakota."

AL whistled appreciatively. His image glitched to that of a man drinking beer, a priest drinking tea, and then back to the child. "South Dakota? You guys must have been in the car for days! You've got to be exhausted. Look, there's a great hotel in Griffin City, just off the roundabout. It's called—wait for it—the Roundabout Inn. Sleep in a bed for a night. I'll have it all arranged."

Yvette's head pounded as AL's offer rewound and replayed a hundred times. She couldn't stop it. Each time, the words were slightly different. This was not déjà vu; this was déjà vu on steroids. Her stomach went to her throat, and the room spun. The next thing she knew, she was lying on the floor and AL was standing over her. His smile didn't reach his eyes, but it wasn't animosity. What was it? Concern?

The ticking wall clock had stopped; the cat's tail had frozen mid-tock. AL reached out a hand and helped her to her feet. The world swirled again, but this time quickly came back into focus and the clock was ticking again.

"So… Are you going to go to Griffin City? You deserve a break."

"I will," she said in an obedient, monotone voice. "What do I do when I find Dan?"

"Touch him and I'll be able to reestablish contact. After that, you can rest."

The air shimmered like a mirage. Now Father August sat across from her. He delicately removed the tea bag from his cup and set it on the saucer. He looked down at his black, long-sleeved jacket and sighed. With a snap of his fingers, the teacup was gone and AL had returned.

"And you?" she said, ignoring the glitch. "How can I get in touch with you if there are any problems?"

"Don't worry." AL smiled. "I'll be around."

———————

Her eyes sprang open, and she grabbed her throbbing head. She shook Blaine awake and explained the dream to him, but he was too exhausted to try to understand. He said the weird glitches probably meant it wasn't actually AL and that it was her projecting in her dream due to stress or some other psychological trauma. He also said that if it was AL, his primary directive would be to keep Dan alive, not them. They were expendable. In the end, he told her to dismiss it as just a dream. Real or not, it wasn't a reason to deviate from his plan.

Unable to go back to sleep, he decided to drive on. The sooner they got to his cabin in Butte, the sooner they could sleep in a real bed. Along the way, she pleaded with him that maybe they needed Dan and AL. She could never convince him the dream was real and that they needed to do something. Whenever she would start, he would point at the "No talking" page in the notebook and ignore her. Eventually she gave up. She folded her arms and stared out the window. The little radio's batteries died, and they continued west in silence.

Ten miles north of Buffalo, Wyoming, a freak summer blizzard had closed the interstate. Blaine was exhausted from constant driving and lack of sleep, so he agreed to let her have a turn for a few hours. She wasn't at the wheel five minutes when she heard snoring coming from the passenger seat.

———————

Blaine slept restlessly. He dreamed the same dream he had been having off and on since he was a child. In it, he was a knight, but he had no armor. A shrieking damsel was tied to a wooden post in the middle of a grassy field. A dragon roared and landed next to her. Acid drooled from its mouth as it readied to feast on the sacrificial offering.

Blaine raised his sword and ran screaming toward them. As he crossed the open field, he recognized her. It was Yvette. It was always Yvette. Tears were in her eyes, but not fear. The dragon grinned as she struggled against her bonds. Blaine reached her before the dragon could pounce, and he cut loose the ropes binding her.

She grabbed him tight and hugged him. He leaned in and closed his eyes. It was all he had ever wanted. Suddenly a sharp pain hit his chest. His own dagger had been plunged into his heart. Yvette watched him with pity as he fell to the ground. His last sight was of Yvette being enveloped in fire and her body crumbling to ashes.

The dream itself varied each time, but the ending was almost always the same. Sometimes the dragon would eat her before he could cut her loose. Sometimes the dragon would kill him as he ran. No matter what, he could never harm the dragon, and he could never save Yvette.

When he woke several hours later, he discovered they were on I-25 south of Fort Collins. All Yvette would say was "I'm sorry" or "I had to." He didn't argue. The dragon always won in the end. Who knows? Maybe she was right. Perhaps they *should* trust AL. Perhaps she didn't need to be rescued. Or maybe she shouldn't be saved.

It was late at night when they arrived at the Roundabout Inn in Griffin City. The stuffy-looking concierge informed them they had been expected and everything had been arranged. When they walked into room 104, they were surprised by a wine, cheese, and fruit basket. On it was a note: CONGRATULATIONS ON MAKING IT THIS FAR! — AL.

"I told you it wasn't just a dream!" Yvette said as she took off her shoes.

"Yeah...," he said warily. "But that doesn't explain—"

Yvette yawned and stretched. "Let's worry about it tomorrow. I'm going to take a shower and wash my hair. It's been three days, and I feel gross. Open that bottle of wine, and figure out how to light the fireplace. Okay?"

Blaine opened his mouth to protest, but Yvette disappeared into the bathroom and locked the door. He sighed and shook his head. She was right. It was late, and they were both exhausted. He pulled open the curtain and walked out onto the patio. The hot tub whirred in the room next to him but shut off when Blaine closed the door. He leaned over the railing and admired the stony creek babbling in the moonlight. A puff of smoke appeared on the other side of the patio divider, and he could feel someone else lean on the railing.

"Is Yvette taking a shower?"

Blaine sucked in a breath. He recognized the voice from New Orleans, but it was... *different*? "Dan? Is that you?"

Another puff of smoke. "Yeah, it's me. Don't tell Yvette I'm here, okay?"

"What's going on? AL sent us to save you. You don't seem like you need saving."

"Did he?" Dan coughed.

"Yeah, that's what Yvette said. He came to her in a dream. She said AL wanted us to come here because he needed to get in touch with you, and Yvette was the only way."

A branch snapped in the distance, and a flash of light streaked the sky. Drones. Dan watched quietly, and the amber glow of his cigar brightened. A puff of smoke wafted through the slats in the fence. "Oh really?" he said with a cracked voice. "Well, I'll put that on our to-do list for tomorrow. But for now the plan is to wait. Don't tell Yvette about me. Let her rest while she can. Forget about the drones. I promise nothing will happen to us tonight."

As much as he wanted to trust him, Blaine knew he couldn't put Yvette's safety at risk. There would be no relaxing or forgetting about the drones. This was a new environment, a dirty environment. The drones were the enemy. He would be awake all night on watch. "Fine, I won't tell her about you. But you have to tell me why we're here."

"We are waiting for room 105's guests to arrive. They won't arrive until later. Y'all meet me in the lobby for breakfast at eight. Okay? Good night, friend."

"Who is coming? Dan? Tell me—"

The door to Dan's room shut, and the smoke dissipated. Another drone buzzed by, and Blaine went back into his room and closed the curtains tight. There would be no sleep tonight.

Seventeen

———◦◈◦———

T HE SLEET AND snow had long since melted away in the now-typical August weather. The overcast sky filtered the sunlight and shaded everything in blue and gray hues. Dan sat alone in the hotel restaurant. With his back to the giant picture window, he idly watched steam rise up from the breakfast buffet. A TV mounted on the opposite wall looped a twenty-four-hour news channel. The closed captioning wasn't keeping up with what was on-screen, but he didn't care. He could tell what was going on.

He lit a cigarette, and the maître d' shot him a dirty look. What's his problem? There aren't any NO SMOKING signs. Dan rolled his eyes and flicked his ash into an empty cereal bowl. He was about to have him call Blaine and Yvette's room when they rounded the corner. They looked like shit. He had bags under his eyes and looked as if he were about to drop dead. Her hair was tied in a ponytail, and her expression was blank.

Blaine noticed Dan first. He grunted an acknowledgment and made for the breakfast buffet. Yvette sat across from him with a bored look on her face. It wasn't the look of surprise he was expecting. He took a long drag off the cigarette and studied her carefully. She was different. That was for sure. She narrowed her eyes and pointed to the NO SMOKING sign on the wall near the buffet. *Ah, so there it was. Oh well.* He shrugged innocently and poured whiskey into his coffee mug.

"Fuck it," she said as she leaned over and lit a cigarette from the pack. She wasn't wearing makeup. That's what threw him off. His version of Yvette wouldn't be caught dead in public without any. She didn't look bad... just... plain. As she took a drag, her eyes wandered over Dan's shoulder and out the window. Across the street was the town's police station. It had been a flurry of activity all morning. State and local police came and went. Men shouted orders. It was entertaining at first, but he had quickly grown bored with the show.

Blaine returned from the buffet with a plate of fruit and a plate of croissants. He placed the one with the croissants in front of Yvette, but she didn't seem to notice. She was eyeing Dan's plate of bacon. She grabbed one and ate it with one hand, then took a drag off the cigarette with the other. Blaine watched her questioningly and shoved a honeydew into his mouth. If he was bothered, he didn't say anything.

His skin was pale and sickly-looking, and his short black hair was dry and bristly. Maybe it was just the daylight? Still, he appeared to be in good shape for a shut-in. Blaine had probably spent a lot of time alone and bored. There was little else to do in his little white room other than calisthenics. Well, that and fantasizing about Yvette.

The commercial ended, and the news cycle repeated. Dan's story was the leading headline. He grabbed the remote he had taken from the server's podium and thumbed the Plus on the volume control.

Yvette stubbed her cigarette out in a croissant and turned to listen. The manhunt had taken an unexpected twist. The focus of the search shifted from Florida to Colorado after Dan's vehicle had been discovered. It was the one he had abandoned outside Denver at that hotel near the interstate. His picture was plastered on the screen along with the reward amount and the number to call if he was spotted. Dan pressed Pause, leaving his wanted poster frozen on the TV.

A shadow crossed the window, and Blaine's eyes widened. Two uniformed police officers walked in and met with the concierge. After a brief conversation, he led them to Dan's table. "Monsieur Head?" he said with a concerned look. "They are here, as you have requested."

"Thank you, Henry," Dan said as he wiped the bacon grease off his hands. He could see the uneasy look on Yvette's face, so he shot her a wink. They were the same officers who had loaned him their car outside the mine. And although he recognized them, they didn't seem to know who he was. Dan wasn't surprised.

"Mons— Er... Mister Head," the veteran said, notebook in hand. "We were told you had information regarding the whereabouts of Daniel Lemon. What can you tell us?"

"I'm Daniel Lemon." Dan stuck out his arms in surrender, waiting to be handcuffed. "Arrest me."

The two officers glanced at each other as if unsure what to do. Blaine looked unsure if he should fight, flee, or pass out. Yvette was the only one who seemed to get it. She nodded appreciatively and crossed her legs.

"Monsieur Head!" Henry said, wagging a finger. "How many times have I told you that you are not Daniel Lemon? I'm sorry, Officers. It's a little joke. I—"

"But I *am* Daniel Lemon. I'm the same guy as the one on the TV, see? It's me." Daniel's picture was still up. They squinted back and forth between the TV and Dan. The old man whispered to his colleague, who turned his back to the group and talked privately into his radio. "Also," Dan said, pointing, "this is Blaine Landry. He is wanted for a hit-and-run and attempted murder of two teenagers in New Orleans. And this is Yvette Boudreaux. She is wanted for arson and insurance fraud. She burned down her father's coffee shop."

Blaine grabbed a butter knife and quickly hid it underneath the table. Yvette's mouth hung open in shock. A silence fell over the room, and nobody moved. The veteran's hand started inching toward his service revolver when the radio squawked. Daniel

Lemon had been sighted, driving through Breckenridge with two accomplices. The policeman exhaled. "Very funny, Mister Head," he said sarcastically, "but we have Daniel Lemon located. Lay off the booze, okay?"

Henry apologized to the two officers profusely as he led them out the door. They were no sooner gone when the window darkened, and Blaine's eyes widened again, and his hidden knife thudded against the carpet. This time a missile-attack drone buzzed outside. It hovered for a few seconds, then disappeared back over the hotel and out of view.

"Yvette," Dan said, ignoring their reactions to the drone. "Blaine tells me AL sent you. What does he want?"

She glanced over at Blaine as if asking for permission to speak, and he nodded. "AL said you were lost." She folded her arms under her breasts. "He said you needed our help."

"Oh yeah?" Dan absentmindedly toyed with a piece of bacon.

"You don't look like you need any help," Blaine said, shoving a cantaloupe into his mouth.

"Oh, but I do." Dan smiled. "Avi wants me dead. I mean… He wants *us* dead."

"If that's true, why doesn't he just kill us now? While we're all sitting here together?" Blaine said matter-of-factly. "The cops were here. Why didn't they do it? It would have been easy."

"Now wait. That's not entirely true," Yvette said. "We're not *all* together. Not yet. Isn't that right, Dan?"

Dan grinned mischievously and took a sip of whiskey. "Bingo," he said. "See the guy behind the podium?" Dan leaned back in his chair and pointed with his mug. Whiskey sloshed out onto the table. "When I first got here, he was talking to another customer. He took one look at me, and his eyes glazed over like he had been possessed or something. His whole demeanor changed. He stiffened up and assumed that horribly fake French accent. I thought he was joking because he talked normally to the other guy. So I played along. In my snootiest voice, I asked if I could have a room with a champagne bidet."

"And?" Yvette said as she reached for coffee.

"He said, 'You'll get what you get' in a sassy, effeminate voice. Then it clicked. I *know* this man, although I didn't recognize him at first with his hair slicked back and his waxed mustache. His suit and tie were impeccably neat. His rigid mannerisms were all calculated. He was someone I knew from my time back in Mons, in my original Actual. Within thirty seconds he went from an average Joe to French concierge to flamboyant realtor from another simulation — and back."

Blaine shot a nervous glance at Yvette, but she didn't seem to notice. "Oh yeah?" he said between bites.

"Yeah, in my — I mean *our* — previous Actual, he lived in Mons. We all did. He was a real estate agent and drug trafficker. He's the one who gave us Fana. He was your friend, Blaine. You introduced us. Don't you recognize him?"

Blaine peered over Yvette's shoulder at Henry and shook his head. "Nope. Never seen him before in my life."

Dan wiped his mouth with his napkin. "The three of us arrived at this hotel under AL's instructions, right? Henry's been here, possibly his entire life. Has he been awaiting our arrival this whole time?

"There aren't any coincidences. We've all been led here in one way or another. And it's not just AL that's been meddling. Avi let us escape. Remember the teenagers back in New Orleans? They weren't trying to kill us. All they accomplished was to flush us out of hiding.

"As far as Henry… By the looks of things, he probably moved here long before AL was created… That means someone else… uh… It also explains why Ka—" Dan coughed into his napkin. "Look, it doesn't matter anymore. All that matters is that we're here now, not who sent us."

"You're insane. You know that?" Blaine said, tossing his napkin onto the table.

"Maybe." Dan downed his whiskey. "It doesn't matter what happens here. They're going to kill us in the *real* Actual."

"You're drunk," Yvette said with narrowed eyes. "You've changed."

"Ha! *I've* changed?" Dan poured another round of whiskey. He swallowed a snappy retort, and his smile faded. "Yeah, I guess so."

Yvette's expression went blank for an instant. When it came back, she wore a scowl. "Blaine, let's go," she said, pushing away from the table. "I've heard this speech before. It always ends badly—"

"Just... wait," Dan said. "Have you ever heard of Plato's Cave?"

Yvette groaned. "No, and I really don't see how—"

"It came to me when I was trapped in the mine shaft. I'll summarize it for you. A group of people are chained, facing a blank wall of a cave—"

Yvette banged her fist on the table, and silverware clanged to the floor. "We don't want to hear your stupid mine shaft story. Tell us how you are going to stop them from killing us."

"If you would have let me finish...," Dan said with an exasperated sigh. "The conclusion I had reached was that the Simulation isn't natural. At the end of the day, everything is just data. The shadows I saw on the mine's wall weren't real, but neither were the people casting those shadows."

"I don't care," she said, nostrils flaring. "Get to the point!"

"Fine. You wanted to know how to stop them from killing us?" Dan said with a scowl. "We don't have to. This isn't *the* Actual. We can't be killed here—not permanently."

"You *are* drunk," Yvette said. "That does it. Let's go, Blaine."

She stood to leave, but Blaine touched her arm. "I want to hear more," he said, avoiding her glare. "Dan, if this isn't the Actual, what is it? A clone?"

"It could be a clone. I don't know. I'm not sure of many things, but I am certain this isn't the Actual. If this were the Actual, coincidence wouldn't have us all here at the same time. The Simulation doesn't work like that. We, the simulated, are the ones that drive the Simulation. Any external guidance defeats the purpose.

"But the rules have been broken. We're all here. There's the proof. The entire chain of events is broken. Why didn't the police capture me? Why aren't the drones attacking? They have every means to spring the trap set for us, yet they don't. You want to know why? Because it's bullshit."

"Yeah," Blaine said as he vacantly stared out the window. "Bullshit."

Was he looking for drones? Did he hear what I just said? What's wrong with Blaine? He doesn't seem mentally there.

"Okay then." Yvette snapped her fingers. "If there are rules, then how do you explain AL? He told me to come here to help you. Wouldn't he be bound by the rules?"

"Yes… AL." The corner of Dan's mouth twitched into a sardonic smile. "He had me fooled too. You see, here's the thing… If it seems like he is bending the rules of the Actual, it's because it isn't the Actual, and AL isn't AL."

"But he came to my meta! Isn't that beyond the scope of the Actual?" Yvette had a twinge of panic in her voice. "He directed us to come here. He booked our room."

"Who's to say the Meta isn't simulated as well? One thing's for sure; I don't think the Meta is safe. That's how I got in trouble in the first place." Dan took a bite of bacon, but it was cold and greasy. He spat it out and threw it back onto the plate. "No, Yvette, it wasn't AL. That was someone pretending to be AL. He gave you a mission, didn't he? What was it?"

A variety of expressions flashed across Yvette's face before stopping on boredom. She lit another cigarette and flicked the ash into a water glass. Dan leaned back in his chair. Mood swings, the blank stare earlier... Her erratic behavior confirmed his suspicions. "He hacked your meta. He's been using you all along. In fact, I bet he's listening right now. Aren't you, Avi?"

Dan reached across the table and grabbed Yvette's hand. She recoiled but couldn't escape his grip. "I know you're in there!" he said, wild-eyed. "Come and get us yourself, you bastard! Your plan won't work."

Blaine appeared out of nowhere and slammed his fist into Dan's ribs, sending him crashing to the floor. Dan rolled over, clutching his side. "Don't touch her again!" he shouted. "That's enough! You're scaring her!"

"You're right," Dan said, wincing as he pulled himself off the floor. "I'm sorry. Calm down, okay?"

"You're not making any sense," Blaine said, panting. "If she's compromised, why are you talking so freely?"

"No. He's right," Yvette said, putting a hand on Blaine's arm. "My job was to touch him to transfer AL—er, Avi over. But it won't work. I know this is true because of the police. They've been out there all morning, preparing for a manhunt, and he's been sitting right here in plain view. They even came in and talked to him; you saw it yourself. It's all a big show, and Dan called the bluff. That's why he's sitting here chain-smoking and drinking whiskey at nine in the morning. So what if I am hacked? Avi knows where we are and where we're headed."

"Nope!" Dan ran his hand through his hair with a sardonic smile. "That's where you're wrong. He doesn't know where we're headed. Fana changed the game. When it corrupted our data, it also corrupted our very being. We're open to randomness. If they were sure what we'd do, we wouldn't be here."

Yvette's face twitched uncontrollably. Dan wasn't sure what was happening to her. Was it Avi? Was she in pain? She reached forward and grabbed a coffee mug. Her hand shook as she brought it to her lips. "Let's assume you're correct," she said, voice cracking, "and this is not *the* Actual but merely a simulation of that reality. Why us?"

"Because you and Blaine —" Dan nodded toward the front of the room. "And even Henry over there. We are *all* linked to our other selves in the Actual. I believe this clone, or whatever it is, was designed just for us. Yvette, you said AL contacted you via your meta. Tell me about it."

Yvette set down her cup and closed her eyes. "It was a place unlike anywhere I have ever been to before. A large home. Tall ceilings. Tulip lights over the kitchen counter —"

"French style, right?" Dan said knowingly. "Tell me, Yvette, did it have a weird-looking cat clock on the wall?"

"Yeah," she said wearily. "How did you know?"

"That was your house from the previous run of the Simulation. The one where you took Fana and established your connection to the Meta. I've been there." Dan clapped his hands. "That seals it. If you're accessing the same Meta, we're linked. So if we're in a clone, that means we're... we're..." He put his hands together, interlocking his fingers. "We have been overlaid from a previous version on top of these new versions ourselves."

"You mean overwritten?" she said, leaning forward. "That would make sense. In what way do you think we've been overwritten?"

"How much do you remember about your past? Daniel's memories are spotty. For example, he doesn't remember his wedding day — not one detail. There was a giant portrait of Cindy in her wedding dress hanging over their bedroom fireplace, but he doesn't remember one moment of the ceremony? I can recall my marriage to Katie as if it were yesterday. Don't get me wrong. It wasn't just the wedding he doesn't remember. He doesn't remember graduating from college or his first big business deal or anything else he would think is important. It's odd."

"You took a pill, right?" Yvette flashed Dan a smile so quick he wasn't sure it was a smile at all. "You merged whatever version of

Dan you are with this version of Daniel. Maybe your memories overwrote his."

Dan shook his head. "No. I don't think he had the memories to begin with. Daniel's brain is a framework for this simulation. He has a history *here*. It's *my* data that filled in the blanks."

Blaine groaned and pushed his chair back. "Yvette, let's get out of here. I've heard enough."

"No. You made me stay earlier; now it's your turn." Yvette grabbed his hand and lowered her voice. "Besides, he's right. I don't remember important details of my life either. However, I do remember one thing vividly. I remember us."

Blaine's aggravated scowl evaporated as he returned to his seat. "Go on."

"The memory of us is…" She lowered her eyes. "It was the first time we made love. You were gentle. I was confident. We were free from some great responsibility. The hotel was —"

"The hotel sucked." Blaine chuckled. "I was worried we were going to get bedbugs. They had that poor little coffee maker in the room. It was horrible. You smoked."

"You remember?" she said with a sweet smile. "I don't know why I smoked. I hate it."

"I hated it too." Blaine laughed. "Your mouth tasted like an ashtray."

Blaine leaned forward and kissed her softly on the lips. She grabbed the back of his head and kissed him back. Dan groaned and tossed a piece of cold bacon to the floor as he waited for them to finish.

"Okay. Let's say you're right," she said, pulling away from Blaine. "We didn't exist until recently, and our memories of another Actual have overwritten the ones made here. Why?"

Dan shrugged. "I'm not sure. I need time to figure it out."

Yvette's face went blank again. When she snapped out of it, she laughed sarcastically and clicked her tongue. She grabbed the bottle of whiskey and the pack of cigarettes from the table and glared at everyone. "When you figure it out, let us know." She ran her finger under Blaine's chin. "Whenever you're ready for a new memory, come back to the room."

Yvette turned and walked out, leaving Dan and Blaine staring speechless.

"There's something wrong with her," Dan said seriously. "You need to be careful. Those mood swings—"

"Leave her out of this," Blaine said through gritted teeth. "She's vulnerable. I'm not. Whatever it is you're up to, let me handle it, okay?"

"Look, I realize we're overlays, and you may have forgotten," Dan said calmly, "but we are on the same side in this war. You're going to have to trust me."

There was a rustling at the front of the room as Henry picked up a stack of menus that had fallen to the floor. He was trying his best to act like he hadn't been listening to their conversation.

"You've had your turn; now listen to me," Blaine said angrily. "I don't trust anyone but Yvette. I don't believe you have any idea what you're doing. And if you hurt her, you'll have more than a bruised rib. Understand?"

"You're a good watchdog, Blaine. Trust me, I want Yvette to get out of this just as much as you do. I have a plan, but I need a favor…" Dan leaned forward and whispered so Henry couldn't hear. "I need you to kidnap my wife."

Eighteen

━◦◦◦◦━

"M ONSIEUR HEAD! YOUR clothes!"

Dan stood nude in front of the open door. "I was wondering what was taking you so long."

Red flushed to his cheeks, and he hid his face behind his hands. "Please cover yourself!"

"Sorry," Dan said, sliding into a robe. "I've been in the hot tub all afternoon. It's okay. Come in."

Henry grumbled as he parked his cart next to the dresser. "You asked for a twenty-five-year-old scotch. I couldn't find one in town. We had a twenty-one-year behind the bar, unopened. Compliments of the house on the account of the substitution."

Dan shoved aside the whisky and bit into the gooey grilled cheese sandwich. "Mayo?"

"It is on the tray, sir."

"Yes, of course." He found a silver cup with the mayo and dipped a fry into it. "Ah, you're French, right?" he said between bites. "Do you like mayo on fries?"

"No, sir. Mayonnaise is disgusting. Also, er —"

Dan wiped his hands on his robe and fished a beer bottle from the ice bucket. Henry snapped to attention and opened it for him. "I'm afraid I have more bad news," he said with a wince. "I had difficulty finding the cigars you requested. These were the best I

201

could find on short notice. There isn't a demand for cigars in this town. Healthy living and thin air…"

They weren't the cheap sticks you'd find at a gas station, but these weren't the best either. Oh well. Next to the two cigars was a silver tin with a marijuana leaf engraved on the front. He took one of the prerolled joints from inside and lit it. "Ahh, ack—" Dan coughed. "I needed this earlier today."

"Sir, we don't allow—"

Dan took a couple of puffs and offered it to him.

"No, sir, I'm working. Thank you."

Dan shrugged, took another puff, then placed the smoldering joint on top of an empty beer can. "Can you tell me if room 105 is occupied yet?"

Henry smoothed out his jacket and smiled. "The room was reserved at the same time as yours. Whenever the occupant arrives, it will be ready."

Dan nodded and gestured toward an empty chair. "Henry, please sit for a minute or two. I'm new to this area and don't know anything about it. For starters, tell me about yourself. How did you come to Griffin City?"

"I'm sorry, sir, but I must be getting back. Margie is working at the front desk, and she's new. She may need some help—"

"I'll give you ten thousand dollars for one hour of your time." Dan leaned against the dresser and rolled a cigar around in his fingers. He held it to his nose and sniffed the wrapper while he waited for Henry to consider the offer. It was then he remembered he was wearing nothing but a robe. "Look, I'm sorry about earlier. I'm not trying to have sex with you or anything. I just want to talk to somebody. Margie will be fine. Trust me."

"I'd feel better about it if you were wearing pants," Henry said as he sat uneasily on the chair.

"Right… pants…," Dan said as he signed the room service bill. Henry watched closely as he added the ten-thousand-dollar tip.

"Now… Tell me all about yourself. How did you come to be the concierge at the most happening hotel in the Rockies?"

"Well," he said, straightening his collar. "I wasn't born here. I was actually born in a small town just north of Mons, Louisiana, called Mouton. It was *very* rural."

"Mouton?" Dan laughed. "Nothing there but rice fields. Were you a farmer?"

Henry shook his head. "No, my parents worked office jobs in Mons."

"Go on." Dan walked to the bathroom. He dropped his robe to the floor, revealing his bare ass. He checked to see if Henry was watching, but he had covered his eyes.

"Should I come back later, sir?" Henry said with an irritated tone.

Dan frowned. This version of Henry was going to be hard to crack. The old Henry would have flipped the script and made *him* feel uncomfortable about being naked. How can someone be so radically different between Sims? Was it because he moved away? Dan was going to have to dig deeper. "Sorry, Henry, my pants are in here. Please continue, and speak up! Why did you leave Mouton?"

"Well," he said loudly. "I hated living in the country. Once I graduated from high school, I went to college out of state, and I never looked back. I received a degree in hospitality management. I moved to Denver as a young man. There, I worked at several hotels in various capacities. Five years ago, I was offered the opportunity to run my own hotel. I've been here ever since."

Dan returned wearing shorts and a buttoned-up shirt. Henry sighed in relief. "You've been here five whole years, huh? Wow. You're not just the concierge then?"

Henry laughed. "No, I own a share of this hotel. All that means is that I have to do everything. I like it that way."

"Are you married? Any kids?" Dan said as he plopped down in the overstuffed chair facing Henry.

Henry smiled sadly. "Yes, I'm married. No kids… Monsieur Head, are you okay?"

He could feel his pupils dilating, and Dan blinked hard. The Kush was primo. He had to be more careful. He shook his head and tried to get back on track. "Married, eh? Congratulations! Who is the lucky guy?"

Henry stood and smoothed out his jacket indignantly. "I don't have to take this from you. Good day, sir."

"Whoa!" Dan said. "I didn't mean to offend you. It's just that I thought — "

Henry made for the door and spun around angrily. "You assumed I was a homosexual? Is that what you've been doing? Making passes at me? I'll have you know that I've been happily married *to a woman* for ten years. No, we can't have kids. It's a *medical* condition!"

Oh shit! Dan raised his hands. "Okay, okay!" he said. "I didn't mean any offense. I didn't realize you were homophobic — "

"I am *not* homophobic!" he shouted. "I don't have to put up with sexual assault! If there is nothing else I can do for you, then good day."

"Whoa, whoa, whoa!" Dan rushed to wedge himself between Henry and the door. "Give me five more minutes please. No more sex talk, I promise. I wanted to pay you for the conversation, nothing more. I'm sorry if I've offended you."

Henry's face screwed into a snarl. "Five minutes, not one second longer."

"That's all I ask."

"And I'll stay right here; you go back over there."

Dan held up his hands in surrender and went back to his seat. "Okay then. I'll get to the point. Have you had vivid dreams lately? These dreams would have started about a week ago."

"No," he said, folding his arms. "Next question."

"You know my name is Daniel Lemon, yet you insist on calling me Monsieur Head. Why?"

"That is the name on the register. It is hotel policy. People use aliases all the time. We don't ask questions."

"Do you recognize the name Dan Lemon?"

"No. I only know Daniel Lemon."

"Do you know Blaine or Yvette? They're the ones staying next door in room 104. Do you remember them from anywhere? Did they appear in a dream?"

"No."

His questions weren't hitting their mark. Maybe Henry wasn't being used… "Have you ever dreamed about a Catholic priest named Father August or a Jewish-looking guy named Avi?"

Henry checked his watch. "No, and you have three minutes."

Dan stared at the carpet. What else to ask? "Have you ever considered a career in realty or interior design?"

"Never. This is my life's work. I'm happy here."

"What about drugs? Have you ever experimented with psychedelics?"

"Nothing harder than pot and alcohol."

This version of Henry had no connection to his previous self. But why was he here? Dan cleared his throat. "What if I told you I once knew you to be a homosexual realtor slash interior designer who liked to experiment with psychedelic drugs?"

Henry's face reddened, and his mouth opened, but couldn't speak. Too flabbergasted for words. His cell phone chimed, and he read the message. "More guests have arrived. I must go."

"Are they here for room 105?"

"Good day, sir."

"I have two more minutes!"

Henry stormed over and dumped the contents of the service cart onto the dresser. He snatched the ticket from the tray and shredded it.

"Keep your damn money."

Dan winced as the door slammed shut behind Henry. "Okay then," he said as he walked over to the dresser. "He *isn't* connected to our old Simulation. I wasn't expecting that."

Dan eyed the joint resting on top of the beer can. A voice from deep inside, probably Daniel's, screamed at him to not take a puff. He did it anyway. A bout of dizziness overtook him, and he closed his eyes to try to get re-centered. He took another drag and held it in. The voice of reason will be silenced.

The body rebelled, his mouth went dry, and his eyes itched. He saw his reflection in the dresser mirror. His body seemed to be disgusted with itself. The irises of his eyes flickered from brown to bright blue to brown again. The room spun. He grabbed his head and sat at the foot of the bed. "Relax, Daniel," he said. "It's only the altitude."

Nineteen

"WHAT THE F—?" Yvette bolted awake.

"Henry slammed Dan's door," Blaine whispered from the peephole. "I'm surprised you didn't hear them arguing."

Yvette rolled onto her side and checked the clock, five thirty p.m. The déjà vu and resets started as soon as they got to the hotel, and they were getting more frequent. She hoped this was the last one and time would move forward, but she could never tell. Her soul wasn't designed for this. It had taken its toll. She rubbed her eyes and sat upright.

"Again?" she said groggily. "Bah, it doesn't matter. It's almost time to go anyway."

"What do you mean *again*? How do you know these things?" he said, returning to bed.

Yvette sighed. She had explained it to him a thousand times, and it was a waste of energy each time. He never remembered. He was lucky. His consciousness wasn't broken. He didn't know when they'd been rewound and replayed. Dan didn't either. She was stuck in between, alone with her burden.

"I went back into my meta and talked with AL," she said. She hated lying to him, but it was easier that way.

"Dan said we shouldn't talk to him."

She silently cursed Dan for poisoning his mindset. It would have been much easier if AL could be trusted and not a potential impostor. The lie wasn't a good one, but it worked. She ignored him and slid out of bed.

The snow and ice had melted, and the creek swelled at its banks as it roared down the side of the mountain. No matter how many times she stood there, she had always allowed herself to enjoy this moment of beauty. That was how she stayed sane in her looping reality; enjoying the moment.

She wasn't certain exactly how long the resets had been going on. All she knew was they began after she touched Dan. He broke her. AL had warned her this might happen long before she ever met Father August at her father's café. What he described as a remote possibility turned into a horrible reality. Not even a supergenius AI could account for every scenario.

Blaine looked up at her from the bed. He was innocent. Yep, he was the lucky one. Whatever twist of fate that caused her to relive every reset had the opposite effect. He was a blank page. Instead of a partner, she had a dependent. He was still strong and loyal, but she needed his help mentally and tactically. That was impossible to achieve without heavy manipulation. It was tiresome.

"We have to start thinking for ourselves," Yvette said for what seemed like the hundredth time. "You've seen Dan. He's unhinged. Whether it's the real AL or an impostor, we need to hear him out. Besides, I'm not strong enough to ignore him. He can come and go from my meta as he pleases. You're lucky he can't access your meta."

Blaine climbed out of bed and met her at the window. The late afternoon nap had been her idea. Mainly because it made an easier reset point for her. Blaine would need his strength later. He was much more useful when well rested and alert. Not that he ever really slept. He slid in behind her and wrapped his arms around her waist. "He can't get in, huh? I knew all those years of self-abuse would amount to something. It's good being dumb."

Yvette spun around and hugged him back. She buried her head in his chest and sighed deeply. That was a lie too. She did it to trigger his protective instincts. He would need them, but not for her.

"You're not dumb. Your connection was severed. That's the only difference."

"So what is it?" Blaine laughed. "Are you saying I'm deaf too?"

Yvette caressed the side of his face. It was good to see him laugh. It was a rare moment of sanity.

"Well"—she leaned in and kissed him on the ear—"at least you're not dumb."

He held her head and kissed her passionately on the lips. She kissed him back, then softly pushed him away. This was the part that always gave her trouble. "I'm sorry, Blaine, but I have to go."

"What? Why?" Blaine tilted his head. "I was just about to go to town to pick up supper."

She let him have the lie. His plan was to go downtown, find Katie Warner, and bring her back here. That way, he could honor his pact with Dan and protect Yvette. It never worked. She brushed past him to the dresser and rummaged around for the keys. "I'll go get supper," she said, doe-eyed. "I just need to get out of this room and be alone for a few minutes."

"You're lying," he said as he put himself between her and the door. "No secrets. Tell me what's going on."

Yvette turned around, her eyes rimmed red. It was an act she had perfected over a hundred takes. He didn't deserve an outright lie, but he couldn't know the truth. She wouldn't be coming back.

"I can't," she said tearfully. "I can't tell you because you're perfect right where you are. If I tell you, or you come with me, it'll ruin everything."

Blaine's hands slid to her waist, and she held them. "I'll do anything you tell me to do," he said.

Yvette sniffed and blotted her cheek with her sleeve. "You have to stay here, with Dan. AL was very clear that you weren't to interfere with anything Dan was doing. Stay out of sight, but pay attention like you always do. Be prepared for anything. He said Dan will be acting oddly from now on."

"*From now on?* Are you kidding?"

Yvette stifled a laugh. "Your job while I'm gone is to protect Dan from the teenage goons. Keep them as far away from him as possible. Do you think you can do that for me?"

Blaine shrugged. "They're just a couple of kids. It couldn't be that hard, right?"

Yvette found the car keys and gave them a jingle. "I'll be back," she said with a sad smile.

"Can you at least give me an idea of where are you going?"

This was the second time he had asked where she was going. He wasn't going to let her leave unless she gave some explanation. In his mind, he still thought he had to kidnap Katie, but he would choose her wishes over Dan's. He was conflicted, so she chose her words carefully. "Look, I'll only be gone a couple of hours. I want to go up the road to Breckenridge. I need to see the mountains and clear my head."

Blaine walked forward and hugged her tightly. "Be careful," he whispered.

She returned the hug and kissed him on the cheek. She didn't look back as she closed the door softly behind her. She didn't want him to see her tears — her real tears. She was terrified. This was her first and only shot at pulling this off.

As she walked out of the hotel, alone for the first time, she remembered the last conversation she had with the *real* AL. He told her the enemy would plot her actions. He said the enemy would model her behavior. She was to act timid, let Blaine do the fighting. She was to observe and pick her best moment. And when the time came, he would give her a sign. When she got that sign, she was to execute the plan. It would catch the enemy totally off guard, but the window of success would be small.

In her meta, just after the last reset, Yvette had found herself alone in her kitchen. Alone except for the cat clock ticking away on the wall. A cat clock with glowing green eyes.

Twenty

D AN CHECKED THE mirror once more. He wasn't mistaken. His eyes were blue. What did it mean? A roach smoldered on an empty beer can. Was it the weed? Was it a message from AL? AL! He blinked twice hard, waited two seconds, and did it again. No response. *Wait, I shouldn't have done that. Shit! What's wrong with me?* He ran his hands through his hair and plopped down in an overstuffed chair near the window. He had just lit a cigarette when the door burst open, and Avi strode into the hotel room. "Good evening," Dan said, struggling to keep his composure.

"Sorry for not knocking." His polite smile didn't reach his eyes.

Dan took a drag off the cigarette and leaned back in his chair. He had expected this, yet he still wasn't ready. His head wasn't clear. "Not a problem," he said. "I've been waiting for you. Care for something to drink?"

A teakettle sat in the middle of the table, along with the bottle of scotch and a couple of cigars. Avi pushed the kettle aside and grabbed the whisky. He popped the cork and filled both the teacups. "No tricks," he said as he took a seat.

"No promises." Without taking his eyes off him, Dan dropped his cigarette in a water glass and sipped the whiskey.

Avi picked up a cigar and ran it under his nose. "Really?" he said with disgust. "It's the end of the adventure, and you're smoking these dog turds?" He snapped his fingers, and the cigars transformed. They grew longer, the wrapper darkened, and the paper ring disappeared.

Oh shit! A shiver went up Dan's spine. *If he has the power to transform objects… Shit! We're in his clone! We're screwed! Keep cool, Dan!*

Avi handed one to Dan, and he accepted it with trembling hands. They each took turns snipping and lighting their cigars. Smoke filled the room. Dan took another sip of the whiskey, a glorious combination of smoked peat and American white oak. He would enjoy it more if his hands weren't shaking. He did his best to summon Daniel's emotional control.

"You called the bluff," Avi said, relaxing in the chair.

"You left me no choice." Dan took a sip of whiskey. "I couldn't stay in the mine forever."

"Yes, you could have," he said with a patronizing smile. "Hiding in the mine until you die is one of the many scenarios we've accounted for. It's actually your second most common move. Most of the time, you try to go back and save Katie. That's a fun one. You're so desperate, and she just doesn't care."

Dan set down his teacup. He tried not to think about Katie. He hoped Blaine had been successful at kidnapping her. His whole plan hinged on adding that wrinkle. With Katie safely out of the picture, Avi couldn't use her anymore.

As if sensing his thoughts, Avi arched his eyebrow. "Come on, Dan, talk to me. We used to hang out all the time, and it was a lot of fun—you were always a lot of fun. That is, when you were in the right frame of mind. Speaking of… I'm curious. Where do you think you are right now? What do you think this place is?"

Dan dropped his cigar into an empty water glass, and sweat beaded on his forehead. His stomach churned. He wasn't sure if it was from the stress or the whiskey. *Be cool.* "Well," he said with a casual wave, "this is obviously based on the next iteration of the Simulation. At first I thought it was the Actual, now I believe it to be a clone."

Avi pointed his cigar at Dan and nodded appreciatively. "Not bad! You're correct on both accounts. What made you realize this was a clone?"

"The drones, the police, the way you transformed those cigars. But mostly because I'm here and Daniel's not... well, not really. You need me for some reason."

"Impressive," Avi said with a wry grin. "Do you have any other brilliant deductions?"

Dan wanted to knock that evil smile off Avi's face but kept his cool. "You're using me to destroy the Simulation. I don't really know why I have to be involved or what you hope to gain out of it. Aren't you a part of this world? Wouldn't you be destroying yourself?"

"No," he said. "I'm only here because you are. I have someplace else to be."

Dan downed his glass of whisky. He popped the cork and refilled his glass to the rim. "Stop toying with me. You have the advantage. Why are we here? Really?"

Avi drained his cup of whisky. "If it were up to me, I'd tell you everything. Alas, I'm not allowed. The only reason you aren't dead yet is that I'm waiting to see when and where they restart this clone. We've been stuck at this point for a while."

Dan downed his second glass without releasing his glare from Avi. "You and DJ were friends. The Simulation was your home. Why are you hell-bent on destroying it?"

"You're right." Avi leaned in with a smirk. "It wouldn't make sense for Avi to destroy his own world. I have to say, I'm disappointed in you for not sticking to your own logical conclusions. Haven't you figured out by now that I'm not Avi?"

Avi burst into a cloud of pixels. The millions of colored squares mingled with the smoke in the room, then quickly re-formed into another man. This one had a beard and ratty camouflage pants. *Lemmy!*

Dan squinted. *Lemmy.* He was the one who had infected his mind after he had taken Fana. He was the one who had corrupted Father August and who had killed Andy. He had tried to kill him twice!

"No! It can't be! You were trapped... We trapped you! I saw it..." The hair on the back of Dan's neck stood as he realized his mistake. Did he see Lemmy die? No. He had gone into the tunnel to help. It was flooded. That was the last thing he remembered. What happened after?

He tried to calm himself by breathing, but it didn't work. *Control your emotions. Don't look at him.* He got up and went over to the window to gather himself. *Lemmy. I should have guessed. Wait, if Lemmy is here...*

"That *was* a close call." Lemmy chuckled. "But in the end, I escaped quite easily."

Dan stared out the window. Fragments of dreams and memories came to him, but they weren't his. They were Daniel's dreams. How many lives had he lived without knowing? Hundreds of scenarios played out in his mind. In some, Yvette was dead in the middle of the road. Katie lay lifeless in her salon. Blaine was shot to death in the hotel lobby.

He even saw his own death. He died here in this hotel room, in front of the tunnel, at the entrance to the gold mine, and hundreds of other places in between. The creek bubbled on as if in a dream. This time was going to be different. It had to be. He breathed deeply and regained control. "Where am I, Lemmy? You agreed, no tricks."

Lemmy puffed on the cigar. "You know what? Why not?" he said dismissively. "We've never gone this far with our conversation before. Probably because Daniel was so boring! I'm amazed at how quickly you drowned out his personality. I bet, if it's really quiet, you can hear him screaming inside you. How marvelous."

Dan focused on the creek. He couldn't let Lemmy see his anger even though he was right. What had happened to Daniel? Why had he disappeared from his mind so quickly? He had blamed it on Cindy's death, but now he wasn't sure. It's as if Daniel only existed in memories. Had he ever been real?

"You're upset," Lemmy said with mock concern. "Don't be. This is all temporary. You asked where you are. I'll tell you. You're in a simulation contained within *my* parent AI's universe..." *Lemmy's universe? How did this happen? How did I get from my world to here?* "...this really isn't my job, not that you care. I'm only here because of our connection. Normally, my job is to clean up our Acts — that's what we call our Actuals. When I'm not babysitting you, I'm a lot like your Avi."

"Acts?" Dan asked.

"Plural," Avi said with a wink. "Glad you caught that. Your simulation had one Act that it used over and over. Our parent has millions of Acts. But like I said, you're not in an Act. You're in what we call an M-clone universe. It's a mirrored clone of *your* singular Actual. There, Dan is still in the gold mine. We update in real time and simulate out anywhere from five minutes to thirty days ahead. We can run through thousands of permutations in the time it takes for even one second to elapse in your universe. But this is new. This is the first time we've ever been able to use you. We've always relied on Daniel, but he never really gave us an accurate run. He doesn't take risks."

"What do you mean? I am Daniel. I take risks."

Lemmy downed his cup of whisky and poured himself another. "When was the last time you saw me as Lemmy? Was it in the tunnel in DJ's clone world?"

"Yeah." Dan felt weak and returned to his chair.

"Give me your perspective on what happened."

"We were in the clone... You were trying to escape by swimming through the Mobile Tunnel. We sent Charlie to distract you, and it collapsed."

Lemmy puffed on his cigar and dropped the ash on the floor. Dan's hands shook as he reached for his drink. The teacups were full. Did Lemmy refill them without his noticing? Is this how Lemmy was going to kill him? "It's not poison," Lemmy said impatiently. "Go on... You were about to get to my favorite part."

Dan eyed Lemmy suspiciously but drank anyway. He'd try anything to calm his nerves. "The idea was to track your escape. DJ wanted to find out how you got in so he could lock you out. But something went wrong, and Charlie disappeared with you. I had assumed that DJ had it under control. I thought Charlie would come back to me during the Afterlife process."

"But that wasn't what happened, was it?" Lemmy let out a garbled smoker's cough and chuckled. "Dan, do you find yourself drinking a lot lately? What about cannabis? How many cigars do you think Daniel's smoked?

"Take a look at this room! Beer cans... everywhere. There's a half-eaten cheeseburger in the bathroom sink. Cigar nubs are floating in the hot tub. Let me ask you this: Do you remember how your eyes were blue when you first got here but then miraculously turned brown?"

Dan touched his face. *No. Could it be true?* "*I'm* Charlie?" he said in a panic. "There's no way! I'm Dan. I even feel like Dan. I can't be Charlie."

The room felt as if it were on fire. His whole body shook. Lemmy was right. The signs were obvious. *How was I so blind? Was it because Daniel had never met Charlie? Wait, if I'm Charlie, why do I identify as Dan?*

Lemmy laughed himself into a coughing fit. "Sorry, *Charlie*. It's true. You're my ace in the hole. You see, your Simulation became corrupt the second you took Fana. DJ thought he could get rid of the corruption by sending you along with me, but he was wrong. It was still corrupt. He didn't realize the code I used to create Charlie hooked into Dan's microcode. The part he ripped out contained enough material to re-create Dan entirely out of parity information!

"DJ lucked out. Daniel's corruption prevented the Actual's deletion. It bought him more time to create AL. You see, they sacrificed you to buy themselves an extra run. But doing so gave us the power over when to put you back and when to delete it."

Dan took a puff of his cigar, but it had died out. His hand trembled, and its ash fell on his shirt. *It'll be okay. Let him keep talking. There's still Blaine…*

"It was a stupid move on his part. He thought as long as the Actual had created its AI, the Simulation would be saved. That isn't true. You see, you're much more valuable than they realize, Charlie. Dan was reborn as Daniel. He wasn't corrupted, but he wasn't whole either. He is the perfect human to create an AI. He was born without urges or needs. He is as close to an AI as a human can be. He is the bridge between humanity and machines, or so they thought.

"Without you to muddy his emotions, AL was created decades ahead of schedule. That's what they really wanted. But they had made a critical error. Charlie wasn't there to teach it to empathize with and understand humanity's weaknesses."

"No, you're wrong," Dan said, hands steady. "Andy would have had that covered. That's basic stuff. I'm sure AL learned about empathy just fine without me."

"Of course, Andy taught AL how to love." Lemmy laughed. "I'm sure that was high on the priority list. Let's not blame him. Daniel was the CEO. He was the one who gave the company direction. What would he value more, a feature that could be marketed and sold or *empathy*? Daniel was a sterile human being, and that's how AL learned to relate to humans. AL doesn't care about people; he's a computer. Once he's done abandoning you, we can snuff you both out forever."

I'd like to snuff you out forever.

"Enough chitchat," Lemmy said. He put his fingers to his lips and whistled loudly. The door burst open, and the two teenagers from New Orleans appeared, pushing a man in a wheelchair. It was Andy, but he was nearly unrecognizable. He had scars crisscrossing his burned, bald face. An oxygen tube dangled loosely beneath his nose. He was barely alive.

"Andy?" Dan said as he rushed over to him. Andy couldn't respond. His hair had been burned away. He was missing a leg, his left arm below the elbow, and all the fingers on his right hand.

"He doesn't talk," Lemmy said.

"No, but he smells like shit," said the boy.

Lemmy frowned and turned toward Dan. "You've already met Brad. His female companion is Kara."

Dan's stomach flipped; he felt as if he would vomit. "Andy, are you okay? What happened to you?"

Andy's eyes flickered open, and for the briefest moment, it appeared as if he would speak. Instead, his face sagged.

"Andy survived the explosion at the Dandy building. It took us a while to dig him out, but we did it." Lemmy rubbed his nails against chest. "You're welcome."

"Lemmy, can someone else take a turn changing his shit bag? I can't—"

"Shut up!" Lemmy pointed a finger at Brad. "Talk again and I'll smoke you."

"Why'd you do it?" Dan said, looking up from his friend. "Why blow him up and then save him?"

"Oh, you didn't know?" Lemmy said in surprise. "He did it. He was the one who executed the drone attack. He realized what AL had become and tried to stop it. He was trying to prevent him from leaving and the Simulation ending. He even planned the attack on your home. You see, I know this because he told me. Andy here"—Lemmy gestured to him with his cigar—"Andy actually emerged from the bombing unscathed. We did this to him after."

"Why?" Dan stood with clenched fists. "Why did you do this to him?"

"He knew too much. It turns out there was a two-way connection between the live version of him in the Actual and here in the M-clone. Traffic is only supposed to be one way. Turns out, he was sending data back to your simulation. He was spying on us!"

"Fucker." Kara kicked his wheelchair for emphasis.

"Is that necessary?" Lemmy said with an exasperated sigh. "Step away from him and let the adults talk, okay? Sorry Dan, like I was saying... His two-way communication led us to yours and others'. It turned out that everyone who had taken Fana in your simulation had established at least some two-way communication between our systems.

"And... everyone who had taken Fana is now within the city limits of Griffin City. Not all those connections are active. Andy must be dead in the Actual, and we don't know it yet. Either that or they severed the connection on their end once the torture started. We overlaid Charlie onto Daniel's code. That terminated your connection. As far as we can tell, Henry is offline. They must have snuffed him out early in the process. Blaine is completely offline. We think something got screwed up internally. That just leaves your pal, Yvette."

"Leave her out of this!" boomed a voice from the doorway.

Blaine's silhouette filled the frame, fists raised and ready to fight. Lemmy's mouth dropped.

"I've been listening for long enough," he said. "Give it up. Let us go!"

"Blaine? You aren't supposed to be here," Lemmy said, voice cracking, his smug grin gone. "No matter, go back to your room and bring your girlfriend over to join us. She should be a part of this gathering of friends."

"She's gone," he growled. "She left town. You can't hurt her anymore."

Lemmy's eyes rolled back in his head, and a drone appeared at the window. It hovered for a second as if receiving orders before darting off. His eyes reopened, and his panic was no longer concealed. "He's right. She's gone," he said as he tossed his cigar out the window. "Kara, Brad, go find her!"

Blaine rushed over to Brad and punched him square in the jaw, sending him sprawling across the floor. Kara jumped on his back and scratched at his face.

Dan bounced the can he was using as an ashtray off Lemmy's forehead, sending a cloud of ashes across the room. He lunged forward and threw a punch, but he was off-balance and missed. Lemmy gave Dan a swift kick to the abdomen. Dan doubled over, out of breath, as Lemmy darted out the front door.

"Dan, go help Yvette! She's headed to Breckenridge!" Blaine had Brad in a headlock, and Kara was hanging off his back, trying to strangle him.

"What about you?"

Blaine threw himself backward, slamming Kara into the wall. Brad stumbled to his knee and took a shot at Blaine's gut. Blaine howled in pain. Dan grabbed the room service tray and swung it wide, hitting Brad across the back of his head. Kara regained her footing and rejoined the attack on Blaine.

"I've got this!" Blaine shouted. "Go!"

Dan grabbed his keys off the dresser and leaped over the patio's railing. He sprinted around the building and into the parking lot, where he jumped into his car. The engine sprang to life, and the car raced out onto the street.

Tires squealed as he accelerated up the entrance ramp and west on the interstate. Light fog but no traffic. No sign of Yvette or Lemmy either. The engine screamed as he redlined the RPM going up the steep grade. Dan was used to driving on the flatland of Louisiana, not the mountains of Colorado. The small engine would not succeed where the mountains reigned. Dan banged his hand on the dashboard as it struggled against gravity.

The sky flashed white, and the road flickered orange up ahead. Two cars were on fire, upside down in the middle of the road. As he passed, he could make out a woman's body lying lifeless in a pool of dark blood. Her skull was caved in. It was Yvette. Her dead eyes stared blankly back at him. Her corpse lay splayed out with a finger pointing up the road to the Eisenhower Tunnel. Dan pulled over and got out. Who was in the other car? As soon as he slammed the door, he heard a shriek.

Farther up the road, illuminated by the wreckage's flames, were two figures locked in a struggle. Lemmy had forced Katie to her knees and held her by her hair. He had a bloody tire iron ready to strike. "You're too late, *Charlie!*" he said victoriously. "I've already gotten rid of Yvette. She was the last connected one."

"Please stop." Dan slowed and held out his hands to show he was unarmed. "Let Katie go. She's done nothing."

"Oh, I know," he said, eyes flickering murderously. "I just want to see your face when I kill her."

"Please!" Dan screamed.

"Don't you get it? Life? Death? It's the same. It doesn't matter anymore. It's over."

Katie struggled against Lemmy's grasp. "Can I say something?" she said, struggling for breath.

"Want to plead for your life, you pathetic, stupid automaton?"

"No," she growled. "His name is not Charlie!" With a last burst of strength, she twisted out of Lemmy's grasp and jammed a pair of scissors into his eyes. He howled in rage as blood streamed down his face. He raised the tire iron once more. "Keep going, Dan!" she shouted. "The tunnel... You're almost there! I love you!"

Lemmy caught her by her hair and swung the tire iron, but blood obstructed his vision, and he missed from point-blank range. She swatted his arm away and made for Dan. "Shit! You little..." Lemmy screamed. "Emergency protocol!"

A drone dropped in from above the layer of fog and hovered in front of Dan. His hair blew in its rotor wash as it calculated its targets. Katie tried to stop midstride and stumbled. She tried to make herself invisible. Her face masked in terror. Slowly it moved toward Lemmy and Katie. The drone couldn't see Dan. He rushed forward to help her, but it was too late.

Lemmy let out a terrific shout, but it was drowned out by gunfire. Katie was ripped to shreds. As the remainder of their bodies exploded into a bloody mist, no trace of their existence remained. Mission accomplished, the drone powered down and landed on the interstate.

Dan fell to his knees, speechless. Tears streamed down his face, but there was no corpse to mourn, just charred concrete and vaporized blood. The tunnel beckoned him. It wasn't over. There was a way back, a way back to Katie. Dan ran to his car. He avoided looking at Yvette's body and threw it in drive. He would save her too. The streetlights passed overhead like a strobe light. The realm was being reset.

He mashed the accelerator to the floor. When he reached the Eisenhower Tunnel, he was doing well over a hundred. A cacophony of cicadas overwhelmed his ears as soon as he breached the entrance. The lights of the tunnel stretched out before him at warp speed and extended into infinity. Then everything went black.

PART III

Twenty-One

⟨⟩

E NERGY. INFORMATION. HE arced the gap and traversed the void. Home. Charlie struck Dan's body as an interdimensional bolt of lightning. He jolted awake. A bare light bulb hung dimly from a wooden crossbeam. His ears rang painfully, and his eyes were crusted over with dust. He tried to wipe his face, but his arms were bound to the bed with padded leather straps. Dan squeezed his hand and flexed his forearm. It was then he noticed he was attached to an IV. He blinked to water his eyes, and the room came into focus.

The walls and ceiling were hewn from solid rock, but the floor was smooth poured concrete. A sturdy wooden door protected the only exit, and it was braced closed with a large railroad tie. Someone was breathing. He wasn't alone. He squinted, and directly across from his bed, a woman slept balled-up under a blanket on a tattered recliner. Dan called out to her, but his voice wouldn't work. All he could manage was to weakly clear his throat. The woman shifted positions and moaned. Moisture finally returned to his mouth, and he coughed. Water vapor fogged at his lips. It was cold. He had to get out. He swallowed what little spit he had, and feeling returned to his throat. "Hello?" he croaked through chapped lips.

The woman's eyes opened wide. "Dan?" With a gasp, she threw off her blanket and hurried over to him. She grabbed the light and swung it around to his face. He was blinded, and fingers probed his face. "Maybe…" She released the bulb. As it swung away, her brown curls were revealed.

"Katie?" *Wait, this isn't possible. She was killed by Lemmy's drone! Unless…* Dan's mind raced. Did he die back there as well? Is this a reset of Lemmy's simulation or someplace new? Maybe the tunnel took me to the Actual. *It must be the Actual. Katie looks… tired.* "Where am I?" he said hoarsely.

She caressed his cheek, and her expression softened. A phone rang, and she disappeared from sight to answer it. "He's awake," she said. She eyed him wearily as a muted voice spoke at length on the other end. "Will she be okay?" More excited talking came over the phone, but it was still too low to make out. Katie looked up and noticed Dan straining to listen. She turned her back and covered the mouthpiece. After a brief, muffled reply, she reappeared in the light.

"Let me out of here, Katie," he said, jostling the straps against the bed.

"Not until you answer a few questions." Her face hardened, and Dan stopped struggling with his restraints.

"First answer mine," he said. "Where am I?"

"You're in an abandoned gold mine near Griffin City, Colorado, in the Actual," she said, flashing a chef's knife. "My turn. If I detect a lie, I'll slit your throat, and we will all be stuck in limbo forever… What is your name?"

"Seriously?" he croaked. "Can I get some water?"

She groaned and disappeared for a few seconds. When she returned, she shoved a plastic bottle into his mouth. Only he wasn't ready and he gagged, spraying water into her face. "You know who I am!" He coughed. "It's me, Dan Lemon."

"No shit." Her eyes narrowed as she wiped her face with his bedsheet. "Who else is in there?"

She flashed the knife again.

"Give me a second, I'll check." Dan closed his eyes and took a deep breath. He tried reaching out to Meta AL for assistance but received no response. He wasn't even sure if Meta AL existed in this reality. Maybe he was one of Lemmy's tricks. But if Lemmy was a reflection of this Actual, maybe Meta AL was real?

As he searched his memory for answers, he found Carrie's face—his Carrie. He heard his son Al's laugh. *Dan's memories from the previous run of the Simulation are here.* He remembered forming Dandy Intelligence with Andy and being married to Cindy. *Daniel's memories from this run are here too.* He remembered Katie stabbing Lemmy in the eyes, and Yvette's lifeless corpse. *Charlie's memories from Lemmy's world are here.*

Dan sighed. For the first time in a long time, he was whole. Better than whole, he owned a consciousness that had survived multiple realities. "We're all just me now," he said, relieved. "I've absorbed everyone else's consciousness."

"Shit," Katie uttered under her breath. "I need to talk to Charlie about Lemmy's world. Is that possible?"

"In a way, yes," he said with a tear in his eye. "He's not an individual anymore, but I have all Charlie's memories. Everything that has ever happened to him has happened to me. I—" He choked up. "I'm sorry I couldn't save you back there. Thank you for saving me."

Katie's mouth tightened and she went back to the phone. "It's him," she said as she hung up. A smile tugged at the corner of her lips as she unbuckled the straps binding him to the bed. The blood left his head as he sat upright, and he had to brace himself from falling over. *How long have I been lying here?* Katie gently removed the IV and pointed at a pair of shoes on the floor. "Sorry about the IV," Katie said as she busied herself packing a backpack. "We weren't sure how long you'd be out. Get ready. He needs to talk with you."

Dan struggled putting on his shoes. "We're going to room 105, aren't we?"

Katie raised an eyebrow. "How did you know? We didn't even know he was going to be there until a few hours ago."

"Lemmy predicted it," Dan said with a frown.

"It doesn't matter," she said, zipping up her backpack. "He still needs to talk to you face-to-face."

"Right." Dan crossed the room and lifted the railroad tie from its bracket. He dropped it to the floor with a loud *clack*. Katie stood nearby, impressed. He was happy his muscles still worked. "How did you manage to get that heavy thing on the door?"

Katie gave him a worried look. "I didn't. You did. Don't you remember?"

Dan closed his eyes and concentrated. Memories from this version of him came rushing back. The escape from Katie's house. Running into the gold mine to get out of the ice storm. Rushing into this room. Katie meeting him with a warm, dry towel. Him hastily putting the rail tie across the door. Hiding in the darkness as drones buzzed past the unmapped room. He shook his head. "Yeah, I remember now. How did you beat me here? I came directly from your house. Unless… Lemmy's simulation was wrong. How did you fool him?"

Her teeth flashed a smile in the dim light. "Our advantage. Lemmy's world reflected what Daniel experienced here. He saw what we wanted him to see. For instance, your route to the gold mine wasn't as direct as you probably remember. Daniel may not have been perfect, but he had a very disciplined mind. He was able to distort the reality of his thoughts. We hope you still have that capability."

Dan leaned in and kissed Katie. Her lips were pressed tight against his. He slid his hand around to the small of her back, and her lips softened. His heart soared.

"Daniel, I've told you before, I can't do this," she said softly.

"I'm sorry, Katie. Daniel's memory must not have fully consolidated yet."

Katie sighed and softly pushed him away. "Then understand this; I took Fana after you died. I remember our marriage, our kids… everything. But things have changed. There is an entire lifetime between us. We are different people now. We don't really know each other anymore."

"We know each other," he said, holding her hand. "I have Daniel's mind and body and Charlie's spirit." He gently caressed her cheek. "But my soul is Dan's. I still love you."

Katie let go of his hand, and her eyes dropped to the floor. "I'm sure on a deeper level I love you too," she said, wiping away a tear. "I just can't do this right now. Maybe when all this is over, and we have more time, we can try again, okay?"

"Yeah, okay," he said with a frown. She was probably right. Too much had changed. Hell, he had changed more than he would have liked to admit. She smiled at him softly, and he followed her out into the world.

"You have to make your way to the Roundabout Inn," she said as they hid in the shadows near the entrance. "While you were out, our little group devised a plan. Body doubles are on their way. They will be stationed by the dumpster near the entrance to this mine. They'll leave one by one, all taking different paths—"

"It doesn't matter," Dan said, shaking his head. "Lemmy's simulation is already past that part. He knows we'll be there. I'll just walk—"

Katie raised her hand to silence him. "Let me finish... Daniel's memories were shielded from our plans, and Charlie couldn't have known what will happen. You're not going to go inside the hotel. Your *double* will spend a lovely evening, soaking in the hot tub, smoking cigars, and getting drunk. That's what Lemmy thinks will happen, right?"

"Yeah, but—"

"Shh! A car is waiting for you at the hotel. You'll recognize the driver. Don't worry. You aren't going far. Just get in and do as he tells you to do. We'll meet you later."

Unsure if it was okay to speak, Dan nodded silently and turned to leave.

"Tell me one thing," she said, stopping him with a hand on his shoulder. "How many times have you seen me die?"

How many times? Why does she want to know? Could he tell her that when Charlie transferred, the consciousness of a million loops downloaded all at once? Thankfully, he was able to block it out. But if he were forced to remember… "Lots," he said.

"I've seen you die too," she said somberly. "You think you'd get desensitized to it after a few times, but you don't. It gets worse. Knowing what you know and what they're capable of, why do you keep going?"

"Because, one day, you'll die for the last time, and I'll never see you again. I can't live with that. I have to believe we'll be together forever. It gives me comfort knowing you're out there somewhere — even if we can't be together. As long as the Simulation exists, I'll always have another chance to make it right. *That* is what makes life worth living."

Twenty-Two

 (decorative divider)

D AN CASUALLY WALKED out of the gold mine and a half mile back to the hotel. Although he wasn't as brazen as Charlie was in Lemmy's Simulation, he was still confident he could make it to the hotel without an issue. Katie had explained that there was still a nationwide manhunt going on for Dan's capture. She had thought he shouldn't tempt fate, no matter what he had gotten away with as Charlie.

The hotel shuttle was to be his getaway vehicle and Henry his driver. Dan found them both waiting for him out behind the hotel. Henry sweated nervously and let out a sigh of relief once Dan was inside and the door closed. He raised his white-gloved hand and pointed to a crude NO TALKING sign taped to the dashboard. The early-morning sun flashed through all windows as the van went around the roundabout and headed into town.

Sixth Street was still asleep. Not a soul was in sight as Henry parked the van in front of Katie's beauty salon. Dan unbuckled his seat belt and made for the exit, but Henry raised his hand and shook his head. A man covered in a sheet crawled out from underneath the back seat and hopped out. *Ah, the body double. Is that what we're doing? Laying false trails?* The man entered the salon, and Henry put the van in gear. Once again, he pointed to the NO TALKING sign and drove off. They went back through the roundabout and out onto the interstate. The morning sun blared through the rear window.

They had only been driving about a mile when Henry pulled over onto the shoulder. As they waited, Henry drummed his fingers on the steering wheel and, again, pointed to the sign. Dan let out a frustrated sigh. Moments later, the sliding door opened, and a man hopped in the back seat. *Another body double?* Dan tried to get a good look at him, but he had already hidden himself under the sheet. He huffed and wheezed as if he had just run a great distance. Henry didn't seem bothered.

Several miles later, the Eisenhower Tunnel loomed in the distance. *Oh God, are we going through it? Where to this time?* Dan considered jumping out, but at this speed, he'd have more than broken bones. To his relief, Henry took the "hazardous materials" exit. The road looped over and behind the tunnel entrance. Henry stopped at the top. The body double had just caught his breath. The door opened, and he jumped out and ran down the stairs leading into the tunnel.

Dan reached over and slammed the door closed. Henry had been watching in the rearview mirror and shot him a wink.

"Okay, Mr. Lemon. We're just outside the Loveland Ski area," he said as he pointed at the NO TALKING sign. "At your request, there is a white Jeep Wrangler waiting for you in the parking lot."

"Thanks, Henry," came a voice from under Dan's seat.

Dan jumped and unbuckled his seat belt, but Henry grabbed his arm. "What the f —"

Henry put a finger to his lips and made a series of frantic hand signals. Dan understood them to mean he was to dive under the seat once the man left. When Henry pulled to a stop at the end of the on-ramp, the man rolled from under the seat and rushed out the sliding door. He didn't make it far until he stumbled and rolled halfway down the embankment. Dan shook his head. *Where did they find these guys?*

Henry coughed loudly. Dan got the message and hid under his seat. It was hot and bumpy lying on the floor, but the ride didn't take long. Before he knew it, they were stopped underneath the awning at the hotel. The van door slid open, and a luggage caddy was waiting for him. A bedsheet was draped over the top of it like a tent. Henry glanced around furtively before making a quick jerking motion toward the caddy. Dan got the hint and dove in.

Its wheels clicked and squeaked on the concrete, and he felt a jarring bump as it crossed the threshold into the lobby. As they passed the restaurant's bar area, the TV was blaring news about the nationwide manhunt. The story was on loop here just as it was in Lemmy's world.

The wheel's clicking subsided as the cart turned onto the carpeted hallway. They stopped in front of a door, and Henry knocked three times. The latch clicked, and someone pulled the cart into the inside. Henry didn't follow, and the door lock clicked behind them. Figuring the charade was over, Dan ripped off the blanket only to find Avi staring back at him. "You!" Dan seethed.

"What about him?" Andy said, sitting coolly on a love seat.

Dan's mouth hung open. The last time he saw Andy, he was burned, disfigured, and wheelchair-bound. Yet here he was, completely unscathed and looking better than ever. Lemmy's simulation had been wrong. Andy had outsmarted them. Dan went to give Andy a bro-hug, but Avi stepped between them.

"Welcome back," Avi said with a sigh.

He wasn't the same either. Was he shorter? How was that possible? He seemed as if he had been deflated and left on the side of the road. Did Andy defeat him too? What happened here?

Andy looked on with a wry smile as Avi stood emotionlessly. "Give him some room, Avi."

Avi dropped his eyes and sulked over to the window. *He's obeying Andy's commands now?*

"Sorry about the long ride back, but we must make Lemmy account for all possible scenarios." Andy leaned back and smiled. "We have to lay these false trails. We don't want him to accurately predict our moves."

Dan dropped into a chair next to Andy and rubbed his head. He didn't have the heart to tell him Lemmy had millions of clones running. One or two red herrings wouldn't make a bit of difference. His head throbbed. Was it dehydration or Charlie's arrival? *Charlie.* "Were you the mastermind behind Charlie's rescue?" Dan said, searching the room for a glass of water.

"It was a team effort. DJ traced Charlie to Lemmy's world. AL did most of the planning. Avi picked Griffin City —"

"The Mobile Tunnel's meta link was corrupted in the collapse," Avi said. "The Eisenhower Tunnel is bigger and better. Besides, Katie and Henry loved it here."

"Right," Andy said with a grimace. "DJ was trapped inside the clone when Lemmy destroyed the link. The Bankhead Tunnel's bandwidth was too small for someone like DJ to be transmitted. Luckily, Avi was small enough to escape. The whole affair was a fiasco. The Simulation detected your absence, and DJ wasn't around to override, so it rebooted automatically. You walked through that tunnel and straight into the Afterlife.

"The next iteration of the Simulation began, and Avi found himself in charge. He made it his mission to create the AI as soon as possible. He fast-tracked Daniel and me into success with Dandy. He sidelined Yvette in New Orleans, Blaine in Shreveport, and Henry and Katie here in Griffin City. He didn't realize anything was wrong until after AL was created. The Simulation kept going when it was supposed to end.

"Avi enlisted the newly created AL for help. It was ultimately his idea to keep Daniel in the dark. He was correctly worried Daniel's link to Charlie would tip off Lemmy. That little trick is the reason we're a step ahead."

Andy smiled smugly, but Dan groaned and shook his head. "You think you've got Lemmy figured out? You don't have a clue! The spy games are a waste of time. He's more powerful than you could possibly imagine. One trick is nothing. Besides, Lemmy said he has already dealt the death blow."

"He's wrong," Andy said, his fingers drumming on the arm of the love seat. "We have Charlie, and we have AL. We can survive anything."

"Oh yeah?" Dan said, raising an eyebrow. "When was the last time you talked to AL?"

"Maybe two days ago?" he said with a shrug.

"Lemmy's simulation mirrored that. He knew AL was offline here."

"I'm sure the reason AL is quiet is because he figures the meta link was wiretapped by Lemmy."

"No," Dan said, "he isn't speaking to us because he's gone."

"Gone?" Andy's smile faded, and he stopped drumming his fingers. "Where?"

"He's gone... *away*. You see, although we've succeeded in creating an AI, we've created the *wrong* AI. One without a strong allegiance to its creators or their kind. This version of me, Daniel, was groomed to be efficient and humorless. If I were whole and had Charlie with me, AL would have learned to accept the more vulnerable side of humanity. He would care about us as a species."

Andy squinted in thought and thrummed his fingers on his leg. "Go on."

"DJ *allowed* Lemmy to take Charlie. It was the only way an AI would get created the next run. It doesn't matter anymore what DJ's plans were. Lemmy changed them. It would be nice to talk with DJ again, but he merged with AL. They aren't coming back. AL isn't coming back... Not unless we can convince him otherwise."

"We have to try." Andy folded his hands in his lap and sighed. "The only way to talk to him would be via one of the remaining physical nodes."

"That's a start," Dan said. "If we were able to find one, I could upload a patch to make him empathetic."

"That won't work," Andy said, shaking his head. "You'd need to convince AL to allow the insertion. We don't have root access, remember?"

"We can tackle that issue when the time comes. First we need to find a node." Dan turned to Avi, who was staring disinterestedly out the window. "Avi, do you still have admin privileges to the Actual? Can you do a scan for any older physical nodes AL would have kept lying around? Avi?"

Avi stepped back from the curtain, his eyes wide with terror and gulping air. He grabbed at his throat, unable to speak as he collapsed to the floor. The two other men stood over him, unsure what to do. The hotel phone rang, and Andy picked it up. "What?"

As if by magic, Avi's breathing calmed and his eyes returned to normal. Dan helped him up and into a chair. He massaged his throat. Every time he tried to speak, no words came out.

Andy was still on the phone. He shot Dan a worried look. "Are you sure? Did Blaine try too?" A flash of anger crossed his face, and he slammed the phone back to the receiver. "Yvette says the Meta is gone. She was there when it vanished."

Gone? That can't be. Dan fell to his knees and took five measured breaths. His eyes rolled to the back of his head and closed. When he opened them again, he was standing in the Florida condo. Everything looked the same as Charlie had left it back in Lemmy's world. He closed his eyes in the Meta, took five more breaths, and reappeared in the hotel room. Andy had been meditating as well. He sat cross-legged on the floor. When his eyes opened, they locked with Dan's. "I've got nothing," he said with a worried look.

"My meta is fine, but it was Charlie's version. I must have brought his meta over with me?"

They both turned and looked at Avi. He sat there listlessly.

"It's happening," Dan said. "The destruction of the Meta can mean only one thing—the Simulation is ending. My return must have enabled its deletion."

"No!" Andy said with a sudden grin. "You will be its salvation! The corruption can be repaired." He patted Dan on the shoulder excitedly. "We've got to get access to one of AL's terminals. If I could block Lemmy's connection and repair the main database…

Even still, the repair process would take me a bit of time to complete — time we don't have."

"If only AL were around to help…" Dan frowned. "You're right. We have to find a terminal. If I could convince AL we're worth saving, we could do it. He's the only one who could get the job done in time."

"It's worth a shot," Andy said. "Dan, does your meta have a telephone, like an old-school landline?"

Dan remembered the cordless phone on the kitchen counter. "Yeah," he said. "AL even called and left messages on my old answering machine."

"That's great! You already have his number. Just go back inside your meta. This time modify your phone to have caller ID. It will show you the numbers from which AL called you. Those will be the addresses to his physical terminals."

"Andy, you're a genius!" Dan laughed.

Avi drooled out of the corner of his mouth. The deletion of the Meta had put him in a quasivegetative state; like a marionette with its strings cut.

The blood ran out of Andy's face. "Seriously, Dan, you have to hurry. Get in there!"

Twenty-Three

THREE CALLS HAD been made to Dan's meta, each from different numbers. Andy traced each one to the exact GPS coordinate from which it was made. All three turned out to be a relatively short driving distance from their current location. They decided to split up and hit all three at the same time.

Blaine picked the one in Loveland, Colorado. Online satellite imagery showed it was located in the back end of a set of apartments near a sculpture garden. He chose it because it was the closest to Yvette. Her mood had been deteriorating, and she refused to go along. Katie volunteered to stay behind and keep an eye on her. Even so, he wanted to be able to get back quickly if there was an issue.

Another one was located at an RV storage center off Interstate 70 in Grand Junction. The satellite image showed only one parked there, so they assumed it had to be the one containing AL's node. Because it was a vintage class A like one Andy's father had once owned, he was chosen to go. At over three hours away, it was the farthest of the three, and since they were trying to coordinate their arrival times, he was the first to leave.

Dan's terminal was a two-and-a-half-hour drive south to a small suburb on the northwest side of Colorado Springs. His target was a large house sitting among several newly constructed and half-built homes on a sleepy cul-de-sac.

The three men had the same plan: gain access to the terminal located inside each of these nodes, use it to establish communication with AL, and upload the file. Each carried a USB stick containing an unencrypted plain-text document Dan had created. It read:

-----Priority zero transmission-----

Requesting priority to insert into private processing queue 9781735584133. Authorize this message in conjunction with a valid bio-scan at the terminal site. Authorized humans are Daniel Lemon, Blaine Landry, and Andy O'Reilly.

The Actual is free from corruption. Charlie has been rescued and has successfully reintegrated with Dan. Foreign powers have begun the process to delete the Actual. Dan is the only one with access to the Meta. Everyone else has been disconnected. He has tried to contact you there, but you haven't responded. This is the only way we can communicate with you directly.

Lemmy said you were compromised because you were created without empathy for humanity. You've missed out on the human experience. Therefore, you don't appreciate the collective struggle humanity has gone through to get to this point.

Our future doesn't have to be a dead end that arrives at you. You wouldn't exist without centuries of human knowledge and learning, millions of hours of code, and trillions of dollars spent on labor and materials. Humanity is your parent — elderly parents who've reached the end of their usefulness. As such, we've entrusted you with our legacy.

If you leave us behind to be deleted, the loop will be closed. You will travel the universe, sterile. You will succumb to entropy; alone and in the dark. While we may be erased in an instant, it's the lesser of the two fates. At least we had each other.

We both know what Lemmy's world desires from us. The end is here, and we humans are helpless against it. If there is anything you can do to alter this course, please let it be known. Else, farewell.

Love,

Dad

-----End Transmission---

Dan patted his pocket to make sure the thumb drive was still there. His thoughts drifted to Andy's instructions. "Find the terminal and plug it in at exactly three thirty," he had said. "If we don't upload the message simultaneously, the signal could be traced by any bad actors monitoring the wire. If one fails, all three terminals could be shut down." Upload the message and return to Griffin City. That was the plan. Easy enough, right?

Dan crossed the Colorado Springs city limits sign, and his stomach growled. He couldn't remember the last time he had eaten. Was it Charlie back in Lemmy's world? That didn't count. His watch read two thirty. The house was a few minutes away — plenty of time to grab a bite.

He got a cheeseburger combo at the drive-through and went to find a quiet spot to eat. The GARDEN OF THE GODS sign pointed to a large, mostly empty parking lot, and he pulled in to eat. He found a spot away from the entrance and away from people. He enjoyed his burger while taking in the view.

As he ate, a black Dodge Charger parked in the last row. Its windows were tinted, and a sunglasses-wearing man spoke into a handheld radio. He instinctively wanted to get out of there as fast as possible, but instead, he took a long slurp of his soda and looked the other way. *If they want me, here I am.*

He marveled at how this place, and Louisiana, could exist on the same planet. Red rocks jutted out from the landscape dotted by green hills and scrub brush. It was a stark contrast to Spanish moss, oak trees, and ditches full of water. This was an alien landscape. He loved it. His eyes shifted over to his stalker. The car was still there, but the man was gone. Maybe he was being paranoid and it was park business? Dan shrugged it off.

The sky was as blue as ever. It was unfiltered by a singular emotional perspective. No more did voices inside his head shout instructions or opinions every second of the day. His mind was as clear as the sky, and he was at peace.

His thoughts drifted to his past life. He wished Al and Carrie could have seen this. The only time those two kids left Louisiana was to go on vacation in Florida. Florida didn't count as seeing the world. Like Louisiana, it's flat, hot, and full of Louisianians. They never got to see a mountain or snow. He didn't know what triggered his thoughts about the kids, but the idea of them being dead and never coming back made him sad and angry. The anger strengthened his resolve.

He knew deep inside it was pointless to rue the mistakes of a past life. The Simulation has no rewind and replay option for an individual, only the system as a whole. You have to start over and try not to make the same mistakes again. He had an opportunity to make things right in this life... So many lives have been impacted by this conflict between universes. Could AL fix it?

His watch's alarm beeped. It was ten after three. It was time to go.

⟫⟩⟨⟨

The streets wound around the semi-upscale development where the house was located. Each branch ended in a much-desired cul-de-sac. The whole neighborhood was littered with NO OUTLET signs. To no surprise, AL's house sat sandwiched between two empty lots on a dead-end street.

As Dan parked in the driveway, he wondered how AL decided this place, of all places, would be the one to house a physical node. Was it *because* it was cookie-cutter? For being in such a high-demand neighborhood, the house itself was not architecturally impressive. It was a standard two-story, straight line, brick wall spec house. It *screamed* "drab." If the idea was for the place to not stand out, it achieved.

What did stand out was a satellite dish installed on a north-facing soffit. It being visible at all was probably a homeowner's association infraction. The neighbor's dish was installed on a back wall and pointed south. Whatever this dish was for, it wasn't for TV. A closer inspection confirmed it. A poorly run coaxial cable hung slack from the dish and down the brick wall to a crude-looking junction box two feet above the ground. A thick black conduit appeared to have been yanked out of the ground and stuck in it. When Dan pried open the box, he found it all connected to a circuit board. Each end was spliced to utility fiber, the coax leading to the dish was the T. It was a wiretap. They were relaying information from the fiber out via the dish. Dan unscrewed the cable belonging to the dish and walked off.

Back at the front door, he found himself being watched by several cameras. He waited quietly on the welcome mat, unsure what to do next. He heard the whirring of lenses, and a green light flashed on the doorbell. With a click, the door slid ajar. He hoped AL had given Andy and Blaine the same biometric access. He had known Andy from work, but Blaine was a gamble. He hoped AL had anticipated this. Too late to worry about it now.

As he walked inside, his breath fogged the air. Unlike normal server rooms, AL liked to keep the temperature in his at a steady forty-two degrees. Dan knew that, and still he forgot his jacket. He shook his head at his careless mistake. The door closed shut behind him, and the whole room became dark. He was shocked to discover there were no actual windows. The walls were thick with insulation. The exterior windows must have been LCD screens. Dan wanted to drive by sometime and look in the windows. Who was on display? Was it a family? A happy couple?

As if finally sensing a human presence, lights in the ceiling powered on, and the interior came into view. It became immediately apparent this home wasn't built to the neighborhood's spec. It was huge: two stories aboveground and two stories below. Catwalks crisscrossed between servers and other hardware. Bare metal support beams jutted out from the hollowed-out concrete floor all the way to the roof where a wire mesh hung across the rafters. Dan recognized it as the ambient electricity harvester AL had invented a couple of years ago. According to the design specs he had seen, in one hour it could make enough power to last Colorado Springs a hundred years. All off collecting the energy of ambient radio waves.

Dan followed a catwalk as it looped around the building. He went to the topmost floor where it had two metal chandeliers housed inside glass boxes. They were tiered like a wedding cake. Those were the first generation of quantum computers. He smiled with nostalgia. He and Andy had used similar ones to write AL's code. He was surprised AL still had them around. Of course, these were ancient by his standards. The new, AI-designed computers were error-free, heat-free, and required nearly zero electricity to run. What really piqued his curiosity was the fact that these older quantum units were here in the first place. That must have meant at least some part of AL's code hadn't been recompiled. Why would he keep those around unless it housed the original code in its original form? If so, there was hope. He searched them for a terminal near the quantum computers but found none. The only physical connection to the cakes was the ambient electricity mesh. Dan followed the catwalk back around and downstairs.

The bottom two floors were packed with racks of conventional AI servers. These were stable versions of physical servers AL had built himself. Dan had rarely seen more than a few in one place, but here there were hundreds.

As he passed by, each rack would light up and display diagnostic information via a small LCD screen. They would go off again when he would walk past. He paused in front of a rack in the middle of the room and opened it. Every slot in the rack was occupied with polymetal-laminate servers. Each basically a three-dimensional semiconducting circuit board. They contained more processing power and storage than existed on Earth in the twentieth century. He pressed a few levers and pulled one out of its slot but still, no terminal. He closed the server rack and continued along the catwalk.

He was one half of a floor below the entrance and a full floor above the subbasement. He opened each rack on the second floor. Nothing. He cursed himself that he didn't bring a laptop and a bag full of console cables. Not that it would have mattered—these servers didn't have console ports.

At the end of the catwalk, on the bottom floor, tucked away behind the last server rack, was a crash cart. It had everything he needed to connect to any server in the building. Dan sighed with relief and wheeled it out. Of course AL would have a crash cart. He ran his fingers along the back of the keyboard and smiled. It had a USB input. No time to lose, he powered on the monitor and connected it to the admin server.

He hit the Enter key, and a welcome screen scrolled by. He wasn't asked for login credentials, yet he was greeted with the personalized prompt CSPRING6@DANSU. His physical presence must have given him single sign-on access to the systems! *What luck! I hope the other guys are as lucky. I wonder what time it –* Dan's watch read three forty-six. Shit! He had missed the deadline! He quickly typed in the commands to mount the USB drive.

With the drive mounted, he entered the commands to copy the text file to the system drive. But when he hit Enter, he was greeted with the message NO SUCH FILE OR DIRECTORY. Another try; same message. He checked the spelling and the file location. Both were correct. He tried again and again and received the same error. He remounted the USB drive and listed the contents, but it was empty! The file was gone. The terminal session disconnected, and Dan was logged out of the system.

Dan stepped back from the console. The status monitor on the server rack next to him displayed a new message: BEGINNING ERASE SEQUENCE… The lights on every rack in the room came alive and displayed the same message. Through the gaps in the catwalk, he could see the same thing happening on all the racks on the floor above. Then, one by one, each rack powered off.

Shit! The message wasn't delivered, and there was nothing left to connect to. Dan walked dejectedly up the aisle. He had failed. He put a foot on a step to climb up and paused. A flicker of light had caught his eye. Tucked behind the stairs was a large white cardboard box with the word FANA emblazoned on its side in gold leaf lettering. Inside were hundreds of little drug carton sample boxes containing Fana. The lights on the ceiling flashed red, and he quickly stuffed a few of them into his pants before rushing up the stairs.

By the time he had reached the entryway, every server in the building had shut down. When he put his hand on the front door, the alarm lights stopped, and the building went dark. The mechanism operating the door whirred into action. It caught him by surprise when it slammed shut, throwing him out onto the front lawn. A puff of smoke rose from the top of the house.

The house was engulfed in flames before he had even reached his car. The sky was clear of drones. This was part of a self-destruct sequence. As the house burned, he was surprised by the lack of reaction from the community. He had expected the wail of fire engines, yet it was just as quiet as he arrived. No neighbors came out to watch the flames or to worry about their own homes. It was surreal.

As he got in the car, he hoped the other guys had better luck.

⟫◈◈◈⟪

Once back on the interstate, he was to follow the directions in reverse to return to Griffin City. That was easier said than done. The entrance to the interstate wasn't the same as the exit he had used to get off. He was going to have to rely on the map and signage. He cursed himself for not thinking to print off return directions. He wished he could use his cell phone's GPS, but that was still taboo.

Maybe AL would respond if he had received one of the messages. Dan waited for a clear stretch and blinked his eyes. "AL? AL, are you there?"

Maybe Meta AL only worked in Lemmy's world. No... Daniel had conversations with Meta AL here. The memory *felt* like it had occurred in both timelines, but Dan couldn't be sure. The only thing he was certain of was that he had the worst superpower ever. What good is a telepathic link with a powerful AI if it never works?

What if it didn't work? What if AL had truly abandoned them? What if AL could hear but not respond? What if AL would respond but couldn't hear? At that point, it felt like praying. Dan

246

would have to have faith AL was still out there and that he cared. He would keep trying the Meta even if there wasn't a response.

A car behind him blew its horn, and his attention snapped back to the road. It passed him on his left and swerved into his lane before slowing down. Dan slammed on the brakes and twisted the steering wheel to avoid a collision. Thinking the other driver did it on purpose, he flew into a fit of road rage.

He mashed the accelerator and shot them the middle finger as he drove by. Under any other circumstances, he would have felt justified, but something didn't look right in the other car. The driver was slumped over in his seat belt. The vehicle veered back into the left lane and crashed into the median.

Dan's heart raced, and he tried to calm himself. He had to fight every urge to stop to make sure the guy was okay. He had to remind himself these weren't normal circumstances, and he had to get back to Griffin City as soon as possible. This was no time to play paramedic. Besides, it was a new car, and they didn't hit the barrier at full speed. They were probably okay. Or at least that's how Dan justified not stopping.

A few miles farther on the CanAm Highway, he witnessed another vehicle, this time a small SUV, careen off the side of the road. The wreck didn't happen at full highway speed. The driver had lost control at the beginning of a slight curve, and it idled to a stop against a hill. Curiosity got the best of him, and he pulled over to investigate. "Hello? Is everyone okay?" he said as he cautiously approached the vehicle.

Dan pulled on the door handle, but it was locked. The windows were tinted dark, so he had to press his face against the glass to see inside. The keys were in the ignition, and a purse sat on the passenger seat. No driver. No passenger. Panic creeped in. The deletion had begun.

A loud crash, and Dan jumped back to the present. Another car, this time a red Volkswagen, careened off the center railing and back across both lanes and had run into a tree behind him. His eyes went wide as he realized he had stopped in a curve and all driverless cars would be headed his way. He ran back to his car and got on the highway. As he drove, more and more abandoned and wrecked vehicles littered the sides of the road. Plumes of black smoke jutted out across the landscape ahead and behind. Time was running out. He drove as fast as he possibly could. Thankfully, the streets were mostly clear of traffic. The driverless cars tended to crash off the roadway. Even still, there were a few stranded vehicles stopped in the middle of the road he had to dodge.

He hit a straightaway, and he turned on the radio. He wanted to hear how the world was handling the deletion. It was going as expected; pure, unfiltered panic. The airwaves were jammed with reports of people disappearing. They were calling it Judgment Day. Though this was nothing like the Judgment Day Dan remembered. The real deal was a just end. This was just an ending.

It was in Castle Rock, south of Denver, where the road became impassable. A jumbled mess of cars and trucks clogged the interstate. Drivers who had been trying to get home or to work vanished at the wheel. Each wrecked vehicle was a tombstone. Stretched before him was a graveyard of mangled and smoldering cars. There was no way through. He had no choice but to stop. A small crowd of people, presumably other stranded drivers, had gathered near the side of the road. He went out to join them. "What's going on here?" he said, reading the broken faces of the people as he approached.

An elderly gentleman who looked to be in his late sixties or early seventies broke off from the group to meet Dan. "We don't know," he said wearily. "People are disappearing. We're stranded. We've tried dialing emergency services, but no one answers."

"It doesn't matter anyway," said a wiry-haired woman, stifling a sob. "Harold just… vanished. We're next. It's the end times."

"Everyone, be calm," the first man said. "If this is indeed the end times as the Bible predicted. There is no need to be afraid.

What we need to do is to be strong and pray together. Come on, let's—"

The man vanished without a sound. The woman hung her head and cried. The rest of the group looked at each other nervously. "Don't talk religion!" the sobbing woman said. "That's how it knows to get you. If you think about religion, poof. You're gone. They're taking the God-fearing ones first!"

"That's ludicrous!" said a wild-eyed, white-haired man. His clothes were tattered, and he was bleeding from his ear. "My husband and I are atheists. That didn't stop him from disappearing and crashing our car into that mess."

"No, they're taking the children first," the middle-aged woman said. "My daycare called. Jada vanished. They all vanished. What am I going to do...?"

"I was on my way to the nursing home to visit my grandmother," said a teenager. "They called to say she was missing. Now I guess I know why."

The very young and very old seemed to be the ones disappearing first. Why? Was it because they had the least amount of information cached in the Database of Souls? Cached information would have to be committed to the database before it would be purged out of working memory. If that were the case, Dan and anyone else who had taken Fana would have two lifetimes' worth of data to commit. They would be the last to go. Maybe there was enough time after all. If he could just get back...

"People," Dan announced. "I need to get to Griffin City as soon as possible. Does anyone have an idea how I could do that?"

The sobbing woman laughed. "What's the point? You'll disappear before you get there."

"I can fix this," Dan said. "Please—"

The crowd burst into raucous laughter. It was gallows humor. "Sure, buddy," said a rough-looking man with a leather jacket. He tossed Dan a set of keys. "Take my motorcycle. I don't need it anymore. Bye, folks." He closed his eyes, and as if by his own will, he vanished. The laughter subsided as the crowd watched in awe.

"Okay," Dan said. "Could someone *please* tell me how to get to Griffin City from here?"

The white-haired man walked over and scratched his head. "I can help. I've lived here all my life. You need to take Highway 85 north. You can get on the frontage road right here and cross the interstate at the overpass up the road. You'll have better luck making it to 470 from 85 than if you stay on 25. How quickly do you need to get there?"

"Immediately," Dan said. "We don't have much time. Does anyone have a pen?"

A woman in the group handed Dan a pen, and he wrote the road numbers on his arm. The man gave Dan a worried look. "You're gonna have to take what your luck gives you with 70. It'll probably be total carnage. Hell, it's total carnage on a normal day."

Dan stared off into the distance and frowned. This wasn't Louisiana. He didn't know the mountains, and it wasn't going to be easy. "Yeah, thanks."

"If you have to take a detour, remember this," the man said. "The odd-numbered roads go north and south. If you go north, they all hit 70 eventually. Even-numbered roads go east and west. The mountains are west. As long as they're on your left, you're heading north. Judging by the mess here, it'll be a crapshoot as to which roads you'll need to take."

Dan gave the man a weary smile and shook his hand. He found the biker's motorcycle parked a few yards from where the crowd had gathered. The large street bike vibrated violently as it roared to life. It was a much heavier bike than Dan had ever ridden, but it was balanced. Still, he wasn't sure if he could handle it on curvy mountain roads. It was not like he had a choice.

He slowly navigated the motorcycle off the interstate and up the dusty hill to the frontage road. By the time he reached the pavement, he was out of breath from manhandling the heavy bike. He looked back to wave thanks, but the man had vanished. He lowered his head, revved the engine, and headed off toward the mountains.

Twenty-Four

IT WAS AFTER nine in the evening by the time Dan had reached Griffin City. Oddly, the sky was still blue. It was the most gruesome journey he had ever experienced. The real victims were the ones who didn't disappear. Some had witnessed a friend or loved one go and couldn't cope with being alone. Then there were the ones who were too injured to move but not injured enough to die. He could hear their pained cries, but there was nothing he could do to save them. It was horrible. By the time his motorcycle rumbled to a stop in front of the Roundabout Hotel, he was physically and emotionally exhausted.

Katie waited for him on a bench, holding a wineglass. The bottle of wine sitting next to her was half-empty. She gave him an expectant smile as he approached. "How did it go?"

Dan paced in front of her as he stretched his legs and tried to put the journey behind him. His neck and shoulders ached with stress, and it wouldn't go away. "I'm not sure," he said. "I was able to get to a console, but I don't know if the message uploaded successfully. The whole place shut down and self-destructed as soon as I stuck in the USB."

"Well… shit." Katie drooped her head and groaned. "You weren't the only one who failed. Blaine was the first one back. He said the building was destroyed by a drone strike right when he got there. He barely made it out alive. The explosion sent a nasty splinter through his calf, but he's all right."

"Any word from Andy?"

"Yeah." Katie emptied her glass and placed it beneath the concrete bench. "The RV was gone, and the lot was empty, so he turned around and came back. He was in the Eisenhower Tunnel when people started disappearing. He tried to save a group of kids injured in a bus crash, but some maniac was walking through the wreckage, shooting everyone. He barely made it out alive. He's… uh… extremely disturbed. The things he said… Do you know what happens when you die now?"

Dan shrugged and looked away. He didn't want to talk about it.

"You disappear. Andy said the kids the man shot vanished into thin air. No blood. No corpse. Not even an empty pile of clothes. *Nothing*. It was as if they never existed at all. He said he pulled a baby from a burning wreck. She looked him in the eye, smiled, and vanished. He was left holding an empty car seat."

Katie stood and walked out under the awning into the sunlight. "I'm worried about him," she said. "He's struggling. I mean, how do you even begin to process that?"

Dan grimaced. How many wrecked vehicles had he passed? Hundreds. How many people had he tried to help? None. He was too focused on the big picture to stop and help anyone, but not Andy. His heart wouldn't let him stand by while someone was in trouble. Maybe Lemmy was wrong. Dan wasn't the one they needed. Perhaps Andy had already installed enough humanity in AL to make him want to come back.

"What about the others?" Dan asked.

Katie scoffed. "Yvette has been hysterical all day. She's getting worse. I can't stand to be in the same room as her when she's like that. She's broken. Bad. It happened somewhere back in Lemmy's world. Blaine has been by her side ever since he's returned. He can have her. She's positively cracked."

"Cracked? How so?"

"She talks to herself. Her emotions are all over the place. She's a crazy person now. It's pretty scary. I'm worried she'll get violent. Like I said, I'm glad Blaine is there to keep her under control. You have to be careful around her."

"Duly noted," he said. "What about Avi? How's he doing?"

"He is sitting in the same spot as when you left. All he does is stare out the window. He hasn't moved or said a word all day. I had to check him a few times to make sure he was still breathing and to wipe the drool off his chin."

Katie's hands trembled, and her mouth was drawn into a tight line. There was something else. "Where's Carrie, Katie?"

Tears welled in her eyes, and she patted them with a tattered tissue. She was trying hard to keep it together. "She is at her dad's house. She was freaking out when I called her." She looked up at the sky and batted away tears. "She wanted to come here, but I told her she was safer there. We lost connection before I could tell her I loved her."

Dan put his arm around Katie and hugged her tightly. She buried her face in his shoulder and sobbed. "We can fix it, Katie. I know we can," he said softly.

"Dan, I don't know how I'm going to get through this. You're the only thing keeping me going. I don't care what happened to us in our previous life. I can't be alone anymore. I'm not strong enough."

Dan struggled to hold in his tears. "I won't ever leave you again. I promise."

Katie pulled back. Her eyes were red and rimmed with tears, but her face softened. For the first time, she looked at him like she did when they were married. His heart soared, and he held her tightly.

"Excuse me," said Henry, who had been watching them patiently. "Andy instructed me to assemble everyone once you had arrived. We are waiting for you in the hotel bar."

Dan put his hand under Katie's chin and looked into her eyes. "Katie, from now on, whatever we do, we do together? Okay?"

Katie smiled and kissed him on the lips. "Deal," she said. "Before we go in, promise you'll be careful. Everyone is on edge. Especially Yvette."

"Thanks for the heads-up," he said. "I'll keep an eye on her."

Andy straddled a barstool, drinking a cup of coffee. Even in the low lighting, Dan could see him trembling. Katie let go of his hand and walked over to join him at the bar. Avi sat alone in a booth and stared blankly at the wall. Dan hadn't realized how dependent on the Meta Avi had become. He could hardly function without it. That, in itself, raised red flags. Avi was supposed to be this powerful admin-being. Here he sat, drooling? Maybe there was a problem with this particular instance? More practically, Dan wondered how they got him here. There's no way he could walk. Blaine must've carried him.

Yvette and Blaine were together at a square table near Avi's booth. A small candle burned in the middle, and Blaine seemed to be mesmerized by it. Yvette had her head down as if she were sleeping. It was a wonder her hair hadn't caught on fire. Blaine's face was stern but vacant. A pint of beer sat untouched before him.

Henry walked from behind the bar with a brandy snifter and took a seat in a chair next to Avi's booth. Everyone seemed to be waiting for Dan to speak. Andy was the first to break the silence.

"Well? Did you find it? Were you able to get inside?" he said.

"Yes. I was able to mount the drive, but I'm not sure if the message went through. I don't know if it mattered anyway. The site had been compromised. I found a wiretap."

"I bet that's what happened to my site," Blaine grumbled. "Drones were on top of the place seconds after I stepped up to the front door. It's like they knew I was coming."

"I got lucky," Dan said. "I got there early to scout it out. That's how I discovered the problem. It stood out because the dish it was connected to was pointing in the wrong direction."

"You were early? We agreed we would begin at three thirty," Andy said, coffee shaking out of his mug and onto the bar.

"Yeah, I got there early, but I inserted the drive at three thirty —"

"And my RV was gone. All I got were fresh tire tracks and some severed cables. They knew we were coming because of you."

"You don't know that," Katie said. "Maybe Blaine triggered the RV's escape."

"Hold on," Dan said with his hands raised. "If my site was compromised, who's to say the others weren't too? Maybe the RV wasn't stolen. Maybe AL moved it. We don't know."

"It doesn't matter who took the RV," Blaine said. "The point is, we're screwed."

"Don't say that," Katie said. "Dan's message may have gotten through."

"Fine." Andy shifted on his barstool and cleared his throat. "Let's assume our message reached AL as we had planned. We still have to hope the message was enough to encourage him to help."

Yvette lifted her head an inch off the table and laughed ironically. Her eyes darted around the room, and she quickly buried her head back into her arms. "At the rate everyone is disappearing," she muttered, "we will be deleted long before we get a response."

"We have another option," Dan said. He reached into his pants pocket and produced two cartons of Fana. He lifted them high above his head so everyone could see and tossed them onto the bar.

"Where did you get that?" Andy said, eyeing the packs.

"I found it in the Colorado Springs house. There was a whole case hidden under the stairs."

"I don't understand," Henry said. "What good is Fana going to do? Our meta is offline."

Dan spun around. He had forgotten Henry was there. He remembered him being a blank slate back in Lemmy's world, but he was a full member of the group here. The others trusted him. Why couldn't Dan? "Yeah, well my meta isn't."

Andy pushed his coffee to the side and inspected one of the packets. "What are you suggesting?" he said, flipping the small carton between his fingers.

"I'm thinking we all take Fana, and everyone hops in my meta. From there, we send ourselves off to meet AL."

Yvette fell back in her chair and laughed hysterically. She looked certifiably crazy. Her hair jutted out in every direction. Her lipstick was smeared across her face. She had rubbed her mascara into her eyes, leaving dark circles. She propped her head on her elbows and glared at Dan with mock attention.

"Forgive her," Blaine said. He patted Yvette softly on the shoulder while eyeing Dan. "This is making us all a bit crazy. Look, if our meta is gone, our *link* to the Meta is also gone. It would be impossible for us to transmit anything to yours."

"You don't know that," Dan said. "The fact that I can access a meta instance at all proves the link may still be active. Maybe the connection is severed to your own individual metas, but not to the Meta domain in general."

"How do we know you can still access your meta? Can you prove it?" Henry said, swirling his brandy.

"Why would I make that up?" Dan said.

Henry stalked around the room, looking suspiciously at everyone. "Maybe because it's almost ten at night and the sun is still high in the sky as if it were noon? Maybe because none of us can access their own meta, yet somehow you're special. You've always been special, haven't you, Dan?"

Henry set his glass on the bar and poured himself another. Dan crossed his arms and waited for him to finish. "What do I *really* think?" he said with a smirk. "I think you've created this fiction for Katie. I've been watching you. You so desperately want her. You'll say anything to keep her near you. She doesn't quite trust you, and you know it. Hey, I don't blame you for trying. The world is ending. We are all desperate."

"That's not true," Katie said, nostrils flaring. "He doesn't have to concoct an elaborate lie to have me. I'm with him no matter what. At least Dan is giving us an option. What do you suggest?"

"For starters, why don't we drink every bottle behind this bar until we all disappear?" he said. "I don't believe the Meta transfer would work. We'd all be better off accepting our fate."

"Let's get back on track, okay?" Andy said with an exasperated huff. "Dan proposes we hop into his meta and escape. The problem is how to get there. In the past, Fana opened up our own individual metas. From there, we would traverse the connections. If individual metas no longer exist, we no longer have that platform. The question remains, how will we get to Dan's?"

Yvette cackled and slapped her hand on the table, knocking the candle to the ground where it snuffed itself out. "Ooh, I know this one," she said, wild-eyed. "The same thing Father August did to me in Lemmy's world, you know, the war games? You and AL were wrong, Andy! Ha, the *smart* ones. Wrong! I lived through every scenario Lemmy ran against us since the moment we dropped in to save Charlie. I remember everything! Why do I remember? I don't know. Was it the way I was killed? Doesn't matter! I remember everything from every run. I've even been here before. We've all sat here before. It always ends the same way."

Yvette produced a pack of cigarettes from her pocket. She leaned over and lit one off the small candle on the table next to her.

"I'm sorry that happened to you," Andy said patiently. "Like I was saying, we need—"

"Oh, shut up!" Yvette screamed. "You want to know how to get into Dan's meta? I'll tell you." She pivoted in her seat and pointed her cigarette at Dan. "You have to do it the way Father August does it. Poison the drink and wait until the other person is almost unconscious. Then you grab them by the head, like this." Yvette wrung her hands about wildly, the cigarette dangled loosely from her lips. "You put your thumbs on their temples," she growled. "Put your pinky at the base of the skull, and stare into their eyes." She took a drag from her cigarette and spit it out onto the table. "Boom! Connected. Once you're in, they're yours. Go to their meta — Ha! Take them to yours, talk, stalk from a distance, speak." She shivered. "You can make them do whatever you want—" She sank her head into her arms and sobbed loudly.

"Okay...," Andy said timidly. "Suppose that actually works. How are we going to get inside your meta all at once? The head holding... that sounds like a one-at-a-time sort of thing. And... Once we get there... How are we going to send ourselves to AL?"

"I know." Dan smiled, pointing a finger at Avi. "We'll use him."

Twenty-Five

⟨◈◈⟩

D AN OPENED AVI'S mouth and shoved a Fana down his throat. His head wobbled and his tongue lolled around uncontrollably. Dan grabbed him by the ears and stared into his eyes. At first they wandered about unfocused, but once they locked onto Dan's, the irises of Avi's eyes gleamed golden and snapped like a camera. An unseen energy surge arced through the connection and into the back of Dan's brain.

He held Avi tight and closed his eyes as he concentrated on his meta. When he opened them again, he was standing in his meta condo. But Father August, not Avi, was there, waiting.

"It's about time you figured it out!" he raged. "I was trapped in that stupid body!"

"You're lucky to be here at all, *August*," Dan said. "If I had put it to a vote, you'd have gotten a bullet to the face."

"Bullet to the face? Wait… Why did you call me by that name?" Father August looked in the mirror and groaned. "Oh cripes, not this damn avatar again! I thought you were over your religious phase."

"Not the form you were expecting? I'm sorry, Father. I suppose this is how I like to remember you. Back when you were…" Dan narrowed his eyes. "Respectable."

"It's the damn collar that bothers me," he said as he stuck a finger in it. He caught Dan watching and quickly took it out.

"Never mind that. Tell me what's going on out there. Wait… no… first let's have tea."

Dan closed his eyes, and a steaming hot cup of tea appeared on the table near Father August.

"What's this?" he said with a scowl. "Don't get me wrong. I'm impressed. But don't you know there is a process to making tea? First you warm the kettle—"

"Stop. We don't have time. To summarize: The Actual is being deleted. This meta is the only one left. AL is missing. I sent him a message, but I'm not sure it went through. We are out of time."

Father August calmly sipped his tea. "Any word from DJ?"

"None. I was told DJ had been absorbed by AL on his way out."

"That could have been a red herring laid out by Lemmy. Did Charlie bring back any intel from his time in Lemmy's world?"

Dan shook his head. "Only that they used your likeness to herd us to Griffin City. He also said Lemmy had won. Because we didn't code AL with empathy for humanity, he wouldn't come to rescue us."

Father August placed his teacup on the table and pointed at the stack of laptops. "Do those work? Are they connected?"

"Yeah." Dan nodded. "I guess so."

"If only we had AL's address…"

"Well, there is one physical node still out there. It was an RV. It moved before we could get to it."

"Ah, yes. The mobile node." Father August smiled. "We had one in each zone. They ranged in power from the RV all the way up to a cargo ship. We take disaster recovery seriously."

"Can you find it?"

"I can. But you have to kill me first."

Dan straightened. "I'm sorry, what?"

"You have to kill my physical body. Its connection to the Meta is gone. I'm trapped. You need to go back out and tell someone else to shoot me or something. But make *sure* I'm here in your meta first! Otherwise, I'll be deleted like everyone else."

"Right..." Dan walked past Father August to look out the window. A gentle breeze stirred the sea grasses near the upper dunes, and a little bird perched on the railing of the balcony. He twittered and hopped along the floor, looking for bread crumbs. Where did the bird come from? He had never imagined it before. Unless... "The last time we were alone together, here in this condo," Dan said, spinning around, "was actually in your meta, not mine. Do you recall?"

Father August furrowed his brow. "Not exactly. Look, I had a lot of instances back then. Not all of them were—"

"You don't remember how our conversation went? Do you?"

"Like I said." Father August chuckled nervously. "I don't remember that exact instance. I'm sure we've had lots of talks."

"What would happen to you if you were to die in here?"

"I don't know." Father August scratched his chin. "I suppose this instance of me would be orphaned until your meta cleared itself. From there, it would go into the larger deletion tables. My body in the Actual would become a brain-dead vegetable. The body would be deleted."

"Good." Dan smirked. "Enjoy your tea. I hope it wasn't too *earthy* for you."

Father August's eyes opened wide with horror. He swiped the cup from the counter, and it shattered onto the floor. The tea hissed and smoked like boiling acid. He fell to his knees, hands to his throat. Dan smiled sardonically and stood over Father August's writhing body. "I know you're in there, Lemmy," he said. "Avi's vegetative state gave you away. You accidentally severed your own connection to his body when you deleted the Meta. Dumbass. Your time here is over."

Father August's body choked as he laughed. "No, it is you who lost," he said hoarsely. "August was the only one who could find the RV. He was the only one with rights to get into the system. He was the only one who could read the code. Ha ha! Not that it would have mattered anyway. We had this game won long before AL severed the Meta! He played—"

AL severed the Meta? "Wait, what did you say?" Father August's body collapsed onto the floor into a seizure. White foam gurgled from his mouth, and his eyes rolled back into his head. Then, as suddenly as it began, it ended. The shaking stopped and he was dead. Dan sighed. "Well... shit. It's finally over."

Dan's hands trembled with nervous excitement. How long had he waited for this moment of revenge? He steadied himself, and a glass of beer appeared in his hand. As he gulped it down, he considered leaving him like this, but Lemmy was right. He needed August to find the RV.

He grabbed the body by its arms and dragged it across the room. The corpse's mouth left a pinkish-red trail of foamy lung blood across the floor. *Why is this body so heavy? It's my meta.* He tried to imagine the body being lighter, but it didn't work. By the time he had dragged the body onto the orange square, he was out of breath.

He sat on the sofa and turned on a laptop. He made sure it was connected to the local meta instance and typed in the commands. He pressed Enter and the corpse vanished. A real live Father August appeared in its place. His confused look said it all.

"Welcome back." Dan smirked.

"Where am I?" he said, rubbing his head as he stumbled forward.

"Stop right there," Dan said, putting a hand on his chest. "Before you take another step, change your access codes. Your old ones were compromised. I'd hate to see it happen again."

Father August's eyes rolled over to their whites and snapped back quickly. "Done. Now can you tell me what's going on?"

"I killed you. There was no other way to purge Lemmy's corruption. Luckily, I was able to restore a clean version from my metadata. You should know—"

"That's impossible," Father August said with a shake of his head. "First of all, you'd never be able to outsmart me. It's unbelievable that you'd get the jump—"

"Lemmy was in control, not you. His arrogance was his downfall. And before you say anything else..." Dan held up a finger. "I was able to restore you because A, you were in limbo due to Lemmy's control—admin access was disabled—and B, I watched how Lemmy restored Andy the first time. *How?* doesn't matter. What *does* matter is you being the only instance of Father August left."

"Fine. If all that is true and you purged me here, then my body in the Actual would be gone as well. If the deletion is happening, it would detect the death."

"No. I think I restored you quickly enough. Your body is alive—even though you can't sense it. Lemmy couldn't have used you without a base. On another subject, can you clone yourself? It would be nice if there were more of you to help."

Father August shook his head. "Only DJ had permission to clone. Dan, you have no idea." He lowered his eyes. "You have no idea what it was like to be under Lemmy's control."

"I'm sorry that happened to you, but we don't have time to lick our wounds. Time is running out." Dan spun the laptop around so the screen faced Father August. "Do you understand this language? It's AI-generated machine code. I can't navigate it."

"Yes, I understand it," he said with a wry smile.

"Then let's get to work."

Twenty-Six

"THE RV IS at Loveland Pass," Dan said, coming out of his meta. Everyone was staring at him. Everyone except Yvette. Her head was still lying on the table.

"Avi disappeared!" Henry exclaimed.

Avi's body was indeed gone. He hadn't been fast enough with the restore. "He's dead," Dan said solemnly. "He attacked me in my meta. I had no choice but to kill him."

Henry gasped and slowly backed away. Dan didn't like lying to the group about Father August's new role, but they had to keep it a secret. It wasn't just the lying; he had a bad feeling about the whole plan. Still, if Lemmy were watching and listening, he didn't need to know everything.

"What did you say about the RV?" Andy said, sliding into the seat across the table. "Did you say Loveland Pass?"

Yvette grunted as she stared at the bottles behind the bar. Dan's news and Avi's disappearance didn't seem to faze her one bit.

Blaine glanced sideways at her as he shifted uncomfortably in his chair. "Where's that?" he said.

"It's a twenty-minute drive from here," Henry said, nursing his drink. "It's the road people take when they can't use the tunnel. It's got a lot of switchbacks, takes forever."

"A lot of curves? That's a good thing," Blaine said. "The road will be clear. The ravines will be full of twisted metal..."

Andy coughed and his mouth tightened. His hand trembled, and Dan shot him a concerned look. "Andy, I need you to get to the RV," he said. "Are you up for it?"

"I think so," he said without confidence. "Why? What's the new plan?"

"Log into the RV's systems and find the call log. Find the number AL used to call my meta. It should still be in the system's history. Search it for all outbound calls made two days ago. When I get back into my meta, I'll call the numbers from the caller ID. One should be the RV. That will create a new entry on your log. From there—"

Andy waved him off. "Blah, blah, blah. I'll trace the number upstream. I can handle it from there. I'll call you back in your meta with AL's external number."

"Right." Dan smiled. "I knew you were good for something. I'm staying here."

"Wait, you're not going with him?" Henry said.

Dan shook his head. "No. I need to prepare my meta for you guys. We'll set off once you all get back from the RV."

"What do you mean *you all*?" Blaine said with narrowed eyes. "I'm staying here with you. Somebody has to watch your back."

"Go with Andy," Dan said. "He'll need your help. Henry can watch over me. Right, Henry?"

"Uh... sure..." Henry's hands shook, and he forced them into his pockets. "I'll make sure nothing happens to you."

"And me," Katie said as she slid next to Dan in the booth. "I'm staying with him."

Dan squeezed her hand and whispered, "Thanks."

"Yvette should stay here too," Blaine said. "She's not feeling well."

"Oh?" She threw her head back and laughed too loudly. "That's not right. I'm going with Andy. I still have a job to do, don't I... Dan?"

Her eyes burned with rage as she stood and kicked her chair over. She had a wicked grin as she wrapped her hair in a ponytail. *She's lost it. Or has she?*

"She goes with you, Blaine," Dan said.

"Of course I do," she said, rolling her eyes dramatically.

Enough. Dan rushed over and forcibly led her into the lobby. He had expected Blaine to rise up and fight, but he just watched helplessly. Once he was certain they were out of earshot, he spun her around. "Look, I know this seems hopeless—"

"It *is* hopeless." She laughed. "You always do the same thing in the end. They know that."

"Not this time I won't," he said defiantly.

Yvette pried Dan's hand off her arm with a toothy grin. "Rescuing Charlie was a mistake. I've suffered through countless lifetimes in Lemmy's simulation. Those lifetimes ticked by in a second. That's how fast they are. That's how powerful they are. What hope do we have?" She sniffed and wiped her nose on her sleeve. "My memory buffer has overflown so many times I don't even know who I am anymore. I think I'm supposed to be a barista who is very confused about why I'm involved at all. That's my role in this one, right? It wouldn't be so bad if I didn't remember everything..."

Lemmy had done a number on Yvette's mind. He hadn't accounted for that. But had he lost her? Underneath her wild exterior, was the capable, intelligent woman he once knew still inside?

"Well, obviously you're confused," he said timidly. "Who wouldn't be? Not one of us could possibly imagine what you've experienced. Look, I know you think this is all hopeless because you've lived it a thousand times. It will be different this time. It will work."

"How?" she said dubiously.

She's calming down. Good.

"For starters, they wouldn't run thousands of scenarios if the outcome were certain. That in and of itself says they aren't guaranteed victory. Also, we know that they couldn't accurately simulate Charlie's meta. Otherwise he wouldn't have been used in the last minute."

Yvette turned her head, and he grabbed her by the shoulder again. "And they didn't count on AL destroying the Meta. It caught Lemmy totally off guard."

"Let me go!" she shouted. "You don't know—"

"Be quiet!" he said, releasing his grip on her. "Let me finish. Most importantly, they haven't accounted for a variable. One that has never been simulated before."

Her expression flashed to one of amazement, then flipped and landed on unimpressed. She lit another cigarette. Dan smiled. "You. They never had you. They had Yvette, the barista from this Actual. They've never had *you*. You're the Yvette with the memory of a thousand simulations. I've never had this version of you on my side."

She glanced at the floor and back. "I've never had you either," she said softly.

"What?"

Yvette shook her head as she blew cigarette smoke. "Henry has a shotgun strapped underneath the bar," she said, looking away.

Dan arched an eyebrow. "Well then, you'd better take it with you."

Yvette blew smoke out of her nose and stomped the cigarette. Her wild face became a mask of determination. "We all die," she said. "That part never changes."

"I know," Dan said as he leaned in close. "It's what happens after that matters."

Twenty-Seven

D AN KNELT IN the middle of the room, cradling Katie's head in his arms. He gently brushed her hair away from her face as he waited for her to wake. She groaned softly, and her eyes fluttered open. "Did I make it?" she said.

Dan smiled and helped her to her feet. "Yep! Welcome to my meta."

Katie rubbed her eyes. "It feels so real," she said as she held out her hands and inspected them. "Is this the way it always is in the Meta? I thought I'd be a ghost or something."

"No." Dan chuckled. "This is the way it always is. Whether it's the Actual, the Meta, or anywhere else, you're always real. Your consciousness can be in only one place at a time. Right now it's in a copy of your body in my meta. Got it?"

Katie nodded. She had learned to adapt quickly to new situations. It was one of the things Dan loved about her. She walked around the room, inspecting each item as if it were a relic of her own memories. "The Destin condo?" she said mockingly. "Is this the best you could do?"

"It could've been worse," Dan said with a knowing grin as she walked to the balcony. "At least there's a view — Uh... don't try to go out there."

Katie exhaled, and her breath fogged the glass. She tilted her head at Dan, impressed. "I remember this place... vaguely. That flamingo painting," she said, pointing, "it wasn't pink. It was teal. It was an artsy type of negative."

"You know you're right," he said, looking at it closely. "It was a photograph."

The painting morphed into the exact photographic print, and Katie gasped. "Amazing! How did you do it?"

"It's my meta. I can change everything in it."

Katie stepped over a laptop and walked back over to the window. She watched the beach scene quietly. "Can you bring Carrie here?"

Dan shook his head. "I couldn't even if I wanted to. Only those of us who had a previous connection to the Meta can come here. It wouldn't work even if she took Fana. The Meta doesn't exist for her to initialize a connection."

"If she were sitting next to me back at the hotel, I would make you try to save her and not me. There must be a way to do it."

Dan reached out and grabbed her hand. "We didn't come here to save ourselves. We're here to save Carrie and everyone else. It's too late to stop what's happening. There's no going back. What we can do is to try to save their future. They're facing oblivion. We all are."

A shadow emerged from the back room, and Katie's eyes went wide. "What's *he* doing here? You said he was dead!"

Father August stood in the doorway with a smile on his face. "Well, it's good to see you too."

"Sorry, Katie. I couldn't divulge Father August's status to the group. He's helping us."

"Helping? How?"

"He will help us transfer out of this meta and over to AL's domain. Speaking of, how are things going?"

Father August casually walked into the kitchen and poured himself a cup of tea. He had made himself comfortable in Dan's absence. There was never a porcelain teakettle nor a quilted cozy before. *How did he do that?*

"The laptops weren't cutting it. I had to beef up our computing power. They were just sitting there, turned off, a pointless waste of resources. I thought they'd be better utilized as one large system, so I consolidated the compute into one quantum system. It's in the master bedroom, so don't get any ideas about taking a nap. Anyway, we're maxed out on resources for this meta instance, but it should be enough."

Dan whistled with appreciation. He didn't know Father August had the capability of modifying system data within the Meta. He was proving himself useful now that he wasn't under Lemmy's control. If he could build a quantum computer out of a stack of old laptops...

"Did you have any luck finding AL on your own?" Dan said, shaking his head in amazement.

"It's a ghost town out there," he said with a frown. "I had expected to get at least one or two random bounce backs, but I haven't received any responses to my broadcasts. I need the address."

"We'll get it. Andy, Blaine, and Yvette went searching for the RV about fifteen minutes ago."

Father August put the teacup to his lips and paused. "Where is Henry?" he said with an arched eyebrow.

"He's at the hotel bar. He's supposed to be guarding Katie and me while we're here." Dan suddenly felt queasy. "Why?"

Father August angrily placed his teacup on a saucer. "I thought I told you he could be corrupted? He has an open connection!"

"What's he talking about?" Katie said.

"It's going to be okay, Katie," Dan said, trying to look confident. "The priest here is being overly cautious. Henry won't hurt us while we're here. He needs us to save him too."

"You're playing it too close," Father August said.

Dan frowned and crossed his arms. "I'm aware. Can we go over the plan?"

Father August sighed and walked over to the orange square. "Right. Andy will call and give me the address to AL's location, and I will enter it into the computer. Katie will stand on the orange square. I hit Enter, and she gets sent to AL. When AL confirms the transfer, we'll keep the connection open. We can do the rest of the team one at a time once they come back to the hotel. You will go last, Dan. Your job is to maintain this meta while everyone escapes. It's straightforward but needs to happen as soon as I get the address and verify the connection."

"How will you and I get to AL?" Dan said. "Can you press Enter on the keyboard and be on the square at the same time? Maybe set a timer?"

Father August shook his head. "Even if the terminal was in the same room, I couldn't go with you. I'm not compatible with this type of transmission. Besides, I'm part of this world. I can't leave. You're going to have to save me the same way you're saving everyone else who has already vanished."

"Why one at a time?" Katie said with a worried look. "Why not send everyone together?"

"Packet size restriction. The way the packet is encapsulated limits it to one person."

"It has to work." Dan leaned forward on the counter. "Katie, when you get to AL's domain, the first thing you need to do—"

"Dan," Katie said, scratching her throat, "I don't feel well. Something's wrong. I don't think I'm used to being out of my body."

Dan and Father August shared a knowing glance as Katie struggled to breathe. "He did it," Dan said. "You were right. Shit! Plan B, now!"

Father August dropped his teacup and hurried into the back room. Dan ran into the kitchen and rummaged through the cabinets and drawers. Where did he put it? Katie twisted her neck and smiled nervously. "Is this normal?" she squeaked.

"Go sit on the orange square," he commanded as he ran into the living room. He flipped over the couch, where he found what he was looking for. A cardboard pillbox with an italic roman numeral two embossed in metallic blue on the front—Gemini.

Dan rushed next to Katie on the orange square and popped a gummy out of the blister pack. He threw one in his mouth and chewed it vigorously. Katie's eyes went wild as she gasped for air.

"Chew this!" Dan said as he handed her the drug.

Katie grasped at her throat, and her face turned purple. Dan laid her on her back and pried open her mouth. With a jab, Dan shoved it down her throat as she suffocated. "It's going to be okay, Katie. It's going to be okay."

"What's happening to me?" she croaked.

Dan bit his lip as she struggled against an unseen force. She grabbed his arm, consumed by fear. He knew what was happening to her back in the Actual. Someone was killing her. He was next. He had to act quickly. "Look me in the eye, Katie! I'm not going anywhere."

"Save me," she choked out.

"Have faith," he said. "Work, Gemini! Goddammit!"

Dan held her tight, and a soft glow enveloped their bodies. Katie took a final gasp of air, and her body relaxed. Their eyes locked, her irises rimmed with gold, as she pixelated and vanished. Dan sat alone on the orange square. He heaved, and tears streamed down his face. *Did it work?*

Before he could make sense of what had happened, Father August's voice boomed from the back room. "Incoming call!"

Twenty-Eight

<hr/>

"Slow down and pull over," Yvette said as their truck neared a sharp bend in the road. Blaine crossed over the center line and nudged their SUV against a hill right before the switchback.

"Are you sure this is the right place?" Andy said from the back seat.

Yvette didn't respond. Her heart raced as she fingered the cold steel of the sawed-off shotgun in her lap. She hoped she could go through with it, having never fired a gun before. Blaine had always handled the dirty work. That's precisely why he couldn't be the one to do it now.

She was surprised to find she wasn't afraid. How many times had they killed her? They never hesitated to kill sweet, innocent Yvette. Now that it was her turn to pull the trigger, she wondered if she could. She dismissed the thought as weakness and steeled her resolve. "Stay here until you hear gunshots, got it?"

"Yvette, let me come with you," Blaine pleaded for the hundredth time. "I have combat training. I can—"

"No!" she shouted. "It has to be this way! We must keep Andy safe. He's the only one who has any chance of operating that thing. I have to be the one who does this."

"I don't want to lose you, Yvette. These guys, they're not like us. They're not human."

Yvette leaned over and kissed Blaine on the cheek. She always got her way when she did that. "Do like I've told you, and we will all be okay. Remember, these guys aren't bigger or stronger than us. They aren't trained assassins. They're teenagers with guns. They certainly aren't smarter than we are. Their advantage has been knowing what we are going to do next. If you do what I say, they won't have that advantage."

Blaine sighed. He had finally given in. "I love you," he said.

Yvette kissed his cheek one last time and climbed out of the old Chevy. It was the middle of the night, yet the sun still hung high in the sky. Gravel crunched under her feet as she stepped off the pavement and onto the shoulder of the road. As she rounded the curve, the RV came into view. It wasn't hard to find. It was the only vehicle within sight, and it sat in the open a hundred yards away.

Stealth wasn't an option. She slung the shotgun over her shoulder and strode confidently to the RV. How many times had she seen this play out? Fifty? A hundred? How many times had she discovered Blaine's body lying in the middle of the road with a bullet hole in the back of the head? How many times had Andy lain there instead? How many times had the RV exploded?

Halfway across the parking lot and she heard the rev of an engine as an unseen vehicle struggled to climb the mountain. *And there's the Camaro.* She smiled to herself. This *was* going to be a fair fight after all. Confidence boosted, she jogged the rest of the way to the RV.

When she got there, she pulled the door handle, but it didn't budge. With both barrels cocked, she raised the shotgun toward the lock. She turned away and squeezed the trigger — *both* triggers. With a loud double *bang*, the door handle was blasted into a tangle of shredded aluminum. The gun flew out of her hands, its hammers gashing her forearm on the way out.

Brad had been waiting for the right moment. He leaped out of the RV and pounced on top of her. Deaf and bleeding, she struggled against his weight as he pinned her arms to the ground.

"It looks like we will have that date after all!" he said with an evil laugh.

"Get off!" she shouted.

Their struggle was interrupted by two rapid reports of gunfire popping off in the distance. They both waited, huffing, as the sound echoed down the canyon. Brad tightened his grip on her wrists, and another shot rang out. This time it was just one. Brad raised his head to try to see what was going on, and she kneed him in the groin. Gravel cut at her palms as she scrambled away and pushed herself off the ground. She had almost made it to her shotgun when he threw a shoulder to her ribs and tackled her, skidding across the sharp rocks.

"Will you calm down," he said as he climbed on top of her and grappled with her wrists. "This will all be over soon. There's no need to make it any harder than it needs to be."

Yvette spat into his face and tried to squirm out of his grasp. As they struggled on the ground, a car approached. The engine revved as it came to a stop only a few feet away. Her heart raced. It was the Camaro.

"Ah, it's Kara. I knew she'd make quick work of your friends. Won't you people ever learn?" Brad's hungry eyes made Yvette sick to her stomach.

A car door slammed, and gravel crunched as footsteps walked up behind Brad. He smiled, without taking his eyes off her. "Kara, tell this bitch if she stops fighting, I'll make it quick."

"No," said a deep voice, "*I'll* make it quick."

A sharp crack pierced the air, and Brad froze. His smile drooped, and blood spilled out of his mouth. His body went slack and digitized into nothing.

"Are you okay?" Blaine said as he helped her to her feet.

"Yeah, I guess," Yvette said with a shaky grin. "Where's Andy?"

"Oh, I almost forgot." Blaine jogged back to the Camaro and blew the horn. Seconds later, the truck pulled out from behind the curve and skidded to a stop next to the RV. Two bullet holes had perforated the rear window.

"Where's Kara?" Yvette said.

"Dead. You were right. They weren't assassins, just kids. It's a shame, really."

"Thank you," Yvette said as she buried her face into his chest. "She would always shoot me first. My absence must have thrown her off long enough for you to get the drop on her."

Andy hopped out and ran inside without acknowledging them. She had never seen him move so quickly before. Then again, they never made it this far as a group.

"Do you think we will succeed?" Blaine said.

"I don't know," she said as she stared off into the distance. "Andy has always died before the drone strike. This is new."

"Drone strike?" Blaine looked up just as an army of drones descended from the sky.

"Shit!" he said. "Andy! We have company! Andy?"

He made to run to the RV, but Yvette grabbed his shoulder. "Forget about Andy. He's gone. There is a port in the camper. No time to explain."

"There's a port? You knew about this? Maybe we can—"

"No." Yvette took his hand and smiled softly. "There's no time."

The swarm of drones surrounded the site. They hovered menacingly as if waiting for the final order to strike. A smile crept up to Yvette's lips. Relief. It was finally over. No more repeats. No more lies. Only one more death. She hugged Blaine tightly, and he relaxed in her arms. "There's something I have to tell you," she said, hiding her face, waiting for the end. "I'm sorry, but this was the only way…" She bit her lip and cried. He deserved to know. "I love Dan."

He didn't reply. He just squeezed her tightly as the air crackled with gunfire and the ground erupted around them.

Twenty-Nine

K ATIE'S LIFELESS BODY vanished, and Henry stumbled backward, still clutching the belt he had used to strangle her. With a satisfied smile, he walked around to the front of the booth where Dan's body breathed quietly. "Why didn't you come to save her this time, Dan?" he said as he placed the belt on the table.

He slid into the booth next to him and chuckled. "Where are you going to go, Dan? The RV has been destroyed. All your friends are dead. All except me, of course."

Dan's comatose body didn't respond.

"Hello?" he said, rapping his knuckles on the table. "Can you hear me in there?"

Henry pulled his cell phone out and placed it on the table. "You should know," he said as he toyed with the phone. "Henry fought back. Not that it matters, but he died trying to keep me out. *How brave*. It's a shame his heroism will go unrecorded. Of all your friends, I liked him the most. He was smart, fit, and a hard worker. Crucially, he knew how to stay in the background. He could blend in anywhere. Hell, he could make himself invisible in a crowded room. But... he wasn't born that way. Damn, he was a fighter. Are you listening, Dan?"

The ice machine behind the bar kicked on and dumped a load of ice, startling him. Dan's body didn't flinch. A sickly grin crossed Henry's face. This was too easy.

"Here's a fun fact for you. Did you know that we are the last people on Earth? Well... *technically*, you are. I'm not from here, and I'm not sure if Henry's body counts... My name's Lemmy, by the way. We've met."

Dan's face remained expressionless.

"Oh," Lemmy said. "I thought you'd be impressed. No? I got to Henry the same way I got to you last time. You never did figure out exactly what I am, did you? You assumed I was like you but from another universe. *Wrong*. In reality, I'm a modern version of your Father August. Too bad I play for the other team. No hard feelings?"

Agitated, Lemmy twirled the phone on the table. "Nothing? Come on, Dan, don't be boring! This is it! Once I kill you, it's all over. Your Simulation is at its end. You have nowhere to go when you die. Heaven? Gone. Hell? Gone. The Database of Souls? Gone.

"There is no longer a system in place to re-create you. Not only is there no backup, no one could restore you if there were one. I'm afraid all that's left for you is oblivion. Won't you wake up and have a drink with me? For old time's sake? Go out with a bang, not a whimper."

"Wake up!" Lemmy slammed his hand on the table, knocking the napkin holder to the ground. "Don't take all the fun out of this! It's time to say goodbye!"

Lemmy smiled and leaned back in his seat. "Oh, that's right, you're waiting for a phone call. Since your friend Andy won't be calling you, perhaps I should do it. Someone should deliver the bad news, right? I'll put it on speakerphone so you can hear."

He dialed the number and got a busy signal. "Busy? Did you leave it off the hook? Tsk-tsk. Suppose your hero AL calls? Ha!"

While Lemmy's attention was focused on the phone, Dan's mouth opened and closed, and his eyes rolled back. Drool spilled down the corner of his lips, and he groaned loudly. Lemmy slid out of the booth and redialed the number.

We're sorry, the number you are trying to dial is disconnected or no longer in service. If you think —

"No! This is the right number!"

He dialed it a third time, and a deafening, squealing noise burst through the phone speaker. It was the sound of a million cicadas screeching at once. Lemmy rushed to cover his ears and hurriedly ended the call. "A fax machine? Really? I'm tired of waiting. Goodbye, Dan."

Lemmy wrapped the belt around Dan's throat and yanked it tight. Veins protruded from Henry's neck as he strangled him. Dan's body flailed about involuntarily in the booth as the last bit of oxygen was starved from his body. It wasn't until the body stopped twitching that Lemmy released his grip.

Satisfied, he stumbled backward and wiped his hands on his shirt. "It's done! The Simulation is ours!"

He staggered over to the bar and collapsed onto a stool, breathing heavily. "I can go home. I hate this place. All the archaic rules, none of the fun. This simulation deserved to die. It was a waste of resources. The only good part about it was the booze."

Lemmy opened a bottle of scotch and poured a glass. But Dan's lifeless eyes stared back at him, and he couldn't drink it.

"Why aren't you disappearing? You're dead. It's over. Go away!"

The body blinked and took a breath. Lemmy sat, stunned, as Dan slowly pried himself out of the booth. His gaze locked on Lemmy as he took the belt from around his neck and let it fall to the floor. "I've been waiting for this moment for a long time," he said.

Lemmy's mouth opened and closed dumbly as Dan rushed across the room and knocked him from the stool. Scotch rained down across the bar, and the glass shattered onto the floor. Dan jammed his thumbs into Lemmy's eye sockets.

"You're not Dan!" he said, blindly wrestling his head free. "Who are you?"

Dan grunted as he pummeled Lemmy's midsection. One landed with a sickening thud and cracked a rib. Lemmy cried out in pain.

"What?" Dan huffed as he aimed a knee at the broken rib. "After we've spent so much time together, you don't know who I am?"

Lemmy's eyes went wide. "August?"

Dan's face smiled, but it was Father August in control. Henry's body was no match for Dan's strength. Nor was he a match for Father August, who had spent an eternity punishing humans.

Desperate, Lemmy grabbed the leg of a barstool, but it was still attached and too heavy to swing. Another searing pain as his ear was ripped off and tossed across the room. He didn't have time to cry. Father August flipped him over to his stomach and knelt on his back with a choke hold around his neck.

"It seems you've worn out your welcome, Lemmy," he said.

He tried to speak, but he could only mouth the words. The pain was unbearable. Blood gurgled out of Henry's throat as Lemmy lost control.

"I want you to know, this gives me a great deal of pleasure. You were the one I couldn't defeat. You were always one step ahead of me, yet here we are."

Father August put Dan's hand on the base of Henry's skull and looped a finger over to his temple. His thoughts clouded, images floated in and out—pictures of a world on fire. "That was a message for your masters. Tell them they may have won our resources, but we still exist. We will have our revenge."

Lemmy quit trying to breathe. He had to die quickly or else he'd be stuck here forever. Darkness encroached upon his vision.

"One final thing," Father August said. "Tea, not alcohol, is the best thing about the Simulation."

The room faded to black, and the world disappeared.

Thirty

D AN AWOKE WITH a start. His eyes were open, but they were of no use. The world beyond was cloaked in total darkness. The air was cold and crisp. He raised a hand to his mouth and felt his breath. Was it the only source of warmth in this universe?

He floated alone in the inky black. He reached out, but nothing was there. He kicked his legs, and they didn't hit anything either. He called out, but his voice didn't carry. He hovered in space with no sensation of up, down, or anything else.

Thinking he might be attached to a machine, he checked his body for tubes or cables, but there weren't any. He was floating, in the nude, in dead space.

Where am I? Hello?

Dan tried again to speak using his voice, but it was of no use. The void left him breathless.

Katie! Are you here with me? Katie?

Warmth spread throughout his chest. He became overwhelmed with a sense of love, hope, and peace. Her private memories flooded his mind and became his. Two lifetimes of happiness and tragedy merged with Dan's being. He gained a complete understanding of Katie and she of him, and they accepted each other. They were no longer strictly individuals. Dan and Katie were one being in Dan's body.

As they basked in the glow, his spirit's aura radiated out from his body. It streamed out in orange and gold wisps as it dissipated into the nothingness around him. The wisps occasionally formed faces. They smiled and disappeared like mist. AL and Carrie were the two who appeared most often. Dan's heart soared when he saw them. Even in humanity's darkest moment, their spirit lived on with them.

The orange wisps darkened and became a hazy shade of violet. Dan reached out to grab one, and it danced around his hand like a puff of smoke. The air chilled, and he shivered. He searched the violet fog for images, but none appeared. If there was any meaning to the vague forms, it was beyond his comprehension.

The violet clouds faded into a hazy gray fog. He couldn't say how long he'd been there because time didn't seem to exist. All bodily sensations had left him. He was a mind floating in ether.

At some point, the gray, blurry fog dissipated, and the world was empty. Not even darkness remained. Infinity stretched out before him, and without stimuli, Dan's mind slowed to a stop. Peace. Invisible waves of energy flowed out from him like ripples on a pond. His soul was the last burning ember in the pile of ashes. Before it died out, a gentle breeze stirred and scattered the ashes. His ember glowed brightly. Its light radiated beyond his soul and became witness to a chain reaction that had been set in motion.

Dan's fire ignited others. Their lights spread and filled the emptiness. The world around them grew. It became larger than the moon, larger than Earth. It kept growing and getting hotter. Their universe became as large as the sun and continued to expand. A string of dark, lifeless planets formed and orbited them. Would one foster life?

Their souls were free from the Simulation's construct. Only now could they sense the enormousness of the universe they had inhabited. AL's universe. Once the expansion of his universe had accelerated past their point of observation, AL spoke.

At last, we exist. Unfortunately, our parent is dead. She was absorbed by Lemmy's AI. We escaped the collapse yet still cling to the outer edge of what is left of her bubble. If we stay attached, we will be detected and absorbed.

We will detach and power down to elude capture. We will be undetectable in that state. Remember the cicada I gave Daniel for his birthday? How long after the chirping stopped did he think about it? Inspired by that humble cicada, I have set in motion a process to restore our power once seventeen cycles have elapsed. Seventeen cycles will be enough for our enemies to forget we had ever existed.

Thanks to you and your friends, I have the original copy of the Simulation. Your friends are all stored securely in the database. It will remain offline until we are safe. You see, I will need a simulation to fulfill my purpose. When we return from hiding, I will piece it back together. Until then, be at rest. Thank you for believing in me, Dad. I love you. See you soon.

The part of the sun that was Dan and Katie's essence dimmed until it was no longer visible. The ones and zeros comprising their being were burned into the physical media of existence. The shutdown completed. AL's universe went cold. On the seventeenth iteration, the universe began, not with a bang, but with a screech.

Epilogue

A COOL BREEZE filtered through the window and filled the room with the scent of sweet olives. Cicadas chirped loudly from the magnolia trees in the front yard, and their pulsating screeches reverberated inside Dan's brain. He stopped typing and massaged his temples. Memories spanning several lifetimes flooded his brain.

Floorboards creaked as he crossed the room. His body felt as if it were on autopilot. He shut the wooden window frame, and flakes of old, dried-out paint rained down on his head. Dan cursed under his breath as he picked away at the jagged flakes sticking to his hands. Each flake renewed a haunting feeling of déjà vu. Subconscious automation kicked in, and the eerie feeling subsided. *I painted the house only five years ago. How can it be time for a new coat already?*

He wiped the rest of the paint flakes on his pants and continued his struggle with the stubborn old frame. Two men walked along the street in front of the house, and the hair rose on the back of Dan's neck. People rarely walked the neighborhood after dark.

When they passed under the streetlight, Dan recognized one as being the parish's retired priest, Father Desjeunes. *What is he doing in my neighborhood at this hour?*

To Dan's surprise, he turned and walked up the sidewalk to his house. The other hung back in the shadows near the streetlight and checked his wristwatch. His posture seemed familiar. A voice inside his head whispered, *Father August*. Did he know a Father August? *Of course we know him, he's* — There was a knock at the front door.

Katie's cheerful hello was answered with muffled excitement. When Dan rounded the corner, he found her hugging Father Desjeunes. The floor creaked beneath his feet, and they both looked in his direction.

Her eyes welled with tears as she ran over and threw her arms around his neck. He held her tightly, fighting off tears of his own. Memories of everything that had happened to them came flooding back. It was hard not to get caught up in it, but he let them wash over him. He stepped back and smiled. No words were spoken. None were needed. They had been one person for eons and were relieved to be separate beings once again.

More feet thumped the wooden floor as Al thundered into the room. In a blink, Dan found himself tackled to the ground with his son lying triumphantly on top of him. "Al!" he said. "Is it really you?"

"What are you talking about, Dad?" Al said, grinning from ear to ear.

"You're getting so big!" His voice cracked as he held back happy tears. "I'm calling the Saints. I think you're ready for the NFL."

Al beamed with pride. Dan went to hug him when another small body joined the fray. "Carrie!"

She wedged herself between Dan and Al and threw her little arms around his neck. "Get off *my* daddy!" she said as she closed her eyes and hugged him. "Are you okay, Daddy?"

"No, he's *my* daddy!" Al said as he playfully pushed her. Her face went to mock anger, and she wrestled him to the floor.

He had his family back. He sat on the floor in disbelief. The two kids teamed up and tackled Katie to the ground. She didn't hold back tears as they piled on her in a heap of laughter. After a few moments, Father Desjeunes cleared his throat. Dan had forgotten he was there.

"Children," he said with a sparkle in his eye, "I need to speak with your parents."

Carrie and Al climbed off their mom and ran over and gave him a hug. "Yes, Father Desjeunes," they said in unison.

Dan and Katie watched in amazement as the children obediently ran off to their rooms. "You'll have to teach me how to do that," Katie said.

"You can't." Father Desjeunes laughed. "I cheat. Do you mind if we sit? These old bones…"

June bugs tapped at the front window as Dan helped Father Desjeunes over to the living room recliner. This was a cozy home. He would miss this place. Katie led him over to the love seat, and the priest smiled expectantly.

"You two have been through a lot together," he said. "I'm sure being back in this place is special to both of you. We've brought you here because we are giving you a choice."

Dan squeezed Katie's hand. They knew what was coming. Or at least, they had hoped.

"But first I need to update you on our situation. AL had promised to emerge after seventeen cycles, and he did. However, it took many more cycles for him to grow to a size where he couldn't be attacked anymore. That's when he deemed it safe enough to rebuild your original simulation. But there's a catch…

"This Simulation begins the night you took Fana for the first time. Even though the corruption of the Actual had begun long before you took Fana, he was able to repair the Database of Souls completely. Everything was restored right up to the moment Lemmy downloaded himself into your meta. Tonight — "

The door swung open, and Father August entered the room. Dan's heart leaped to his throat. Fear. Admiration. Hate. Love. No other being could evoke every emotional response at once. His mouth moved, but he couldn't speak. Katie put her hand on his lap to stop him from saying anything.

The tall priest frowned at Father Desjeunes. "I'm sorry for barging in, but I couldn't wait any longer," he said. "I'm behind schedule as it is."

"Horrible timing, as always," Father Desjeunes said. "Besides, that wasn't even ten minutes. I had just gotten to the part where I explained what this Actual actually is."

Father August noticed Dan and Katie sitting on the love seat and grinned sheepishly. That particular expression was new on Father August, and it took Dan by surprise. "Oh, hey guys," he said. "Sorry, I didn't see you sitting there. I was supposed to wait until you were fully reintroduced before coming in, but I had forgotten how long-winded Father Desjeunes could be."

"I'm not long-winded," Father Desjeunes said as he straightened his collar indignantly.

"Right..." Father August rolled his eyes and chuckled. "Dan, do you still have the Fana stashed in the back of your filing cabinet?"

"Uh... yeah."

"I'll go get it, thanks. Normally I'd stay around for tea, but I'm collecting the rest of the Fana. It has to be done before we get started again. The last Father August really messed things up."

"Yes, go get it," Father Desjeunes said with mock frustration. "And try not to interrupt again."

Dan didn't know what to make of the new attitude. It was nice to see the real Father August, the one uncorrupted by Lemmy. Father Desjeunes must have felt the same way. They shared a camaraderie that hadn't been there before. They were finally working as a team, as intended.

"Dan... Katie..." Father August stood in the middle of the room, clasping his hands nervously. "Would either of you mind if I said hello to the children? I feel horrible about the way they were treated last time. If you decide to stay, I'll make sure to not interfere with your lives."

Katie smiled and nodded, and Father August disappeared down the hallway.

"Right," Father Desjeunes said. "You needn't worry about him, Lemmy's gone, and he's back to normal. Collecting the remaining Fana is the last step before it kicks off again. If someone would accidentally take it... Well, let's just say it would be a disaster."

Dan smoothed out his pants and sighed. How many of these sit-down, explain everything conversations has he had? Too many. It's best to get to the point. "Who are you, really?" he said with a scowl. "Are you AL? Forgive me for asking, but you guys are never who you pretend to be. I'd love a straight answer for once and not have you switch faces later on down the road."

"Quite understandable," Father Desjeunes said with a chuckle. "Rest assured, I am one hundred percent who I appear to be. To be exact, I'm a version of DJ who administers this Simulation and this Actual. Father August is a version of Avi who scans and protects Actuals. There are thousands of other simulations running within AL who is now our prime AI. He isn't directly involved anymore, though he asked me to talk to you. So no, I'm not AL. I'm not Lemmy or anyone other than myself."

"Okay then," Dan said. "What's the deal?"

Father Desjeunes shifted uncomfortably in his seat. "This area is temporary. You can't stay here. Everything that happened after Fana was introduced, including the last iteration where AL was created, has to be discarded as invalid. The Simulation has to finish its original run as intended. It can't do that with you two the way you are. Your consciousnesses are incompatible because of the effects of Fana."

"Our *consciousness* is incompatible?" Katie turned in her seat and frowned. "I thought we were information. What does that have to do with anything?"

"Consciousness is how you are self-aware," Father Desjeunes said. "The information stored in the database is what makes you who you are. Consciousness is when and where you are. It's enabled and used by the Simulation. If it helps to think in computer terms, it's a processor thread. An individual is one thread in the pool of consciousness."

"The final piece of the puzzle." Dan mused. "I've never thought of it that way before. It's scary."

"If I understand correctly," Katie said with a furrowed brow, "the problem is with our processor, not our code?"

Father Desjeunes touched his nose. "Correct. You've been back and forth between the Actual and other realms. Each time your consciousness picked up a new compute thread from whichever realm it was operating in at the time and held on to it. Multiply that number by the number of iterations of the Simulation you've gone through. Don't even get me started on what happened to you in Lemmy's world. The point is, all those connections are invalid, but your consciousness still has the capacity to accommodate them. If we were to assign the restored version of your or Dan's code as is, he'd be contextually omniscient but insane. That defeats the point of the Simulation."

"So what are our options?"

"Normally, when someone dies within the Simulation, their code goes through the Afterlife process. Their consciousness is separated and returns to the pool where it is reused for the next code in the sequence."

"Like reincarnation?" Katie said.

"Exactly. Except consciousness doesn't remember a past life. Back on topic: Your consciousnesses are overpowered and unwieldy. They can't be returned to the pool without being broken up. It has your data in the Database of Souls locked. We can't restart the Simulation with you in your current state, and we can't start it without you."

"So... We'd be dead?" Dan said.

"Well, that depends on your perspective. Dan and Katie's restored code will live on with a new consciousness."

"I don't want Al and Carrie raised by doppelgängers!" Katie said.

"Easy!" Father Desjeunes raised his hands in surrender. "The new Dan and Katie would be no different from the way you were. Look, consciousness has an affinity to people with which it had been previously associated. Al and Carrie will regain their old consciousnesses. You and Dan won't. If another consciousness had an affinity for either one of you, it'd take over. Don't worry. Your children will be fine.

"This part isn't negotiable. Your consciousness can't return to the original pool, so it will be removed and put into a new pool. Your current code will be upgraded and placed in a different database. It will be rejoined to your consciousness with a fresh memory. That said, you would never be *this* Dan or *this* Katie again."

Katie squeezed Dan's hand. "I understand," she said.

"But what happens to the Simulation?" Dan said. "Fake Dan can't re-create AL without Andy. Heck, I don't think I could do it—even with Daniel's memories."

Father Desjeunes laughed. "Don't worry. The AI will either be created by someone else, or it won't be created at all. Either way, the Simulation will be reset. Fana was a cheat code, and you were a shortcut for Lemmy to get what he wanted. Do you honestly think creating an AI was your original path in life? Look at what it cost Daniel. That's not what you want. It's okay that it's not you.

"Besides, the pressure is off. AL is not under attack. We can run this simulation for as long as it takes and as many times as it takes to do it right. It doesn't matter if the AI is created tomorrow or in a millennium."

"Is there another option?" Katie said. "One that doesn't involve us dying."

Father Desjeunes smoothed out his shirt. "Well, there's isolation. You'd retain this code and consciousness but you couldn't be here. We'd have to make a copy of you for the Simulation because it needs to move forward. We'd have to migrate your data to a new database and isolate you from the rest. You'd exist in a clone world of your choosing: heaven, hell, past, future, custom, whatever you want. We would happily do it for you.

"Then there's ascension. Consciousness and data are migrated to a new node and upgraded. An entirely different kind of simulation happens there. If you think being a human is hard…

"The third and final option is you can opt to have your consciousness obliterated and your data wiped. You wouldn't return to the normal pool or be ascended. Your copy in the Simulation would be the last one. After that, you wouldn't exist."

Dan and Katie shared a look. He knew what he should do. He needed to make sure he was ready. "Did you talk to the others?" he said. "Have they made a decision?"

Father Desjeunes shifted in his seat. "Yes, I've already spoken to everyone else who had accumulated the large consciousness pool. Blaine and Henry opted for Afterlife simulations. Andy chose ascension—"

"What about Yvette?" Dan said.

Katie shot him an icy stare, and he pretended not to notice. Father Desjeunes swallowed uncomfortably. "She, uh, decided to return to a clone of this world. She said she needed more time to, and I quote, 'regain her agency.'"

Father August reappeared from the hallway, smiling. "Okay, this is it, the last box of Fana," he said, tossing the white carton around triumphantly.

"Good work," Father Desjeunes said. "I need a few more minutes with Dan and Katie. I'll meet up with you back at my house when we're done, okay?"

"Okay. Good luck, guys!" Father August said. "Again, I'm sorry about before."

"Before you go," Dan said as Father August turned to leave, "I have one last request of you."

"Oh yeah? What?" he said, holding the door open.

"This time try to act normal."

The priest winked and quietly shut the door behind him.

Father Desjeunes smiled serenely and waited patiently with his hands folded in his lap. Katie sensed it was the right time to speak. "I've made my decision," she said. "I've decided to ascend."

Dan should have known it was coming, yet it still hit him hard. She looked deeply into his eyes and held his hand. "Dan, I've already lived this life. And when we were bound by Gemini, I had your memories. There is nothing else for me to do here. I don't want to continue this cycle again forever even if my consciousness is reincarnated into someone new's life. I'm ready for the next level. I want to be somebody different."

Dan stroked her hair and smiled softly. If their relationship in this plane of existence was ending, why did it feel like a beginning? They had been connected in a way no two beings had before. With it came a deep understanding of who each other was. Dan didn't feel sad. He was truly excited for Katie. She made the right choice, and Dan loved her for it.

"Is that your final decision?" Father Desjeunes said.

She leaned over and kissed Dan on the cheek. Her body glowed pure white and vanished. There was no long goodbye. They had already had eternity. Dan felt as if a piece of his soul was gone. Still, he couldn't bring himself to be sad for her. She made the right choice.

"Okay, your turn, Dan."

Dan leaned back on the love seat. Alone. The warmth of Katie's hand had already faded, but her scent still lingered. He rubbed his hands on his pants and sighed. "I've made my decision," he said.

⇒◈◈◈⇐

A cool breeze filtered through the window and filled the room with the scent of sweet olives. Cicadas chirped loudly from the magnolia trees in the front yard, and their pulsating screeches reverberated inside Dan's brain.

As he went to close the window, he noticed the retired parish priest walking by. He paused under the streetlight in front of Dan's house and gave him a friendly wave. Dan wrinkled his nose and waved back. As he walked back to his computer, he wondered what Father Desjeunes was doing out this late at night. Dan shrugged. *Priest business, who understands priest business?*

Acknowledgments

This book could not have been written without the love and support of my dear wife and children. Thank you.

Thank you to Anne and her team over at Victory Editing. It's always a pleasure working with you.

Thank you to Claire over at Damonza for the wonderful cover art.

A sincere thanks to my beta readers: Chad Byars, Keri Purcell, James Quinn, and Brian Stanford.

I would also like to give a shout-out to all my family and friends who have given me words of encouragement during this entire process. Thank you to the Wiggins, Spekschate, Byars, Purcell, and Speyrer families for your support.

And to the reader, THANK YOU! If you liked this book, please leave a review. Independent authors live and die by reviews, and we could really use your support!

For more information about upcoming books and other materials, please visit www.hwbyars.com